When Love Isn't Love *is a story about heartbreak, resilience, triumph and the undeniable power of faith. Evil is not carrying a flashing red sign; it smiles while quietly whispering in your ear. It is clear from Lisa's journey that no matter how far you feel you are away from God, no matter how dark the road you are traveling becomes, God's mercy is always with you. I experienced a rollercoaster of emotions: anger, fear, joy, love and relief page after page. I saw myself in Lisa every time she wanted to scream or speak out but couldn't. I also saw myself in her when she found her voice. I was literally on the edge of my seat unable to put it down. I recommend this book to any woman who has ever struggled to be heard and to young women who are struggling to find themselves in an uncertain dating world where one misstep can land you in a battle over your own soul with real-life evil.*

Kaleema Overton Ameen
Columnist, Author - *Hidden in Plain Sight*

WHEN LOVE ISN'T LOVE

a novel by

Tracy M. Fagan

ISBN 979-8-9871593-0-9 (print)

Names: Fagan, Tracy M., author.
Title: When love isn't love : a novel / by Tracy M. Fagan.
Description: Lone Tree, CO: Kingdom Publishing, LLC, 2022.
Identifiers: ISBN: 979-8-9871593-0-9 (print)
Subjects: LCSH Man-woman relationships--Fiction. | Romance fiction, American. | Christian fiction, American. | BISAC FICTION / Christian / Romance / Suspense | FICTION / Women | FICTION / Romance / Contemporary
Classification: LCC PS3606.A2652 W44 2022 | DDC 813.6--dc23

Table of Contents

Dedication

This book is dedicated to my Lord and Savior, Jesus Christ, the author and finisher of my faith.

But He said, "The things which are impossible with men are possible with God."
~Luke 18:27 NKJV

Preface

Ahhhh, the feeling of being in love. The excitement of everything a relationship can possibly be. The fairytale marriage and the happily ever after. So many times, people are more focused on the wedding day than the health of the relationship and the preparation for covenant of marriage. It is evident because statistics show around half of all marriages end in divorce.

Even when divorce brings an end to a toxic marriage, it's still extremely destructive; with a ripple effect that impacts more than just the couple. After personally experiencing the pain of two divorces, my deep desire is to decrease the divorce rate.

When I asked God for strategy on how to go about doing that, He said it isn't about fixing bad marriages, but not getting into them in the first place. Hopefully through this story, you will be able to see red flags and warning signs that might help you or someone you know exit a toxic relationship before it's too late.

When Love Isn't Love addresses some very common, yet painful issues in our society. The characters in this book experience pornography, sexual abuse, and emotional abuse. I share this here because for many, this can be a trigger. If this is something that has impacted your life and you haven't addressed it, please seek help. There is healing available for you.

Pornography and sexual abuse are so pervasive in today's society. For many, it drives an insatiable lust that can destroy marriages. If you are caught in this web, there is a way out. Start by confiding in someone you trust. Speak to a counselor, a doctor, or a pastor. God wants more for you.

I pray that you enjoy this book and stay focused on God to help understand and experience true love.

Chapter 1
A New Beginning

The bright green grass and the huge pink hydrangeas bask under the warm sun; the well-known gray Portland skies didn't receive the invitation for graduation. The vivid colors remind me of the Land of Oz, where dreams really do come true. Instead of ruby red slippers, I have my ruby red dress hanging in the closet, ready to go under my black graduation gown. It is the perfect day to end my four years of college.

"Oh my gosh, Lisa, can you believe we are graduating today? We made it through four years!" Nicki said as she rolled sections of her long black hair over the hot rollers.

"I can't believe how fast these four years have gone. It's crazy...college is over," I replied as we stood side by side, getting ready for the day's festivities.

"Tell me about it! I am bummed that you are going back to KC. I am really going to miss my BFF. Are you sure you have to go back?"

Nicki and I had become best friends the second day of freshman year. Despite the fact we can't look any more different, we have a lot in common. Nicki is tall and slender. With her stunning hazel eyes and beautiful long black hair, she could pass for a model. I, on the other hand, stand just over five feet tall with a slightly athletic build. My creamy caramel hair is usually styled as a messy pixie cut; today, however, I have it slicked back and sophisticated for this transition into adulthood.

"I'd love to stay in Portland, but I have that job waiting for me back home. I'll come back and visit. It's just a three-and-a-half-hour flight away. Don't worry, we will stay in touch. And who knows, maybe I can get transferred back here someday."

"Now THAT would be awesome if you could get transferred back here."

"I probably have to be in my job for at least six months to a year before

I can look at that possibility. After I get started in my job, I'll see what it would take."

"I'm sure we will still be here and we can figure out living arrangements. There's always room for you, Lisa."

"Honestly, I am not very excited about moving back in with my parents. I mean, they are really cool and very generous to offer me a place to live. The thing is, I have a hard time being me when I'm with them...especially living with them."

"See, that's why you need to bail on that job and stay here with us!"

Her offer is tempting, but so irresponsible. Who walks away from a corporate job waiting for them right out of college? That would look horrible. Besides, the overall path of my life has been planned out since I was a little girl: high school, college, find my prince charming, get married, have a family, and live happily ever after. It's pretty cut and dry...well, because in my mind, that's what life is supposed to look like. The side plots, such as where I will live, my job, and my friends are insignificant variables.

"Hey, Nik, can I ask you a serious question?"

"Yea, Lisa, you can ask me anything. You know that."

"Do you worry at all about actually making it? I mean, landing a real job that will pay the bills?"

"To be honest with you, sometimes I get a little scared thinking about it; then I look at some of the scatterbrains that graduated before us that are making it. When I start to worry, I say to myself, 'If Suzie Evans can make it, I know I can figure it out!'" Nicki answered.

"Well, you do have a point there," we both giggled.

"Hurry up and get dressed. We need to get going so we're not late for the ceremony."

As Nicki and I make our grand entrance into the quadrangle, we hear the greetings of our sorority sisters. It's strange to see all of our friends in their caps and gowns. After many hugs, the deans line us up in the proper order and we parade into the fieldhouse for the ceremony.

As with any graduation ceremony, the speeches are inspirational, encouraging each graduate to launch out into the world; a thought that makes my stomach lurch. A deep breath is enough to momentarily suppress that feeling as I'm called to walk across the stage.

"Lisa Byrne, Bachelor of Arts in Telecommunications," the announcer called. The feelings of accomplishment that explode from inside are audibly matched by the holler and whistling that come from my family and friends.

I can't believe I'm actually done with college.

The monotonous reading of the remaining 743 names causes my mind to ruminate on the conversation Nicki and I had earlier. The job I have waiting for me back home came out of the interning I have been doing over the past few summers. If I had to go through the application process, I'm not sure if I could actually land one. According to my parents and my grades, I am a very capable, above-average, adventurous young lady; but on the inside, I have never really felt very special, capable, or confident.

Before getting too far down that road, I am pulled back to reality just in time. "Nicole Stratford, Bachelor of Arts in Sociology." As my bestie parades across the stage, I give out a yell. I'm really going to miss her. I do wish I was staying here in Portland.

After sitting through more names monotonously being called, I never knew how happy I would be to hear Ned Zeller's name. My butt is hurting and I am starving! To celebrate, my parents are taking me and Nicki out to lunch at The Point, one of Portland's nice seafood restaurants right on the Willamette River.

The four of us are seated at a table right next to the window.

"I don't know about you ladies, but after sitting through all of those names, I am HUNGRY!" my dad confessed.

"I am right there with you, Dad. I never thought Ned Zeller's name would be such sweet music to my ears," I said with a chuckle.

"Never a truer statement mentioned!" Nicki chimed in.

"So, Nicki, what do you plan on doing now that you've graduated? Your major was in sociology, right?" my mom asked.

"Yes, ma'am. I am hoping to get a job in the corporate world doing research on the impact of racism in the marketplace."

"That sounds interesting. Do you have anything lined up?"

"I've applied for a couple of positions; one with the state and one with a company that does outsourced HR work. I'm still waiting to hear back on both of them. Until then, I will keep serving up lattes at Common Grounds. I'm sure something will come up."

I am so proud of my friend. That is what I love about her. Along with being pretty, she is smart and personable. She will have no problem making it in life.

Dinner was perfect. We had our share of delicious food, soul-nourishing laughter, and conversation. It's a beautiful way to end this chapter of my life.

After dinner, my folks dropped us off back at our house, aka *The Ladies Lair*, for one last night. Our plans are to get changed and head out to an array of graduation parties.

While looking at my outfit in the mirror, I catch the eyes of the young woman staring back at me. I drift back to the thoughts that had distracted me during the ceremony. I feel like I am living a double life. Growing up, I made some pretty bold decisions.

Like in eighth grade, I was bound and determined to explore Europe with a small group of teachers and my prepubescent friends. Or even how I found myself in Portland for college. I picked Lewis & Clark College for two reasons: it was beautiful...and no one there knew my big sister, Anna. Tired of being "Anna's little sister," I packed up and went 1,800 miles away to freshman year, never visiting the school. So why am I petrified to jump into my adult life?

If I am honest, I'm afraid to disappoint my parents. They've given me so much; I don't want them to feel like they've wasted their efforts on a failure. My mom and dad seem to have mastered life. Our family has never struggled financially. I can count the times I have seen my parents fight on one finger. They have it all figured out. I'm not sure if I have what it takes to duplicate their success.

Maybe if I follow their path, my life will turn out perfect like theirs. The problem is their path doesn't always seem right for me. However, if I go my own way and it doesn't work out, I don't want to receive that look of disapproval or hear, "I told you so."

I've read the profound quotes that say "failure is only failure if you don't learn from it," and "failure is a part of life." As good as that sounds, it seems like everyone in my family except me has found a way to live life without failing. So instead of the possible humiliation of disappointing my parents, I try to do what they tell me: follow their lead, and do what is expected.

Then there is my sister, Anna: the smart, popular one. She walks down the path of success with ease. She excels in school, makes friends, and collects boyfriends without any struggle at all. Me, not so much.

Despite the underlying sense of competition between the two of us, I do love my sister. I really wish we had a closer relationship. Don't get me wrong: when push comes to shove, she is there for me. That's what family does. It's the day-to-day relationship where I think we are too different to really connect. It doesn't surprise me she's not here for my graduation. Nevertheless, I'm bummed she didn't make it.

Nicki interrupts my self-reflection, "Come on Lisa, you look beautiful! Let's go. We have places to go! People to see! Things to do! Parties to attend!"

Welcome to the first day of my life as a college graduate. Life as a real adult. It's kind of surreal. Having my friends and family see me walk across the stage to receive my diploma was momentous. The anticipation of my future is exciting and scary.

I've been working as a marketing intern with Edge Cable every summer since I started college. They offered me a full-time position after graduation. The only thing is, the position is back home in Kansas City. The offer is really good for someone coming out of college, so it is stupid for me to pass it up. After all, where I live and the job I do are minor details. The real focus of the next chapter of my life is finding my prince charming. Maybe God has my husband waiting for me in KC.

My parents pick me up from The Ladies Lair so we can make our flight. Heading home with my parents after graduation reminds me of the last day of summer camp. It's like when you said good-bye to all of your friends and go back to life at home. It feels so strange. Although I've been living "on my own" for four years, I don't feel like I have the confidence or the voice to step into adulthood. I'm always second guessing myself; and the torment of "What if I make the wrong decision?" is ever present in my mind.

It's hard because the people around me see this bold, strong, beautiful leader; a young lady with the world at her feet. While I see myself as a frumpy, scared, unqualified girl who has somehow managed to hide the reality of who I really am.

I am grateful my parents have always been so supportive of me. Part of me is excited to be back home; the other part of me wishes I was somewhere else.

I shower, get dressed, and venture downstairs for the first day at my new position.

"Good morning, Baby Girl," my mom's sweet voice greeted me as I came into the kitchen.

"Good morning, Momma."

"You look beautiful. Are you ready for your first day of your first adult job?"

"I guess so. It kinda doesn't feel much different than going in for any of my internships. Don't get me wrong; I am grateful I have a job. It just isn't really new and exciting."

"Well, keep your head up. Your future holds a lot of great things for you. And you don't need to stay in this job or with this company forever. It's a great opportunity for you right out of college."

"Thanks for the encouragement, Mom."

I appreciate my mom's kind words, and even the fact my parents are allowing me to stay with them while I get on my feet. However, it's so strange living back in my parents' house; in my old bedroom, reporting to work at the same location I have every summer for the past four years. Even though I'm in a new chapter of life, it feels like nothing has changed. How do I meet new people? I don't want to go back and hang out at the old high school hot-spots, and I don't want to go to the bars by myself. I also feel this pressure I need to make a big impact on the world, which is hard to do while feeling so insignificant on the inside.

"Lisa, do you have any plans for this weekend?" my mom asked.

"I don't know. I don't really have any friends here; and doing anything downtown is a thirty-minute drive."

"Well, you have to do something...anything! You're a beautiful young lady. Go out and try something new. Take a class or find a group of artists and keep up with your painting. You aren't going to meet anyone sitting here at home with your dad and me."

That struck a chord; I have always had a hard time making friends. I mean, don't get me wrong, I have many acquaintances.

In high school, I would bop through the halls and talk with people in all of the various cliques—the populars, the jocks, the band kids, the stoners…etc.; but I never really fit in with any one of them. If a group was getting together, I could ask to join, and the answer was usually "yes." However, I was rarely included in the initial plans.

In my college sorority, I fell into the same pattern. There were groups of girls that became really close. These girls would develop friendships with groups of guys in the different fraternities. Again, when I asked if I could join, I was welcome, but always felt slightly out of place.

That makes me feel like a farce; so many people would look at me and see this beautiful strong woman, while I see a weak, desperate, clueless girl.

Over the next couple of days, thoughts of Mr. Tall-Dark-and-Handsome cross my mind several times. *Where did he go to school? What does he do for fun? What does he do for a living? Is he really interested in me? It seems like it. I wonder what he's doing right now? Is he thinking about me?* I can't wait to get back to Capoeira class.

At the end of the second class, the hottie who has been taking up space in my mind approaches me. Even though I am tired and sweaty from the workout, I can feel the butterflies in my stomach come to life. I am rattled back to reality by his deep, booming voice. "Hi, my name is Andres. What is yours?"

"I'm Lisa. It is nice to meet you."

"Would you like to go get a cup of coffee or something sometime?"

A cup of coffee? That is so polite. A cup of coffee is much safer than going to a bar for a drink. I really like that.

"Thank you for the kind invite. I would like to get a cup of coffee with you sometime, Andres." I replied.

"Great. Are you available after class next Tuesday night?"

Knowing I don't have any plans, no matter what night he wants to go out, I replied, "Yes. That would be great!"

I race home and bust into the house.

"Mom! Guess what?!"

"What?" she replied.

"Not only did I make a new friend tonight at Capoeira, buuuuuut…. he asked me out for coffee!"

"Oh, Lisa. I am so excited for you. Tell me about him."

"Well, I don't know much. I do know his name is Andres. He is very cute and has beautiful hazel eyes," I respond, completely twitterpated.

"Well, just make sure you let me know when and where you are going for coffee. I don't want to sound like a mother, but I am your mother. I am happy for you. I just want you to be safe."

"Thanks, Mom," I said giving her a big hug. "I'll let you know."

My parents have a wonderful marriage. They work hard and play hard. I have watched them go on international adventures about every three years since I was in middle school. This time, they're getting ready to jet set off to Italy.

I love watching them prepare for their trips. They have been taking "Italian for Travelers." My dad practices his Italian, using this goofy accent whenever he can. I can see the love my parents have for each other in the way they live. It isn't the cheesy "I 'heart' you" and butterflies in the stomach love; it's the action of cherishing one another: like they promised in their marriage vows—to have and to hold, in good times and in bad, in sickness and in health. My dad is a provider and a protector; my mom is the nurturer and the helpmate. Our house always feels safe.

That's what I want for my marriage...for my life.

Chapter 2
And They're Off

The alarm clock is blaring waaay too early. I am my parents' dedicated chauffeur to the airport for their Italian adventure. Although I'm excited for them, I'm even more excited for myself. I get to be a "real adult" for two whole weeks. I have the house to myself. I can come and go as I please and don't have to answer to anyone. However, the thought of them being gone already makes me feel kind of lonely. Coming home to an empty house and having no one to share my day with intensifies the reality of my current friendless season. The saddest part is I am not thrilled about being with the one person I can never get away from: myself.

I try to lift my spirit by remembering the next step in my life is to find my husband and get married. I just need to find a good husband; one to love and protect me. Then we will live happily ever after.

As the loneliness begins to weigh on me, I remember my next class of Capoeira is in two days...and Andres and I are going to hang out after class. Maybe, just maybe Andres is the reason I am supposed to come back home versus stay in Portland. The thought he might be "the one" is enough to make me smile and make it through another day.

I muddle through the next two days of work. Finally, it's time to head to Capoeira. Honestly, I am more excited to hang out with Andres afterwards than go to practice.

After class ends, Andres walks over. "I'll meet you in the lobby in 15 minutes. Then we can decide what we're going to do."

His hazel eyes and deep voice got me twitterpated. "Okay. I'll be out ASAP."

Heading into the changing rooms, his comment about deciding what we are going to do hits me. His initial invite was for coffee. It meant a lot to me that he invited me for coffee versus drinks. I feel safer getting caffeine versus alcohol on a first date, especially since I don't know this guy at all.

Lisa, stop it. You are making this into much more than it needs to be! It's totally normal to get drinks for a first date.

He is waiting for me as I walk out of the changing room. He's hot. I can't believe he actually asked me out!

"So, I was thinking of heading over to Little Eddies. We can get some drinks and a bite to eat. It isn't too far from here."

"Um, ok. That works," I lied. I don't want to sound like a prude. And if I said no, would he make a scene? It's easier to just go with the flow. It isn't like I DON'T drink.

We get to the bar and order a couple of beers and a plate of nachos. Despite my initial disappointment, things are going very well. The conversation is easy and the laughter is plentiful.

"Tell me about one of your family traditions for the holidays?" I inquire.

"Just the usual. My mom puts up a tree. She cooks dinner for the two of us on Christmas Eve and we open gifts. My aunt and her annoying family usually come over for a little bit on Christmas day. We can't wait for them to leave. After that, I go over and hang out with my friends, and usually go to a movie."

Hearing his rendition of Christmas day is depressing. The fact that they can't wait for the family to leave makes my heart sad. I didn't even know the movie theatres were open on Christmas day.

To further the conversation, I answer my own question.

"Our family tradition is a little bit different. On Christmas Eve, we go to Mass and enjoy dinner with just the four of us. We open all of our gifts on Christmas morning. Since our extended family is back in Indiana, we spend Christmas Day with close family friends. Everyone hangs out, we eat way too much food, and end the night playing games and laughing."

"That sounds like fun. I've always wanted to be a part of a big family," Andres confessed.

I got really excited at the thought of being able to share the joy and love of my family with him. Don't get me wrong; my family is far from perfect. At the same time, our love and grace for each other allows the imperfect to be, well, perfect.

Andres and I enjoy the rest of the evening talking, laughing, and drinking. When we go to leave, he walks me to my car and gives me a kiss goodnight! I'm on cloud nine. Then he asks if I want to hang out tomorrow after work. Since my folks are gone and I have no other friends or plans, I jump at the opportunity.

The pattern of being together after work continued for the next week. I can't believe we have been "a thing" for eight whole days! Andres is fun to hang out with. At the same time, he is kind of a bad boy. Not that he robs banks or anything, but he pushes the boundaries and thinks that not all rules apply to him. It also bothers me when his mean, snarky side comes out. Instead of getting upset, I'm choosing to focus on the potential he has to be an AMAZING boyfriend, and eventually my husband.

I am excited for my parents to come home so they can meet Andres, and for Andres to meet them. This is so perfect! Life is going as planned...I can almost hear the wedding bells in my future!

Andres is really into cars. He drives a beautiful metallic blue Honda Civic with many mods. He loves it because of the cambered racing suspension, aftermarket wheels, low profile tires, cross-drilled brakes, and so on and so on. It is all new to me. It makes him happy, so it makes me happy.

He's picking me up tonight after I get home from work.

"Hello, handsome!" I said, greeting him with a huge hug and what planned to be a passionate kiss.

"Hey," he said dismissively, deflecting my affections.

"What's got your panties in a bundle?" I teased.

"Panties? I don't wear panties. I am pissed off. This guy at work is out to get me. He's mad because he's an idiot and keeps messing things up.

He tries to blame me for it," he started to unload.

"And then, every stupid idiot was on the road between work and here. Nobody knows how to drive any more. One guy cut me off, and this other guy almost hit me," he fumed.

Trying to shift his mood, I interject, "Well, I am glad that you are okay, and your car didn't get hit."

I don't really want to hang with him if this is how he is going to be all night.

"It sounds like it was kind of a rough day. Do you still want to hang out tonight?"

"Why wouldn't I?" he snapped. "What? Just because I had a bad day you don't want to be with me? What kind of girlfriend is that? Do I always need to be in a good mood for you? Is that what you expect from me?"

"Um, no. I was just thinking if you don't feel like hanging out, I totally understand." I tried back-tracking and explaining myself. Nevertheless, I feel like I am digging a deeper hole.

"Well, that's just rude. If I wanted to go home and be alone, I wouldn't have come over here. Whatever. Come on, let's go for a drive."

As much as I want to say no, I feel like I have no choice. I grab my purse and head out the door with him.

We are cruising down the highway, his agitation transferring over to his driving. He's weaving in and out of traffic, slamming the car through the gears. I begin digging my fingers into the seat, afraid of his reaction if I ask him to slow down. He must have sensed my fear.

"Lisa, relax. I'm a good driver, and this car is built to handle this kind of driving."

With that, he noticed a bolt from the bike rack on top of the car come loose. It bounced on the road, almost hitting the car behind us. With that, he starts yelling, slamming the car into a lower gear, causing us to lurch forward with a burst of power. He keeps accelerating and more aggressively weaving in and out of cars. I'm holding onto the side handle on the door, scared speechless, praying for him to slow down.

After what seems like several minutes, in a very shallow, weak voice, I squeak out, "Please slow down, you're scaring me."

As soon as he hears my whispered request, he slows down and apologizes.

The adrenaline dump from his antics has made me nauseous and numb.

Andres looks over at me, "I said I was sorry. You really have nothing to worry about. I am a good driver."

I'm not worried about his driving; I am worried about his anger. That was scary, and a behavior I am not used to. So many things tonight aren't adding up. He said he cares about me, but the stunt he just pulled off put both of us in danger. Up until this point, we've had so much fun together; although no amount of fun is worth what I just experienced.

Now that he's driving like a normal person and the nausea is gone, I choose to accept the excuse that he was having a bad day. It was an inappropriate reaction, but it never happened before. We made it out ok...and when I asked him to slow down...he did. So over all, it wasn't THAT bad—it's definitely better than being alone.

Chapter 3
Family Insight

Early the next morning, I awake to my alarm signaling the start of a new day. As I lay in bed, flashbacks of last night's car ride run through my head. I dismiss the magnitude of the traumatic experience as quickly as I can. That behavior isn't a part of my "happily ever after." If I ignore it, maybe it will just go away. I mean, I made it home okay, right? I just need to love him enough, and that part of him will change.

Hmmm, can I really change him? How long will I have to wait? What will it entail on my part?

These thoughts are way too heavy to be thinking about at 6:00 a.m. I need to get up and get ready for work.

As the water of the shower washes over me, the thought crossed my mind, *Maybe I can just spend time with myself tonight. Get a bite to eat and go to the mall. Maybe Andres and I need a little break from each other.*

The idea actually excites me. Getting a little breather after last night is probably needed. Plus, a little retail therapy always does a lady's heart good!

My productive morning at work is interrupted by my phone. The handsome hazel eyes staring at me from the lock screen inform me that Andres is calling.

"Hey, babe," his voice booms out of my phone.

"Hello, gorgeous. How are you doing today?"

"I'm good. Hey, want to come over to my house for dinner and a movie tonight?"

I hesitated. "I was actually planning on getting a bite to eat and shopping by myself tonight."

"What? Do you have another date? The way you hesitated makes it sound like you are trying to hide something."

"Um, the only date I have is with myself. I have spent the last eight nights with you, and you are worried that there is another guy? Really?"

"Well, my mom invited you to join us for dinner. She wants to meet you; but since you have other plans, never mind," he sneered.

Guilt swept over me. I don't want him to be mad at me; or even worse, think I am cheating on him. "I can go shopping any time," I concede. "I'll head over after work."

"Good. Don't be late. See you tonight."

What just happened? In that short conversation, I was accused of cheating and guilted into changing my plans. I'm kind of excited to meet his mom, so I guess it isn't that big of a deal. Although, the whole exchange left me feeling some sort of way.

Girl, snap out of it and get back to work. You have PLENTY to do on this project. I am sure dinner will be fun tonight; and you can go shopping any time.

I'm excited and a little nervous all at the same time. I have always had a way of hitting it off with my friends' parents. This however, is different. This woman could be my mother-in-law. That's crazy to think about. It also puts a lot of pressure on the whole evening. I wish I had known before I left for work I was going to be meeting his mother. I would have brought a change of clothes and my makeup to freshen up. I really want to make a good impression.

The day flew by. I can't believe it's already 3:50PM. I am supposed to be off at 4. I have many loose ends I need to tie up. Then I hear Andres' voice in my head, "Don't be late." That stresses me out. He lives across town, so I need to get on the road before the traffic gets bad.

Lisa, take a deep breath. He'll understand. It isn't like you have tickets for an event. It is dinner. Buckle down, get things tied up, and head out.

I'm really proud of myself. I got it all done, and I'm only ten minutes late in getting out of the office. I should still miss the main brunt of rush hour traffic.

Walking out of the building, I call Andres. "Hi, babe. Just wanted to let you know I am headed your way."

"You are just leaving now? You were supposed to be on the road ten minutes ago."

"Uh, I'm sorry. I had a couple of things I needed to get finished up before I could leave. I got them done as quickly as I could."

"Well, now you are going to be late. Thanks," he scolded.

"I should still be able to miss rush hour. I will try to make up time on my way over."

"Whatever. I'll see you when you get here."

Then he hung up on me.

I stood there stunned. Really? Did he just get angry about me being ten minutes late from work? And no concern about my safety on the drive over to his place. *Lisa, you are being too sensitive. It isn't that he doesn't care about your safety; it's that he is excited to see you.* I take a deep breath. Better. It feels good to be wanted.

I flip on 105.4 KIXX and get lost in the nonsense of the afternoon drive-time show. Before I know it, my GPS is directing me into Andres' neighborhood. Butterflies start flitting around in my stomach. I had made up four minutes, making me only six minutes late. I have a feeling it will still be an issue. At least it's better than being ten minutes late. *Is this normal? Obsessing over being six minutes late?* I asked myself, and then dismiss the thought.

Waiting for me out front, Andres walks over to my side of the car and opens my door. "You're late. I told you not to be late."

"I made up four minutes on my way over here; and I got here in one piece," trying to make an excuse that would make it acceptable to him.

"Whatever. Come in. My mom is waiting inside."

I walk into his house and I can smell the garlic and onion of dinner cooking. My stomach growls. Andres leads me into the kitchen.

"Hey, Mom, this is Lisa. Lisa, this is my mom."

A cute woman with spiky blond hair turns from the stove. "Hello, Lisa! It is so great to meet you. I have heard so much about you. You can call me Linda. I'm so glad you could join us for dinner tonight."

"It is nice to meet you as well. Thank you for having me. I'm sorry for being late. Is there anything I can do to help?"

"Oh, you aren't late. Dinner isn't even ready yet."

Andres interrupts her, "She doesn't need any help. She's got it. Let's go downstairs."

"Lisa, thanks for offering. I'm just making spaghetti tonight, so it's easy, and almost done. You two go hang out. I'll call you when it's ready," Linda offered. It feels like she is trying to make Andres' rude behavior ok.

"Come on, Lisa. Let's go downstairs."

As he turns to lead the way, I give Linda an apologetic look. I was looking forward to talking with her. I guess Andres has other plans.

"I'll show you my room. It's downstairs."

This makes me feel really uncomfortable. My parents have always been adamant about me not hanging out in a boy's bedroom. It opens up the opportunity for "things" to happen. I think I'll be ok; his mom is upstairs.

"I took over the whole basement when I moved into the room down here. It's more like my own apartment," Andres explained.

I'm relieved there is more than just his bed down here. We head over, sit on the couch, and turn on the television. He starts randomly flipping through the channels.

After a few minutes, I finally speak up. "I was looking forward to talking with your mom and getting to know her."

"What? Don't you want to hang out with me? You'll be able to talk with her over dinner."

Despite the fact I was looking forward to going to the mall and getting a break from him, I wasn't about to admit it. I know that would go over like a lead balloon.

"Of course I want to hang out with you," I lied. "When you invited me over, you said it was to meet your mom. So, I guess I had expected to spend time talking with her. That's all."

"Don't worry, you'll get more than enough time to talk with her over dinner," he said in a condescending tone which made my heart twinge. He is so rude in talking about his mom. If he really wants a big loving family like he says he does, he needs to be nice to the people who are a part of it. I dismiss yet another small red flag. I know my love and example will be enough to get him to change.

"Andres! Lisa! Dinner is ready in eight minutes!" Linda bellowed from the kitchen.

"So, should we head up and help your mom?"

"In a minute. I want to watch the end of this show."

I look at my watch. "Uh, there is still about fifteen minutes left, and your mom said dinner's almost ready."

"She won't start without us. Just relax and stay here with me. The show is almost over." With that he grabs my shoulders and pulls me back into him so I can't get up. Plus, it would be kind of strange for me to just head upstairs without him.

"Andres….Lisa...come on up. Dinner is ready!" Linda yelled again from the top of the stairs.

"Be there in a minute, Mom," Andres yelled back while remaining planted on the couch.

He is being so disrespectful to his mom. It doesn't make sense. He says family is important to him, yet he is just rude to his mother.

"Come on up, kids. Dinner is getting cold," Linda called again.

"We better go upstairs," I said. "That is the third time your mom has called us."

"Ok," he acquiesced.

Andres sits down at the table. I just stood there waiting for direction on where I should sit. Over the awkwardness, I turn to Linda, "Do you need help with serving?"

"Lisa, you are such a dear for asking. You're the guest here tonight, but it would be nice if you could help me pass out the plates."

I have no problem helping since I am designated "passer-outer" in my family.

Linda and I sit down after serving up the spaghetti dinner. Andres and Linda dive right in. At our house, we always said a blessing before we ate. I never realized how accustomed I've become to that practice. It seems a little strange to not thank God for the food.

"Lisa, is everything ok?" Linda asked.

"Oh, yes. Everything is fine," I quickly reply, picking up my fork, and diving in myself.

I am feeling more at ease, enjoying the dinner conversation. Linda is very curious and asked me all about my job, interests, hobbies, and family. However, Andres seems to be practicing for a speed eating contest. It's like he can't finish his dinner fast enough.

"Andres, would you like seconds?" Linda asked.

"No, I'm good. Lisa, hurry up. We are going to go for a drive after dinner," he stated.

I'm confused. "I thought we were going to hang out with your mom tonight? And weren't we going to watch a movie?" I asked.

"You got a chance to meet her, and there is something special I want to show you."

"Ok. Let me help your mom with the dishes first. That's the least I can do."

"No, she's fine. She can do the dishes," he answered for her.

I'm shocked at how rude he is being towards his mother. Pushing back, I playfully say, "She cooked, we clean."

"Thank you, Lisa," Linda chimed in.

Andres gives a slight huff, then realizes he isn't going to be able to make the quick escape he had planned.

After the final pan is placed in the dishwasher and the counters wiped, I look to Andres. "Ok, so I am ready to see that special something."

"Let's go," he says, heading towards the door.

"So, where are we going?" I ask as he starts the car.

"Just for a drive."

"I thought you wanted to show me something special."

"Well, I want to go for a drive, and I want you to go with me."

It is nice he wants me to go with him, but he invited me over for dinner, a movie, and to meet his mom. And now we are going for a drive; which, after last night's antics, is not my first choice of activities to do with him. Well, I guess technically I did meet his mom; so he isn't lying to me. Maybe it will be a short drive and we can come back and watch a movie.

"Ok," I agreed, hoping this won't be a rerun of last night.

Chapter 4
Two Worlds Collide

I'm getting off work early this afternoon to pick up my parents from the airport. I am excited for them to come home. I miss them...and I want to hear about their amazing adventures. I also can't wait for them to meet Andres. We have gotten so close over these past two weeks. We have spent *every day* together. Fortunately, there have been no other incidents as bad as when he lost his temper while driving.

I think it would be a good idea to have him come with me to pick them up. He insists on me going alone.

Seeing my parents' faces in the sea of inbound travelers makes my heart happy. They are an adorable couple. After seventeen hours of traveling, they both have a smile on their faces, and love and concern for each other in both their voices and actions. Seeing them again reminds me of being that little girl in a safe, happy place.

The ride home is filled with great stories of St. Mark's square, the funny singing gondolier, and my dad convincing several restaurant owners he is writing an article about where to find the best Cioppino in all of Italy. I'm bubbling with my own excitement. I can't wait to tell them how my relationship with Andres has blossomed while they were gone.

After hearing about their many experiences, I butt in. "I have something exciting to tell you! Andres and I are officially going out. I'm so excited for you to meet him."

The atmosphere immediately shifts. Awkwardness clings to every ounce of air in the car. Honestly, my heart is broken. Why aren't they excited for me? They don't even know him and they are already making judgments about him and our relationship. All I want is someone to do life with... like them. I am determined to show them this relationship is a good thing.

We stop and pick up a pizza for dinner. Wanting to show them this wonderful, budding relationship, I ask the worst possible question ever. "Could Andres join us for dinner?"

It was my innocent yet desperate attempt to make the heaviness in the air go away. It totally backfired.

My mom is always polite, and this time isn't any different. "Oh honey, not tonight. Your dad and I are really tired and have been traveling all day. We'll make plans to have him over soon. I'll make a nice dinner and make an evening of it."

I'm crushed. Not only will my parents not get to meet him tonight, but I won't get to see him either. That is going to ruin our 13-day streak. I hope that won't make him mad.

When I call to let him know my plan of him coming over for dinner isn't going to work, he responded, "See, I told you they wouldn't like me."

I try to convince him that wasn't the truth. It's a tough sell because I am trying to convince myself of the exact same thing.

After dinner, I go up to my room and lay across my bed; the tears start to flow. Why does this have to be so hard? Why can't they just accept him like they accepted all of my sister's boyfriends? Why can't they be happy for me?

A few days later, staying true to her word, my mom asks, "Lisa, would you like to see if Andres could join us for dinner on Monday night?"

"That sounds good. Let me ask him." Honestly, my heart is torn. I really want them to meet, although I have a strange feeling it isn't going to go well.

I mask my trepidation and dial his number. "Hi, handsome; what are you doing on Monday night?"

"I don't know. Why?"

"My mom and dad want to have you over for dinner."

"I don't know if I want to come. They don't like me."

"What do you mean, 'they don't like you'? They haven't even met you—hence the invite to come over for dinner. And just for the record, I didn't ask her, she asked me."

"But still. I am not what they want for you, and I am not sure if I want to sit there and get grilled. I don't have a college degree yet, and I am just not the kind of guy they want for their daughter."

"That isn't true. You are going back to school. You are a hard worker, and a nice guy. They just need to get to know you. Please, will you do this for me?" I can feel the stability of this relationship beginning to crack.

It doesn't make sense. I have the big family with lots of love that he claims to want. However, in order to have that family, he has to be willing to meet them. I am confused and hurt by both my parents and my man.

"I don't want to. If I really have to, I guess I will," he finally replies.

That is the worst "yes" I've ever received. My trepidation just grew three sizes. I'm trying to convince myself this dinner is just the thing to get the relationship with my parents and Andres back on track.

Who am I kidding? It was never on track. Why...why does it have to be like this? I just want to live happily ever after. Nevertheless, I already feel like I'm being torn in two.

Even with Monday night's dinner looming, Andres and I still manage to fill all of our free time with each other. People at the Capoeira school are starting to notice we are a thing. It feels good to be a part of a couple, even if there are interactions that don't feel quite right.

Capoeira practice is becoming more fun. Andres and I practice some of our moves on each other when we are hanging out away from the school. It is so cool we have this in common. I also like how Andres challenges me. Sometimes it gets a little scary because he moves faster than I'm comfortable with, or he will add in a kick or a punch he knows from his karate training. He's never hit me, but seeing his fist or his foot show up out of nowhere freaks me out. When I ask him to stop, he tells me he is just doing it to make me better.

One thing I love about my parents is they are always gracious hosts;

doing the little things to make guests feel welcome in our home. Mom is making my favorite lasagna for dinner on Monday night. I'm nervous for Andres to come over. I feel like this dinner is the "make or break" between my parents and my man, ultimately my future.

I really hope this dinner will bridge some gaps and start building a good relationship between them; and that my mom and dad keep in mind how intimidating it can be to meet your girlfriend's parents. I wish they could see what I see in him; and that Andres would believe me when I tell him they hold nothing against him.

He might be kind of rough around the edges, but he's just a guy that wants to be loved...and I know I can do that...I can love him enough to make everything better, so we can live happily ever after.

At the Saturday breakfast table, my dad asked, "Hey, Lisa, what does Andres like to drink?"

"His favorite beer is Corona."

"Ok. Anything you want from the liquor store?"

"No. I'm good with whatever you've got at the house."

I am already concerned I'm being too much of a bother with wanting this dinner; I don't want to ask for any more. I can tell my parents aren't comfortable with how fast our relationship has progressed. However, I am grateful they are getting on board and taking the time to meet Andres and see what is so special about our relationship.

Monday night is finally here.

Ding dong.

I run to the door with great excitement and anticipation. I open the door to my handsome man standing there with a beautiful bouquet of flowers. I'm so excited! This is going to earn him some good points with my parents!

As I welcome him into the house, I sense a hesitation and an agitation from him that isn't good. In my mind, I'm thinking, *I get it; things didn't start off the best with my parents. In reality, they are really good people; and they are opening their hearts and their home to you. Let the past go and see the good thing that is right in front of you.*

"You look handsome tonight. That is sweet of you to bring my mom flowers."

"They're not for her, they are for you. How long do we have to stay here after dinner?" he replied.

"Um, I don't know. I am sure we can go out for a little while after we eat. It is a work night, so not too late. Come on in. My dad made a special trip to the store to get you Corona beer, which I know is your favorite."

"Oh, good. I need a drink."

We make our way into the kitchen where my mom is putting the final touches on the meal. My dad comes in from the back porch, greeting Andres and offering him a drink.

This is off to a GREAT start! I think to myself.

My mom started the conversation. "Andres, what do you do? Are you working or going to school?"

"Right now I am working construction. Next semester I will be going to Community College in the city to work on general credits. Then I will transfer to the state university to complete my degree."

I'm glad he is so future-focused. Out of high school, he tried going to college. He spent too much time partying and not enough time studying; so he decided to take a break from school and work. Now he is getting his life together. He says he wants to get his degree, get married, and have a family. It is going to be perfect; I just know it!

Throughout dinner, I can sense an uneasy tension. My mom and dad continue to ask questions, trying to get to know him. Andres is getting more defensive with every inquiry. He is beginning to annoy me.

They are taking interest in you, and you are getting angry because they are asking questions in hopes of getting to know you.

As soon as we finish dinner, Andres asks, "Lisa, do you want to go for a drive?"

I could tell he just wants to get out of here. It crushes me. My parents really put forth effort to get to know him. It was like he didn't even TRY to engage with them. He was angry and defensive, just buying time so he can say he came over for dinner. I get it. He has experienced the rejection of his dad and other people in his life. But he says he wants a loving family...and loving families hang out together. They ask questions about your life. They take the good and the bad. They spend time together and stick with you through everything.

"Dad, Mom—is it ok if we head out for a little bit?" I asked. "I know I have work tomorrow, so I won't be late."

My dad looks at me and nods with a sad look of disappointment. He desires better for me. The better isn't about choosing someone with a college degree or a high paying job. He wants me to pick someone who knows how to love and cherish people, especially his daughter.

My mom verbalizes my dad's nod. "Sure, sweetie. Don't worry about the dishes; your dad and I will take care of them. Just don't be too late... and be safe."

We get up from the table and Andres sprints to the door.

As we get into his car, I enquire, "Why did you want to get out of there so quickly? My parents were just asking questions to get to know you,"

"Didn't you see it? They were totally judging me because I don't have a college degree already and I haven't started in my career," he retorted.

"WHAT?!?! That totally isn't it. They were asking about what you are doing and your plans for the future. They are trying to get to know you. You are on a good path; that is nothing to be ashamed of."

"No, they were totally passing judgment on me. I am not good enough for their daughter. I will never be able to do enough or be enough for them."

That isn't true. I know they weren't passing judgment on him. As parents, they want my future spouse to be able to provide and take care of me. Andres is taking the steps to do just that. My parents realize it is a process. They have told me many stories about when they were just starting out with little money, working to make ends meet. There is no judgment on where he is in life; they just want to know his plans for the future.

"Did you see the way your dad looked at me when I said I was going to a community college? And your mom kept asking questions about the construction work I am doing—like I'm totally incompetent. They have an issue with me because I come from a broken home on the other side of the tracks, and I don't have any doctors or lawyers in my bloodline."

I sit there stunned at his take on the situation. I know my parents, and that is not them. They have never looked down on or talked bad about people for their chosen careers. Being raised in the Catholic Church, they have taught and demonstrated to my sister and me that we should love all people. They have friends who aren't doctors and lawyers and they don't treat them any differently. This is how my parents raised me.

I will admit, dinner was awkward. Maybe Andres is right. Maybe my parents are being judgmental. I'll just have to work a little harder to get my parents to see that Andres is a good guy...and get Andres to realize that my parents are good people, too.

Chapter 5
On My Own Two Feet

"Mom, I am so excited. Andres and I are celebrating our two-month anniversary!" I exclaimed as I bounded down the stairs for breakfast.

"That's nice, sweetie. I've noticed you two spend a lot of time together. Have you met any female friends at work or at Capoeira?"

Her response strikes me as strange. She spends a lot of time with Dad. And since Andres and I are on the path to building a life together, shouldn't we be spending a lot of time together?

"All the women I work with are older. I talk with few of the women at Capoeira, but not much more than that. Besides, Andres gets irritated when I train with other people," I explained.

"Have you reached out to Janice at all? You two were so close in high school. What about rekindling that relationship?"

"We talked a couple of times. It was good, but since we don't have the same interests we did in high school, it's different. Still good; just different. Plus, our schedules don't really line up to spend much time together."

"What about your sorority? Do they have an alumni chapter here? That would be a great way to meet more women your age."

"I don't know if they do or not. I'm not sure if I even have time for something like that. With work, Capoeira, and Andres, I don't have a whole lot of extra time."

Where is this coming from? Maybe Andres was right; they DON'T like him. The problem is, they don't know him like I know him, and he is not giving them that opportunity. I have to say though; my parents are trying in their own way. However, Andres keeps pushing back and refuses to open up to them. It's frustrating. I have the type of family he says he wants, but he is pushing that opportunity away. I just need to stick with him, encourage him, build him up, and love him enough for him to realize my parents are really good people.

The fact I am still living at home makes this whole thing more difficult. It's like I am an adult-kid. I have a real corporate job, a serious boyfriend, a college degree...and I am still living in the same room I've lived in since kindergarten.

My parents are cool, but I want to be on my own. I want to be a "real adult" and come and go as I please. Yet as my mom keeps pointing out, I don't have any female friends to get a place with. I want the freedom of living on my own; however, I am not sure if I really want to live by myself...that sounds lonely. I don't want to move in with Andres because I don't really believe in living together before marriage...even though we have already been sleeping together. Andres is really pressuring me to get my own apartment; that way I wouldn't have to drive as far to see him. I think the bigger reason is so he would have less of a chance of running into my parents.

Linda greets me as I walk into his house after work. "Hi Lisa: how are you?"

"Meh. I'm OK."

"Just OK? What's going on?

"Well, I'm getting tired of living at my parent's house, but I don't know the first thing about living on my own."

"Didn't you live on your own in Portland?"

"Well, kind of. My parents took care of paying all the bills. I'm not complaining. I just don't know how to do it on my own. And I don't want to ask my parents for help because I think they would rather me stay there a while longer and save up some more money."

"I'll help you figure out a budget. I've been a single mom raising Andres on my own for years. I'm a master at budgets!"

"Really?" I asked with excitement and embarrassment.

"Sure. Go to the store and buy a ledger book and we can sit down and figure it out tonight. Once you get your budget done, then the rest will just fall into place."

Linda, Andres, and I sat down that night and worked out my finances. Now I know how much I can spend on rent and groceries. I'm excited! Seeing it in black and white makes it seem like I can actually move out. At the same time, I am dreading telling my parents. I have a feeling they won't approve of my moving out just yet.

Now that I have a price range for my apartment, Andres and I start looking around for my new place. He wants to make sure it's halfway between my work and his mom's house, so it would be easier for us to see each other. I finally select a 525 square-foot, one bedroom apartment, with old shag carpet. There is a family room, a small nook for the kitchen table, a hallway back to the bedroom that is fully decked out with avocado green kitchen appliances. I don't want to seem ungrateful; I know everyone starts somewhere, but I'm not very proud of my new place. I don't know what I imagined for my first apartment; however, this wasn't it.

The hardest part of the whole process is I haven't shared any of it with my parents. It makes me sick to my stomach when I think about it. My parents have been so good to me. When I try to talk about it with Andres, he tells me I am an adult and I don't need their permission. He is right in that I don't need their permission. What he doesn't seem to understand, though, is that healthy and loving relationships share major life events. Here I am excluding my parents from this rite of passage in my life. The plan is to get everything set up, sign the lease, and then I will go back and tell my parents the "good news." I know this will crush them; on the other hand, I don't want to lose Andres.

It's always easier to talk to my mom first. I know my dad loves me, but he gets this look on his face when I do something he disapproves of. That "look" coupled with my mom's disappointment is too much. The plan is to start by telling her; then she will help break the news to my dad.

I'm so glad to find her alone in the kitchen when I get home.

"Hi, Mom. I have some exciting news to share with you," I said in an unconvincing, wavering voice.

"Hi, Sweetie. Well, what is it?"

"Well, I found a cute, one-bedroom apartment and I am going to be moving out this weekend. I have thought about it, and I am now an adult. I have a good job. I worked out the budget and I know I can afford it. It isn't much, but I will be on my own," I continued to ramble, trying to convince myself more than her. "You and Dad have been so supportive by letting me live here; however I really need to get out and stand on my own two feet. It's only 20 minutes from here. And like I said: it isn't big, however, it is a start. A great first place, and um…yea."

As I run out of words, the wave of guilt and uneasiness that had been building crashes over me. I can see just by the look in my mom's eyes she is crushed she hadn't been a part of the process. It isn't that my parents don't want me to grow up and move out; they want to make sure I have a good foundation. As for my mom, I think she wanted to be a part of the process and excitement of picking out my first place. She has always strived to be the best mother she could possibly be to my sister and me.

"Well, ok. So, you have already signed the lease on the place?" she asked, pretty stunned.

"Yes. I pick up the keys on Friday."

"Where is it?"

"It is a cute little studio apartment right over by Park Field Mall. It's close to shopping, restaurants, and walking trails," I spewed, mimicking the leasing agent. "And I'm on the third floor, so it's safe for a single female."

"Are you and Andres moving in together?" she asked hesitantly. I wasn't surprised by the question because I knew they didn't approve of living together before marriage.

"No, Mom. This is MY place. I am able to pay for it all by myself. And no, Andres is not moving in." I feel I have to reiterate that point for her to believe me.

With that she gives me a hug. And with great sadness and disappointment in her voice, she says, "Well, it sounds like your mind's made up. You will need to tell your dad tonight. We love you so much and only want the best for you."

"Thanks, Mom. I love you, too."

This is supposed to be exciting... So why does it feel so horrible?

I am sad for the strain I put on my relationship with my parents. The issue isn't my moving out, but how I chose to do it. If I stop and sit in my truth, I admit I am sad that I don't have any girlfriends. I really miss Nicki. I feel like Andres is starting to control a lot of time and decisions in my life. But according to the plan, the next thing I am supposed to do is get married. I need to be with a man to get married, and Andres clearly likes me.

If I end it with him, would any other man want me?

I am grateful the phone rang and interrupted my thoughts. Instead of addressing any of these issues, I am pretty good at sweeping them under the rug, putting a smile on my face, and hoping they will somehow get resolved.

"Hello, this is Lisa."

"So, how did it go telling your mom?" Andres' voice boomed on the other end of the line.

"It went ok," I said in a sad voice.

"Lisa, don't let her put you on a guilt trip. You are doing nothing wrong. They just don't want you to grow up. And they definitely don't like you hanging out with me. When you move out, they lose control over you. You have every right to move into your own place. And see, you did this without their help. We did this together."

Being in my parent's house is awkward. They are showing as much support as they can muster. I can tell they don't want to ask any questions that will precipitate an answer they don't want to hear.

I am doing my best to not ask for anything from them because I want to "do this on my own." I don't want to ask them to support something I know they don't agree with.

It's finally Friday! After work, Andres is coming with me to sign the lease and get the keys to my new place. It's exciting to walk into my own apartment for the first time. I guess when it's actually your own place, the avocado-colored appliances look a better shade of green.

Andres helps me move the furniture I have been collecting into my new place. It feels better now that I have my stuff in here. My plan is to have it all together before I invite my parents over to see it. I want them to be proud of me.

"Hey, Lisa, I know this is your place, but it would be a good idea for you to give me your extra key, so in case you get locked out, or need me to come over and take care of the place, I can get in."

I'm not really comfortable with the idea although it does make sense. I'm not going to give a key to my parents because I am adamant about being self-sufficient. I slip one of the door keys off the ring and hand it over.

I am excited to spend the first night in my very own place. Without an invitation, Andres stays the night with me.

I didn't plan on the sun streaming in the bedroom window, waking me up early. Despite my lack of sleep, I'm looking forward to today. It's going to be a great day of adulting. I get to go shopping for the household items I discovered I'm lacking.

Our first stop, Target. I need everything for my kitchen: plates, bowls, silverware, pots, pans, you name it. A filing cabinet is also on the list. I want be an organized, responsible adult. We grab a simple, two-drawer filing cabinet, the kind that comes in a flat box and warns, "some assembly required."

We get home and Andres carries it up the stairs and offers to put it together for me. It kind of bums me out because I enjoy assembling that kind of furniture. Nevertheless, he insists. I let it go. I guess that is part of the give and take in a relationship—sometimes you have to give up the things you want for the other person. So, I focus on getting the kitchen organized and leave him in the front room to put my new cabinet together.

I hear him tear into the box, then some banging, some hammering... and then some expletives. I come around the corner and find part of the cabinet put together. Andres is holding part of the drawer in his right hand and another piece in his left. His face is red. He is angry and yelling at the file cabinet.

Trying to diffuse the situation, I ask, "Honey, what's going on?"

"This #%#$%@#$% stupid filing cabinet. This piece should have gone in before I glued these pieces together. So now the whole thing is ruined. I just #%@#$% up the whole thing!"

"Take a deep breath. Can't we just pull those pieces apart?" I offered in a calm voice.

"NO YOU CAN'T. I said it is all #%@#$% up. Ruined!" he snapped back at me.

"Here, let me try," as I reach for the piece that was glued together.

"IT'S NOT GOING TO COME APART!!! SEE..." and with that, he yanks the two pieces, and the cheap particle board breaks in two, not where it was glued together. Then he throws down the destroyed pieces and storms out of the apartment, slamming the door.

Standing there in complete shock, I want to cry; but I can't muster up the tears. I want to scream, yet nothing is coming out of my mouth. I want to fix the file cabinet and make everything better, but I can't. I am so confused and out of my element. We never had anger outbursts like this in my house growing up. This is crazy and unacceptable.

I walk through the heaviness over to the door and lock the deadbolt. I stand at the door looking at the chain. He has a key, so he can get back in if I just lock the deadbolt. The question is, do I want him to come back in? Do I want a relationship that has this kind of anger? I don't like my new stuff being destroyed. I don't like feeling scared. I hesitantly slip the chain lock into place.

As I start cleaning up the mess of the broken file cabinet, I begin thinking, *What if he never comes back?*

The thought of rejection triggers an overwhelming pain in my heart. If he doesn't come back, it's because I am not enough. Something like this would never happen to my sister. She always knows how to do things the right way, which is why everyone loves her. If I was enough, I would know how to act to not make Andres mad. If we broke up, it would say to my parents...and the world...that I am a failure. That I can't do what it takes to create a successful relationship. It would be like a divorce.

Divorce. That dreaded "D" word. It brings up many gut-wrenching thoughts. Not that I experienced it personally, but I remember the horrible divorce of one of our family friends: so much fighting and angst. Not to mention the fact divorce is wrong...well at least that's what I was taught growing up. Just thinking about it is petrifying!

I am a total wreck of emotions. The conflicting thoughts of wanting him to stay or go have me so confused. I've already invested so much into this relationship; I'm not sure I could actually end it even if I wanted to.

About twenty minutes pass. I jump out of my skin when I hear the key rattling in the lock. I quickly run to the door to remove the chain. I know Andres' fear of rejection; the chain lock would definitely tell him he's not wanted. I am afraid of his reaction if he knows I had locked him out. And by the way, what girlfriend locks her boyfriend out? I mean, we are on the road to marriage; wives don't lock their husbands out of the house. As he fumbles with the lock, I gingerly remove the chain...just in time.

He opens the door and we are face to face. I feel my heart rate quicken and my breathing becomes shallow.

"Did you really lock the door with the chain?" he asked me in a calm, yet perturbed, voice.

"Um, I wasn't sure if you were coming back...or um, if you were going to your mom's house," I said, sounding like a guilty child. The truth is:

I am scared of him. I don't like the anger and the yelling...but that is something we are working on.

"I can't believe you would do that. If you put the chain on, I wouldn't be able to get in," he scolded.

"I'm sorry. I just..."

"Well, I am sorry about your file cabinet."

"Your apology is accepted. It is just stuff. It can always be replaced. When we get a new one, please let me put it together...or at least promise you will read the directions."

There was a shift in the atmosphere...for the better. The tension released like a deflating balloon. I can breathe again. That was intense. A level of intense I don't want to experience again.

"Andres, can I tell you something?

"Sure."

"I want you to know, one thing I am very afraid of is divorce."

"Really? Why?"

"I was really afraid when you walked out of here that you were never coming back," I confessed as tears began to run down my face. "I know people get in fights and need their space, but please promise me you will never use the word 'Divorce'. I mean, you can say, 'I need some space,' or, 'I need a break,' or anything like that. However, promise me you will never threaten me with the word 'DIVORCE'. Please promise me: if you do use the 'D' word, you say it with your bags packed and one foot out the door."

"Yea, sure, Baby. First of all, we aren't even married. But don't worry; I'll never leave you," he said as he wrapped his arms around me to try offering comfort.

Chapter 6
International Promotion

I can't believe it! Tonight is troca de cordeós, the changing of the chords ceremony at our Capoeira School. It is extra special for us because it is our batizado, which is considered our introduction to Capoeira. It means we are now official students of this art. Up until this point, we have been wearing a white cord at practice. Tonight, we get our new white and yellow cords. I never thought I would receive any kind of official ranking in any type of martial arts. Not that a yellow and white-stranded cord is a MAJOR accomplishment; it's still pretty cool.

I love that studying Capoeira includes the study of the culture as well as the martial art. The drive of the music is so powerful, you can't help but to get your body moving. The twang of the berimbau, rattle of the caxixí, the driving beat of the tall drum; when I hear it, I am reminded of my experience traveling to Brazil in college. Back then, I never thought I would be doing the dance I watched practiced in the parks of Salvador.

I am nervous as I wait for my turn to be tested. The newbies are the first to go; I am the second one up. We have to "play" with one of the teachers for about four minutes. They will test our knowledge and ability to flow by calling out the names of the top ten Capoeira movements. I am so glad I gave this a try. It is a great new addition to my life! And I am really excited because this is something that Andres and I can do together.

The thing that makes our school so unique is the main instructor, Mestre Lucas Mota. He is from a small town outside Salvador, Brazil. He loves breaking bread and sharing his native culture with his students. To continue the celebration of the promotions, he hosts a potluck at the school. Mestre Mota will most likely bring Feijoada, a popular stew-like Brazilian dish made with beef, pork, and black beans; and Picana, a Brazilian barbecue specialty. Most everyone else will bring typical

American potluck dishes.

I'm bringing one of my favorites, a red velvet Bundt cake with cream cheese frosting for our contribution to the feast. Even though I know I could walk into this potluck by myself, it feels better being with someone; someone who can protect me.

It's fun to talk with the other students we have been training with over the past several months. Many fascinating people practice here. Sarah is a curator at the art museum downtown; Frank is a high school biology teacher; and Larry is the owner of HP Construction, the company building several new apartment complexes around town. When we are practicing, they are just people like me, trying to learn Capoeira.

While I am talking with Larry, I notice Andres sitting by himself in the corner.

"Hey, Andres, did you know Larry is in construction, too?"

"No."

"Come over here," I said, motioning for Andres to join the conversation. "Larry was just telling me about the apartment complex he is building on the corner of 13th and Poplar."

I turned to Larry. "Andres is right now working construction as he is getting ready to head back to school."

Hesitantly, Andres comes over and joins the conversation. In watching the two of them start to talk shop, I notice Andres is uncomfortable and intimidated. I don't understand. Larry is easy-going and the conversation is about a subject Andres knows well. It breaks my heart Andres has such a hard time talking with people he doesn't know. The most difficult part isn't the fact he is shy, but when he doesn't talk, he comes across as rude. It's something I can live with until I can convince him that he is special and loved; then he will change. After enough of my encouragement, he will be able to carry on a conversation with anyone!

Chapter 7
Moving Towards a Point of No Return

I can't believe I've been on my own for about four months now. Well, not REALLY on my own because Andres has pretty much moved in. I mean, I guess it's cool even though I can't remember the last time I even spoke with Nicki. And I haven't had any time alone to meet new friends. I am so busy with work, Capoeira, and Andres. He also gets irritated when I even talk about hanging out with Janice. It's like he's afraid of me cheating on him; which is weird because I have never cheated on anyone...and how could I? I am always with him.

Even though I feel pretty restricted at times, we are still doing well. We do a lot of things together, and for the most part, have fun hanging out. I think his heart is softening. He is even okay with going over to my parents' house for dinner about once a month. It isn't much, but at least it's a start.

I do wish I could have more mommy-daughter time; however, it always seems to be an issue. Andres gives me a hard time, and ever since I moved out, there seems to be a wedge between my mom and me. I know she still loves me. Nevertheless, it's like she's always on guard, waiting for me to drop some new unbearable news on her.

"Hey, Lisa, I know the lease on this apartment is ending in a couple months. This place is kind of a dump. Since we practically live together already and don't really have anything else planned for today, why don't we go take a look at some other apartments and officially move in together."

A dump? I thought to myself. *That is rude. When we first looked at this place, I made a comment like that and he defended it saying, 'it wasn't that bad' and 'it is nice for a first apartment.'*

"I don't know about actually moving in together. I know my parents would really flip out."

"Lisa, you are twenty-two years old, making your own money, paying your own bills. You can do what you want. You don't need your parent's approval! Stop being so worried about what they will think!" he snapped at me. "Come on, we are building a life together."

The truth is I don't know if I want to move in with him. Like every little girl, I have this fairy tale idea of being swept off my feet by prince charming. I'm already feeling kind of smothered. However, he is right: we are building our lives together. And we have already been together for almost eight months...it feels like so much time.

If I say no to moving in together, he will most likely leave me. And if he leaves me, I will not only look stupid, but I will have no one. I couldn't go back to the Capoeira School because he would be there. I don't really have any friends.

Memories of fifth grade heart-break start flooding back. I was infatuated with Carl. So was almost every other girl in my class. There was something about his messy, sandy-blonde hair and cocky attitude that had all the girls swooning. It was skate night for our school at SkateLand. I always had a love-hate relationship with those events. I wasn't very coordinated, so it was a toss-up as to whether or not I would come home aching and bruised. The nights that ended without any major wipeouts made me feel like a roller-derby queen. This night however, the pain didn't end in a black and blue mark; it was a deep gash to my tender heart.

From the beginning of our skate session, Carl and his side-kick Christopher were giving me and my friend Kelly more attention than usual. I was excited yet cautious of their affections. I was flailing around the rink, trying to get used to the skates. Carl sped by me, swiping the hat off my head. It was playful with just a touch of cruelty. I didn't care; it was attention from Carl. Even though it didn't make sense, I still was excited about it.

"All right, folks, go grab that special someone...it's time for couple's skate!" the announcer boomed over the loud speaker.

My heart jumped. My head was on a swivel, waiting for Carl to come up and ask me to skate.

"Kelly, there he is." I pointed to the fifth-grade Fabio who was now about ten yards away.

He noticed my pointing, and then, yelling so he could be heard above the love song that was playing for the couple's skate, "What makes you think I would EVER skate with you?" He turned to Christopher and let out a sinister laugh and skated off.

I was mortified.

I would have rather fallen and cracked my head open. That way I would have been able to leave, even if it was via ambulance.

I can't believe I was so stupid to even think that Carl would be interested in me. Now that the whole school knows I'm not "Carl-worthy," they all know the truth: I'm really a total nothing.

I shudder thinking about the pain of Carl's words. The rejection I felt that dreaded night at SkateLand returns to taunt me again. If Andres left, I would be all alone…again. Not good enough for Carl, and not good enough for Andres. That seems so painful.

If I break it off with him, what will I do? How will I face my parents? The last thing I want to hear is, "I told you so."

My current apartment is in a strange part of town far from my job. The only reason we selected this area of town was to be closer to where Andres was living. Moving in together is a step I don't really want to take. Then again, I can't say "No!" To top the whole thing off, I have lived in the same house since I was five years old. This concept of moving every six months just doesn't seem right.

"I am not sure if I am ready to move." I answered, telling a half truth.

"What do you mean? This place is so tiny and crappy. Your commute is way too far. We can move in together and get a nice two-bedroom apartment, much closer to your work. I can help pay the rent. It will be great. Come on; let's go take a look."

What can it hurt to go look? Maybe that will appease him. "Ok, we can go, but we are just going to LOOK."

Begrudgingly, I get ready and we head out to scour the city looking at apartments.

The day was long and laborious. I think we toured almost every apartment complex in a ten-mile radius. I honestly had no idea there were so many! I felt guilty every time we would go into a leasing office and they would ask, "Are you married?"

In my mind I would answer, "No, just shacking up together." Why is this such an issue for me? I haven't been to church since before I left for college. Still, there is something about it that doesn't feel right. Maybe it's because I see it as another "point of no return" in my mind.

I will admit: these other complexes make my apartment look like a dump. This one place has a pretty lake and fountain on the property. The apartment model was pretty and clean. The floor plan the property manager showed us is twice as big as my current place. I slip into my own little world, pondering my issues of "officially living together."

Suddenly, I am jarred back to reality by hearing Andres say, "So the two-bedroom on the first floor will be available in two months? Perfect. We'll take it!"

WAIT! WHAT!! No! I didn't say yes to this thing. The plan for the day was to just look. I mean, moving in general is something you plan out and think about....let alone moving in together. The nervous pit in my stomach started inching its way into my throat. I struggle to put a smile on my face, let alone show any excitement about the turn my life just took.

Leaving the leasing office, he grabs my hand and says, "Come on! Let's go walk by our new place!"

I am still in shock. I'm on a fast-moving train headed to an unwanted destination. I can't find the courage to jump off.

Andres senses my hesitation. "Hey, what's wrong? Why are you being so weird? This place is so nice! I can move out of my mom's house. You will be closer to work. We will be close to the school. It is perfect!"

Protecting my heart, I offer up only part of my feelings. "I don't know.

This just seems like a big decision; a big move. And it's happening so suddenly. I thought we were just going to look today."

His mood shifts to anger immediately as he spews the excuses he gave before. "What do you mean, 'suddenly?' Your lease is coming due. The place we are in now is a hellhole. It is far from your work and the Capoeira School. This place isn't going to cost much more, and I will help pay the bills. So, what is your issue? I can't believe how ungrateful you are. This is the perfect place for us, and you are too busy worrying about what your parents might think. You are a grown adult. YOU DON'T NEED THEIR PERMISSION!"

His words cut me to the core.

What is wrong with me? Why can't I just 'go with the flow' and enjoy the ride? Am I letting my parents influence me that much? I really miss them, and I know this decision will drive a deeper wedge between us. In reality, it isn't just them; I am not sure if I want to move in with Andres. I don't like these anger outbursts. They scare me....but if I didn't care so much about what others thought, and was able to just trust Andres more, he wouldn't have the anger outbursts.

After quietly pondering what he said and completely ignoring the root concern, I confess, "I'm sorry for ruining the excitement. This place is much better than my current apartment. And my parents: well, they will just have to deal with it."

Chapter 8
A Costly Move

It is official: I hate moving! This is such a pain in the butt. After a long day at work, I need to find boxes and pack everything up...I just did this six months ago. And I find it interesting: whenever I ask Andres to help, he is too tired. Or he says, "This is your apartment."

The other part of preparing to move that sucks is I still haven't told my parents. They are going to be crushed. I feel like every time I talk with them, I manage to disappoint them. I just want them to be proud of me. Maybe I am as screwed up as Andres says I am.

Taking a break from packing, I decide to call my mom. "Hi, Mom. How are you?"

"Hello, Sweetie. It is so good to hear from you. How are things going?"

Not knowing how to break the news, I just blurted out, "I'm good. Andres and I are moving."

I hear the verbal punch land on her heart and knock the wind out of her. "Um, where are you moving?"

"Actually, we will be moving closer to you guys." Not that it really mattered because we very rarely saw them anyways. "We found a place kind of by Tinker Park. It's a newly renovated, two-bedroom apartment. The complex has a small lake with a fountain in it. It won't cost much more than what I am paying now." I rambled on, trying to convince myself just as much as I was trying to convince her.

I continue babbling because I don't want to give her an opportunity to ask any questions; specifically the question about us living together. I really don't want to answer it.

"That sounds nice," she politely responded. "When do you move?"

"Next weekend."

I don't know what's more devastating: the fact I am moving in with Andres or that I have pushed my parents so far away, I'm afraid and ashamed to share my life decisions with them. They have always been there for me. Despite the fact our relationship hasn't been perfect, their love for me always covered any imperfections.

"Thank you for letting us know. We love you so dearly. We just want what is best for you," she said with a palpable pain.

Another wave of guilt washes over me as it hits; she would have to be the one to tell my dad. It's always been easier to talk to my mom and then let her tell him. I feel bad knowing how much pain that three-minute conversation will cause them.

Then I hear Andres' voice in my head telling me, "You're a grown woman. You don't need their permission or approval. You can do what you want."

Alone with my thoughts, boxes, and packing tape, I continue to pack up my small apartment. I keep going back to something I said to my mom. "It won't cost me much more than I am paying now." The reality is, this move is going to cost me everything.

My phone rang with my mom's ringtone. "Hi, Momma."

"Hi, Sweetie."

"It is good to hear your voice. How are you?" I said, afraid to ask. I can only imagine how she is doing with the news I broke to her last night.

"Your dad and I were talking, and we would like to buy you a couch for your new place."

I was shocked. "Really?"

"Yes. Let's set a time for you and me to go down to The Design Center and look at couches. With the way you describe your new place, that futon you have won't be big enough for your new living room."

I am blown away by my parent's generosity. Although it is exciting to think about having a new couch, I'm more excited about having some special time with my mom. And she is a talented interior designer, so I know she will help me select something beautiful.

"I am pretty sure I can take off from work early next Tuesday and meet you down there. Does that work?"

"That works, Sweetie."

"Ok. Wow. Thank you again. Please tell Dad thank you, and give him a big hug and kiss for me as well. I'll confirm once I am sure I can get the time off work."

I am so excited. I hope Andres sees the kindness and generosity of my parents, and realizes that they aren't the "bad guys" he paints them out to be. I can't wait to tell him tonight!

"Hey, Honey!" I greet Andres at the door with a big hug and a kiss; brimming with excitement about the news I have for him.

"Why are you in such a good mood?" he questioned.

"I have some EXCITING news!"

"Oh, really? What's that?"

"My mom is going to take me to The Design Center to pick out a new couch for our new place!"

"So, she is going to take YOU to pick it out? Am I not invited?" he snapped.

Ouch. That verbal punch hit me right in the gut.

"Um, I don't think she was intentionally excluding you. My parents are offering to buy us a couch; and well, my mom and I haven't spent much time together recently...and The Design Center is only open during the week, and you have to work...and I just know growing up, my dad never really liked shopping, so my mom was asking me to go." I tried throwing out many different reasons other than the conclusion he'd already settled on.

"Fine. Whatever. You go pick out YOUR couch with YOUR mom. Don't you see? This is just another way your parents are excluding me and trying to cut me out of your life?"

WHAT?!?!? I thought. *That is the stupidest thing I have ever heard. I see this as a peace offering. Nevertheless, whatever they do, he turns it against them. I will just have to convince him this time with my mom is not a slight towards him. I'm really looking forward to time with my mom. I am not going to let him ruin it.*

I love driving into the city. I'm so glad I was able to get off work to go shopping with my mom. The Design Center is such a special place with so much creativity and beautiful home furnishings. As I pull up, I see my mom waiting for me under the iconic statue in front of this magical place.

"Hi, Momma!" I greet her with excitement.

I hear the love in her voice as she responds, "Hello, Sweetie!" and approaches me with open arms to give me the best mom hug I've had in a very long time. "Are you ready to go look?"

We head inside and start going from showroom to showroom. We found everything from traditional brown leather sectionals to some modern, asymmetrical black and white striped loveseats with a splash of color. With every moment that passed, the tension I had been feeling dissipated. It's so good to be with my mom again.

After a couple hours of shopping, we found the perfect couch. It is a deep chocolate color with brightly colored throw pillows. It will look perfect in the new apartment. Even on clearance, it is still more than I had ever imagined spending on a couch. Mom gives me a big smile and says, "Your dad and I want to treat you to something special. If you love it, it is yours."

"YES! I am so excited to tell Andres about this. You two are the best! Thank you, Momma!"

"Great. We will have it delivered to your new place on the Saturday you move in. We love you, Lisa."

I head home, excited to share the news with Andres. We are going to have a real couch in our new place, not the futon that manages to keep sliding down whenever you sit on it.

"Did you have fun with your mom?"

"Yes, we did. It was really good to spend time with her," I shared. "And, I have some great news! We found the coolest couch ever!" I said showing him the picture of it on my phone.

"Poo brown? That's kind of ugly. How much did it cost?"

Ugly? I thought it was really pretty and it would fit with the rustic pine coffee table we picked out. For the price, well, I am kind of embarrassed to admit how much. Granted, it is a lot of money from our perspective; however, if my parents want to spend it on us, who am I to say no. I don't want to tell Andres because he will make a big deal about it and turn it into an issue instead of a nice gift.

"Well, it was on clearance, and my mom got her designer discount, so it wasn't that much," answering as vaguely as I could.

"But how much was it?"

"What does it matter? It's a gift. It was the couch I liked and picked out."

"Yea, but how much? We should have just gone to Dave's Furniture World and bought our own couch. Then they wouldn't have anything to hold over our heads."

WHAT? It is a gift. From my parents. Why did he have to turn this great time I had with my mom and this generous gift from my parents into an issue? Every time my parents try to reach out, he seems to create a bigger rift.

Moving day is finally here. It feels like just yesterday we were hauling all of these boxes up three flights of stairs into this little apartment; now we are hauling them back down.

I have to admit I am warming up to the new place. The discontented feelings I had about living together have been shoved deep down and silenced. As Andres pointed out, it does seem like everyone is doing it these days.

The move went much better than planned. Even though I had prepared myself for Andres to be irritated, he held it together. We found a few friends to help us and got everything moved in by 2:00 p.m. I am feeling much better about this relationship. Maybe it is really becoming the "happily ever after" I knew it could be!

Chapter 9
Anniversary Surprise

"Hey, Babe, do you know what's happening in two weeks?" Andres asked.

"Um…" buying time, searching the deep crevices of my brain, "no, I don't."

"Really? You don't know?" he said in an agitated tone.

"Really, I don't know," I confirmed.

"It is the one-year anniversary of our first date," he boasted.

Oh, man. I don't even remember the date when we first went out. I hold my breath, waiting for him to get angry with me, but he doesn't. That's strange.

"Take Wednesday and Thursday, the 12th and 13th, off from work. I have a special surprise planned for you," he announced with a smirk on his face.

Well, ok. That sounds like fun. I'm still surprised he didn't get mad at me for not remembering our anniversary. Regardless, I'll take this reaction any day. "I'll work on getting it off. What else do I need to know?"

"Plan on wearing something nice, like that pretty red dress. I am going to take you on an adventure."

The excitement for our big date grew over the next two weeks. Even though I try to guess where he is going to take me, he won't budge on telling me anything. It is fun joking around with him. This is the kind of relationship I was hoping to build. I am so happy!

Wednesday the 12th finally came. I wake up early, like a kid on Christmas morning! I poke Andres awake. "Happy Anniversary! What are we doing today? Will you tell me now?"

"Stop it. Why did you wake me up so early?" he snapped.

What is his problem? I didn't expect that reaction. Today is supposed to be a happy day. I slip out of bed and go into the kitchen to get a cup of coffee to start my morning.

About an hour later, I hear him holler from the bedroom, "Hey, Lisa, where are you? Get back here in bed."

That is probably the least romantic way to try and seduce your partner into some anniversary fun. But I know if I don't comply, it is likely to set all of the plans for today on a major course of destruction. When I get back to the bedroom, even though he was more awake, he was still very grumpy.

Throughout the morning, he is agitated and distant. I am getting so frustrated and about ready to call off dinner. He is just being rude and absolutely no fun. I am sick of it. I'm also upset I actually wasted my vacation days on this.

The plan is for us to be all dressed up and leave at 4:30 p.m. By the time I start to get ready, Andres is on my last nerve, so I decide to get ready in the second bathroom. The whole time I'm murmuring to myself, "He better clean up his act, or this is going to be the anniversary of the end as well."

"Are you ready to go?" he called, standing at the front door.

"Almost. I just need to grab my purse."

As soon as he sees me walking down the hallway, his eyes get big and his jaw drops open. "Wow, you look beautiful."

There is a sweet softness to his voice I haven't heard all day. His kind words and the fact he looks very handsome melts my heart; and makes up for the jerk he's been all day. After a sweet kiss, we head out together on our anniversary adventure.

"Where are we going?" I inquired.

"You will have to wait...just a little longer," he responded, a little gleam in his eye.

The conversation was pretty minimal. Andres wasn't irritated so much anymore; now just kind of distant. At least he is being nice; so I allowed myself to get caught up in the anticipation of the surprise he has planned for us. He exits off the highway and heads towards the high-end area of downtown.

"We are a little early for our reservation, so let's just walk around for a little bit," he says as he helps me out of the car.

Downtown. Fancy clothes. Reservations. I have to admit; I feel pretty, loved, and special right now!

The excitement and energy of downtown radiates off the streets as we walk hand-in-hand. Our jaunt ends at the Downtown Hilton. I am delighted, twitterpated, and confused...and STILL cannot figure out what he has planned.

We walk through the lobby and down towards the ballrooms. A frantic woman greets us. "I think something life-changing is going to happen in the ballroom right over there! Hurry over to see what's going on!"

Andres boldly follows this woman's suggestion. Now I am really confused. As we enter, some of the puzzle pieces start to fall in place. We check in with the person at the front table and are handed a packet of information. Once we find our seats, Andres gives me a section of the packet.

The top reads, "You are Scarlet. Your best friend, Jane Waterson, who also happens to be 'America's Movie Sweetheart,' was murdered and we are all here to help solve her murder mystery. BEWARE! You are in GRAVE danger. The killer believes you are onto them and now has their sights on you!"

"What is this? I am confused," I inquire. "Am I a target in a murder mystery? Is that why you asked me to wear my red dress?"

"No, I asked you to wear your red dress because you look hot in it," he flirted. "I thought it would be fun for us to do a murder mystery dinner party for our anniversary."

Wow! Just wow! This is cool, and so thoughtful. Now I feel bad for being so angry with him about being a jerk. He was planning all of this for our anniversary. At the beginning, I didn't even remember it was our anniversary. Andres really IS a good guy. For the moment, all the struggles melt away; the fairytale relationship I have always imagined is coming to life!

As the murder mystery starts to unfold, I quickly realize I'm cast as one of the main characters. Interestingly enough, Andres is not overly involved in the storyline. Poor Scarlet is really in need of a Prince Charming to come in and save her from the murderer. As a collective group, we are close to narrowing it down to the one who did it.

The plot takes a strange turn. Scarlet is called out to sit on a chair in the middle of the room for a "deep interrogation." As soon as I sit down, a bright spotlight flips on, almost blinding me. Now I am really feeling awkward. With that, Andres walks into the spotlight, gets down on one knee, pulls a small box out of his pocket, and asks me to marry him.

I am in shock. I had absolutely no idea this was my anniversary surprise. We had talked about marriage a few times, but I didn't know he was this serious about it. As everyone continues to cheer for us, a huge pit begins to form in my stomach. After all of this planning, how can I say "no"? My mind is reeling; my heart is beating out of my chest. All eyes are on me.

The chatter going on in my mind was interrupted by Andres, "Well…"

"YES!" I said. Partially because that's how the conversation is supposed to go; partially because I don't want to find out what he would do if I said anything else.

Upon my answer, the theatre erupts with applause. Flash bulbs are going off. Despite all of the excitement, I think I am the only person in the room who isn't happy.

The feelings of excitement and dread are battling for my mind. The pit in my stomach is growing in size. I try to put a smile on my face, hoping that ignoring the conflict on the inside of me would cause it to resolve itself.

Irritated, Andres prodded, "What's wrong with you? Why aren't you happy?"

"I am happy. It's just a big step, and I really had no clue that you were going to propose to me. I mean, you did an AMAZING job of it...truly a night I will never forget. But..." I can't bring myself to admit the pain the conflict between Andres and my parents causes me. Having a contentious relationship between my husband and my parents is not a part of the happily-ever-after plan.

There is so much going on in my head right now. Instead of trying to sort it all out, I'll just enjoy the rest of the evening and deal with all of that later. The reality is, no relationship is perfect; and just look at all Andres went through to make this proposal so special.

He really does love me! Lisa, quit being so selfish!

After dinner, Andres had booked a room on the top floor at the Hilton. I walk in and see a dozen red roses, champagne, and chocolate-covered strawberries. I feel like a princess....until the thought of telling my parents creeps into my head. I try to thwart it with a gaze at the roses or a sip of champagne, which helps, but only for a moment.

It feels exciting waking up with my fiancé next to me in the bed.

"I want to thank you again for making last night so special. My ring is absolutely stunning!" I brag as I ogle the new rock on my finger.

"I'm glad you like it. I wanted to make sure it's big enough so everyone knows you are taken."

"Did you ask my dad for my hand in marriage? Do they know?"

"No. Why would I ask them? You're a grown adult. We don't need their permission, so why did I need to ask them? You said in the conversation we had a few weeks ago it wasn't important for me to ask your dad."

What I remember of the conversation is that he didn't want to talk to my parents by himself. Either way, I need to tell my parents we are engaged to be married. All I know is this isn't going to be a good conversation. I can already sense the separation that has been growing between us and them is increasing.

"Hi, Mom," I greeted her when she picked up the other end of the call.

I know my voice is timid and nervous. I really hope Andres isn't within earshot. If I don't "stand firm and stand up for our relationship," he'll get angry with me. At the same time, I fear if I don't show my parents some level of respect, I could lose them. And here I am, stuck in the middle. This is supposed to be one of the best times of my life. And yet, I still have that pit in my stomach, tears ready to drop any second, and absolutely no peace in my spirit.

"Good morning, Sweetie. Is everything ok?"

"Yes, everything is great," I squeaked out in an unconvincing voice. "I have some exciting news to tell you...Andres proposed to me last night. We are engaged!" I tried adding some excitement in my voice, hoping she would join me by at least faking it.

Instead...silence.

"Engaged?" I can tell from that single word she is crushed.

"Yes. He did an amazing job planning the proposal. He took me down to a murder mystery dinner and they worked the proposal in as part of the murder plot."

I was trying to make a case for him, knowing the fact he didn't ask them, or even talk to them about his plans to marry me was a slap in the face. A decision that would create one more obstacle to overcome in order to be the "one big happy family" I had dreamed of.

"I don't know what to say."

"Mom, I hoped you would say congratulations, and give us your blessing."

"I can't do that right now."

The hurt and pain in both of our hearts was palpable. I just want to be a grown-up, moving forward in building my life with the love and support of my parents. My mom and dad want me to move into adulthood and build a successful life as well; except they saw the relationship I was in was headed towards destruction.

"Ok. Well, I still love you," I said.

"I love you, too."

It doesn't make sense. If my mom loves me, why can't she be happy for me? I know Andres is a totally different person around them than he is around me. But if my parents love me, couldn't they just TRY a little harder to see what I see?

Maybe this relationship isn't the right thing. Maybe I should just end it. The question is, though, how would I ever find a new relationship? And we have so much invested together now: a year of our lives, a new lease on this apartment, and now an engagement that so many people witnessed. I can't back out now. It would just look bad.

My thoughts of hopelessness and desperation were momentarily broken.

"Hey, Lisa, I got some wedding magazines to cheer you up. We can start focusing on planning our perfect wedding. It is going to be beautiful!"

Chapter 10
Wedding Planning

The process of planning our wedding is gut wrenching.

From my understanding, in most weddings, the bride does the majority of the planning with her bridesmaids. Not that the groom doesn't care about the wedding, but he lets his fiancé "do her thing." That is not the case for us. It is Andres' wedding, and there are certain things that he wants...well, a lot of things actually.

"We should go look at the Montview Castle as a venue for the wedding. It looks really cool, and we can do the ceremony and the reception at the same place," Andres said.

"Ok, sure. That sounds good," I numbly respond.

"And since the venue only rents out in three-hour blocks, we should do a buffet because it will be a cheaper and quicker way to feed people. Also, I want a four-piece string quartet to play as guests arrive and during the service; and a DJ for dancing at the reception."

My head is spinning. I am still just trying to digest the idea of getting married, and he has his list of demands for his wedding. Question is: who is going to pay for all of his wants? I haven't even spoken to my mom since the phone call that shattered her heart...and I really don't want to talk to my dad. Not that he would get mad or yell at me; it's just he has this tone in his voice, and a look of disappointment that would crush me.

My dad is an amazing provider for our family. My parents want nothing less than the best for me. However, my dad has always been very opinionated. If you line up with his beliefs, all is well. When you don't see life the same way he does, it becomes uncomfortable, quickly. As his little girl, one who has reaped the benefits of his hard work and generosity, I feel an obligation to please him. Not to mention I hate any feeling of conflict or disapproval.

"Hey, Lisa, snap out of it. What is your issue? Why are you letting your parents ruin our happiness and joy? Is this what I have to look forward to for the rest of my life?" Andres said as his anger begins to rise. "Are you going to allow your parents to hold the strings to all of the decisions that are ours to make? Really? Because if that's how it's going to be, we are not going to have a good life."

Hearing his reaction, coupled with my already fragile state, I begin to beat myself up.

What is wrong with me? If I can't stand up for my relationship as a fiancé, what kind of wife will I be? Am I being a rebellious and rude daughter? Or am I just growing up and making my own decisions? They just happen to be ones my parents don't like. I'm so confused...and I can't seem to make anyone around me happy. I just want to keep the peace. Andres hates my parents, and my parents hate Andres...and I am stuck in the middle. I wish they would just stop and be nice to each other so I don't need to choose a side.

The thought of doing what I wanted never crossed my mind.

"I can't take this anymore. Planning our wedding should be fun, and this...this is crap. Once you realize you are a grown adult and you don't need to do everything your parents want you to do, then OUR relationship will be back on track. Don't you see, the only time we start fighting is when your parents are involved?" he scolded, then grabbed his jacket and headed for the door.

"Wait, don't leave. Let's start planning again. I promise I won't let my parents influence me anymore." I am so torn. Honestly, it would be so much easier if he just left. However, the thought of that rejection and failure is just too much.

The door slammed. It's torment not knowing when or if he is coming back.

His leaving really shook me up. It's already hard enough that I feel I have to choose between my parents and Andres. It's like I can never do enough to please Andres. It has to be his way or no way. I am grateful I can talk to his mom. She is always supportive in helping me process my feelings.

"Hello, this is Linda."

"Hi, Linda, it's Lisa."

"Why, hello, Lisa. How are the wedding plans coming along? Are you getting excited?"

"No, Andres and I…" no longer able to hold in the tears, I begin to sob. "Andres and I had a fight. He told me that I need to basically not care at all about what my parents want or our relationship will end. I don't want to lose him, but I love my parents."

"Oh, Lisa, it is going to be ok. Andres loves you. He isn't going to leave you. He just doesn't always know the best way to communicate. Have you two tried talking about it?"

"Yes, but it always ends with him accusing me of siding with my parents and caving into what they want, and not fighting for what is best for our relationship. Having my parents in my life is important to me. Andres doesn't seem to understand that."

"Have you two thought about getting counseling?"

"What do you mean by counseling?"

"Many couples get pre-marriage counseling. They go and talk with someone who helps them learn how to communicate better and discuss issues that come up in marriage. They give you tools to handle them when they do. Counseling can help make a bad relationship good, and a good relationship great."

"Really? The only thing close to that I have ever heard of is a marriage retreat I remember my parents going to when I was in middle school. I do remember them being more in love with each other when they got back."

"Counseling is kind of like that. A lot of people go. In fact, counseling was one of the best things I ever did for myself. I also believe that Andres' dad and I would have never gotten divorced if we went to counseling together. I can give you Brenda's number. She is the woman I went to. Andres has heard me talk about her."

"Sure. I'm willing to give it a try. Right now, I am willing to try anything to make this relationship feel better."

"I am confident Brenda can help you two. I just wouldn't approach him about it when he is angry. You know how he doesn't accept new suggestions very well when he is in that state of mind. It might be best if I suggest it to him. If you suggest counseling, it might make him afraid things are really wrong and you are going to leave."

"Thank you for helping us. Oh wait, I hear Andres coming back in. I better go."

I hope he didn't hear me say goodbye to his mother. Even though she is one of our biggest advocates, sometimes he gets perturbed when I talk with her. Other times it is no big deal. The problem is I don't know when he will get annoyed and when he will be fine with it.

"Who were you talking to?" Andres commanded as he walked in.

By the tone of his voice, I sensed my talking on the phone could lead to a continuation of our fight.

"I was talking with your mom," I confessed. "This whole situation has been hard and stressful for me. I just needed someone to talk to."

"Well, if getting married to me is so 'hard and stressful', let me make it easy for you and we will just call it all off. I know that will make your parents happy...which will make you happy," he threatened.

Call it off? What is he talking about? I am trying to share my feelings with him. What would it look like if this relationship ends? After all I have done to stand up for him. Also, if we break off this engagement, I might be single for the rest of my life.

I don't get it. He says he loves me; and all he did for our engagement; and now he is talking about ending it. I know I can get this relationship back on track; I just need a little more time and to try a little harder.

"No, that is not what I am saying. I don't want to call it off; I just don't want to keep fighting about everything. I want the tension and stress to stop. I just want us all to be happy. That's what I was talking to your mom about."

"Well, what if the fighting doesn't stop? I have a feeling if the fighting doesn't stop, eventually you will leave me and choose your parents. How do you think that makes me feel?"

WHAT? I am so confused. First of all, in my mind, marriage is forever. Divorce is not an option. My parents are not bad, mean people. I don't understand why Andres can't and won't just let the past go and TRY to build a relationship with them. Although my parents have shown their disapproval of him in the past, they are willing to bury the hatchet and build a relationship with their soon to be son-in-law. Andres seems to keep pulling that hatchet out of the ground and swinging it...hitting and hurting anyone who is close.

Taking a deep breath, I answer. "I am sure that feeling isn't good, but I am not going to leave you."

As I said that, I remember the conversations we had about the multiple father figures in his life who had left him. Just thinking about the rejection he must have felt as a young boy hits me at my core. That brings a better understanding of the root of his controlling behavior. I know if I just love him enough and prove I will never leave him, I can heal all of that past hurt and give him the love he desires.

"I don't know. We'll see about that," he responded, almost as a challenge.

That night as we climb into bed, he turns his back to me, shrugging off any form of comfort or reassurance. Reacting to this rejection, I roll over and cling to the edge of the mattress on my side of the bed.

I am just as terrified of being left and rejected as he is. I don't want to disappoint anyone, especially my fiancé. If I can't be the woman he wants me to be, I am afraid he will leave. Since I seem to be failing at pleasing him, it makes me wonder if I am marriage material. I don't want to be alone for the rest of my life. My pillow is becoming wet as tears of loneliness and desperation silently stream from my eyes.

As we wake up the next morning, things are better; but there is still some residue from last night. Will this ever get easier? At least we have training tonight after work. That always helps both of us feel better.

The next few days were on a pretty even keel, probably because there was no wedding talk.

Andres approaches me as I cook dinner. "My mom and I were talking, and she suggested we look into getting some pre-marriage counseling. Maybe it could help us get through this wedding. What do you think?"

"Well, I've never been to counseling before, but I think it sounds like a great idea."

"My mom suggested we give Brenda a try. She is over by my mom's house, but at least we know she is good."

That was easier than I expected. I guess Linda spoke to him at a good time. "Sure. Do you have Brenda's number or should I get it from your mom?"

"If you can get her number and set up our appointment, that would be great. I am just so busy."

"Yes. I can do that." *I am busy, too. However, getting help means so much to me, I'll make time.* I take a deep breath. It feels like there may be some relief in sight!

Chapter 11
Counseling

When I contacted Brenda, she said she wants to meet with us individually at first. Then she'll have us come in together. I hope her rules won't upset Andres to the point of changing his mind about going. I'm excited and nervous about this counseling thing. I thought only crazy people go to counseling. I have to admit: this relationship sometimes makes me feel crazy. It's like I'm always doing something wrong and I can never do enough...ever!

"I'm headed off to see Brenda," I called out from the front room early Saturday morning.

"Ok. Get in here and give me a kiss," he demanded while still lying in bed.

It was a good thing he couldn't see me roll my eyes.

Why don't you get your lazy butt out of bed and come say good-bye to me... and you better not pull me back into bed or I'll be late.

As I head back to the bedroom, that thought translated to, "Hold on, I'm coming. Just a quick kiss, nothing else. I don't want to be late for my appointment."

I pull up to Brenda's house. An older woman with a kind demeanor and softness about her greets me and invites me into her home office just inside the front door. The furniture is dated and the walls are covered with a dark wood paneling. I can feel my heart rate increase as I sit down. I am so nervous to share about myself; I don't want to hear from one more person that I am doing everything wrong which is messing up my life. I am already trying to please Andres, my parents, and Linda; I don't want to add one more person to the list of people I need to appease.

As I start filling out the intake paperwork, waves of anxiety begin to crash over me. I feel my breathing getting shallow. My now-clammy hands begin to shake. I am paranoid about her finding that something is really wrong with me...like I can't navigate and create the beautiful harmonious life everyone else is living. Or my inability to make everyone around me happy.

Her sweet, soothing voice interrupts my thoughts. "Lisa, why are your hands shaking? Take a deep breath. You are ok."

There is something about her voice and demeanor that put me at ease. I can tell, even though I am paying her to listen, she genuinely cares about me; no ulterior motives.

As the words, "You are ok" reverberate in my head, I break down in tears. *No, I'm NOT ok. I am a mess,* the thoughts rage in my head. *I am trying to live the dream, which is more of a nightmare. I feel all alone. I am just not enough to be everything that each person in my life expects me to be.*

Before my feelings make it out of my mouth, I shove them down into the depths of my heart. I don't know her well enough to know what I should share and what I should keep to myself. I can't let her see the true relationship I am experiencing. If I am honest, I am embarrassed by it. However, the last thing I want is for this stranger to see I really am an utter failure at life.

After I complete the paperwork, she asks, "So, tell me what happened inside when I told you, 'You are ok'?"

Through a second wave of tears, I try explaining I feel like I'm never enough. It's like I'm in a tug-of-war between being what Andres wants me to be and what my parents want me to be. The expectations of everyone around me are just more than I can live up to.

"Well, what about just being you? You are OK just as you are. You don't need to change into what others want you to be."

We talked a little longer and she gave me homework. I am supposed to come up with a list of ten things I like to do. When she first gave it to me, it seemed pretty simple. As I start thinking about it on the drive home, it's sad how hard it is for me. Despite the challenging assignment, I feel more hopeful than I have in a while.

Things at Capoeira are going really well. Both Andres and I are not only improving in our skills, we have also caught the attention of Mestre Mota. He is generally friendly to all of the students that come in, but he has noticed we both are interested in taking our training to a new level. There is a small group of students around our age that have this same desire. Randy has a few more years of training under his belt than we do, and is always happy to help us learn. Mestre Mota lets us keep the jogo (game) going after the class is done. He will even come out and play with us sometimes.

After class, Randy calls us over to the back corner of the office. "Mestre Mota wants to know if you two would like to stay after for dinner tonight."

"Yes! That would be great!" Andres replied immediately for both of us.

"Cool. He has cooked up some traditional Brazilian food to share with a small group of us. Go get changed and just kind of hang out. Don't say anything to anyone. Not everyone is invited."

Wow! What a special opportunity. Our extra effort here at the school is paying off in ways I never imagined.

As the last students leave, Randy locks the front door and leads us into the back room. Mestre Mota is there with the table informally set, and a large pot of a reddish colored stew.

"Come, sit down. I am sure you are hungry after practice," Mestre Mota said. "I have made Moqueca, a Brazilian fish stew, for dinner."

The smell of chili spices and coconut milk make my mouth water as he dishes up our plates. The first bite was amazing! This meal tastes as good as it smells! As we enjoy the delicious cuisine, Mestre Mota starts teaching us about Brazilian culture.

"One of the biggest celebrations of the year is carnival. It happens in February, and is an outrageous street party that takes over the city. It is the last big celebration before the forty days of lent. Do you know about lent?"

"Yes. Lent is the forty days before Easter. It is celebrated in the Catholic Church. It is when you give something up as a way to begin preparing for the celebration of the death and resurrection of Jesus," I answered.

As I responded, Andres shot me a look that could have killed—along with a swift kick under the table. I returned it with a confused glance, not understanding why my response wasn't acceptable to him.

"You are correct," Mestre Mota responded. "There is a lot of Catholic influence in Brazil. It was the religion brought over by the Portuguese when they colonized it in the 1500s. There is another religion in Brazil called Candomblé. It is based on African beliefs that were brought over with the slaves. When forced to accept Catholicism, these people used the images of Catholic saints to represent their gods."

By the end of dinner, my love of Brazil was completely rekindled. Learning more about the roots and culture of Brazil made studying Capoeira even more exciting. The school is really beginning to feel like a second home.

After taking a few weeks off from wedding planning, we decide to try again. We picked up right where we left off...with the plans and the fighting. In following tradition, my parents are planning on paying for the wedding. With that, they understandably want some say in the plans. Andres keeps saying that it is OUR WEDDING and OUR SPECIAL DAY, so we should be able to decide how things go. To be honest, at this point, I am agreeable to just about anything: just get this stupid day over.

"Did you talk to your mom about getting the deposit sent over to Montview Castle to secure the space?"

"I did, and she is concerned about having it in the middle of the week. Most people get married on a Saturday."

"I don't care what most people do for their wedding. I want to get married on the anniversary of our first date and our engagement. And it doesn't matter what priests do about weddings because we are NOT getting married in the church," he exploded.

Cowering back from the sting of his words, I try reasoning. "I totally understand about not getting married in the church, but I agree with her that having it in the middle of the week will make it difficult for people flying in."

"That is the stupidest thing I have ever heard. If people want to celebrate our wedding, they will be here. If it's too difficult, they won't. I mean, isn't it so cool to have the wedding on the anniversary of our first date and our engagement?"

"Yea, that would be cool," I agree verbally. However, in my head I thought, *You know what would be even more cool? You being able to compromise on at least SOMETHING with this stupid wedding!*

"Ok, so we have the date, the venue, and the colors selected. Now we need to figure out the menu. Did you set up appointments for us to talk to the caterers yet?" he ordered.

"No, not yet. I was thinking it would be nice to see if my mom wanted to join us for the meeting and tasting with the caterer. Are you ok with that?" I asked.

"Sure, I guess that is fine. As long as she realizes I want Beef Wellington at the wedding, and she can't talk me out of that...or the fact we want a buffet, and not a sit-down dinner."

Why is he acting this way? I mean, really? I will admit that at first, my parents really didn't like him. I also understand they went away for a two-week vacation and came back to this guy always hanging around their daughter. However, they are trying...really trying, and he is being a jerk.

I never really had an idea of my ideal wedding, but I know this isn't it! I feel stuck. I want to make it all stop. How can I? I have already said yes to this man. Wearing my engagement ring and making these plans makes me feel I'm past the point of being able to back out.

Chapter 12
Making Headway

pick up my ringing phone. "Hello?"

"Hello, Lisa! How are you doing today?" It was Linda. I am so blessed to have such a loving and caring mother-in-law to be.

"Actually, I am doing pretty good today. We had our first couple's session with Brenda yesterday. I think it went really well."

"That is good. What types of things have you been learning with Brenda? Don't worry; I don't expect you to share the details."

"I have been learning that one of the main reasons I've really lost myself is I try to make everyone around me happy. I have a tendency to be a people pleaser. In doing that, I chameleon myself into being what others want. One of the things I have realized is I don't even really know me."

"I get it. I was in that place, too. Keep working on finding the real you. You are a special and beautiful woman."

"But what if Andres doesn't like the real me? What if I don't like the real me?"

"Well, honey, when you love someone, you accept them the way they are: the good and the not so good. It isn't about changing to make them stay with you. When someone really loves you, they appreciate your good qualities and focus on those. They will support you in working on the 'not-so-good' qualities you choose to work on."

That sounds wonderful. I am excited to work on that type of relationship. I want to be in a marriage where I don't have to be perfect; one where I am appreciated for who I am, just as I am.

Her words remind me of what Brenda said in one of our sessions. "Sometimes loving yourself means choosing to leave the relationship."

Leaving sounds more painful than anything.

My thoughts are interrupted by Linda's next question. "So, what's your homework from Brenda? I know she gives homework almost every session."

"Oh, I am really excited about our homework!" I exclaimed. "Sometime this week, we are supposed to write each other a note to tell the other person three things we appreciate about them, and one thing we specifically want to work on together. She said it doesn't have to be long or elaborate; the effort alone is enough to fill up your partner's love tank. Pointing out one thing we are committed to working on together shows our commitment to make the relationship stronger. Just the thought of receiving a note like that makes my heart really happy."

"That's a good homework assignment. You are right; receiving a note like that brings so much love and a sense of commitment."

"I think I am going to write mine out and then leave it on the windshield of his car while he is at work. I want to make it a surprise for him."

"That's so thoughtful. Lisa, I'm really proud of you for jumping into counseling with both feet. It isn't always easy. However, if you work through the process, it leads to a much healthier and happier life!"

"Thank you for your help and encouragement. I really appreciate it!"

I'm in a happy place when I get off the phone with Linda. Andres and I are getting the help we need. Tomorrow, we are going to the big welcome home celebration and potluck at the Capoeira School. Bobby is returning from Brazil after being there for a year as part of the exchange program. He will show pictures of his trip and tell about his adventures at the party. The idea of going to live in another country, let alone Brazil, is so exciting! I can't wait to hear all about it. I'm so blessed to be a part of a school that offers so much more than just teaching a martial art. It is extra special I can share all of this with Andres.

I am excited about this week's homework. I'm glad we have Brenda's help on making our relationship better. Her insight has helped me see some of my behaviors from a different perspective.

I only have about forty-five minutes until Andres gets home from school and we will need to head down to Bobby's welcome home party. So instead of the elaborate card I was planning to do, I'm going to settle for something meaningful and simple.

Hmmm...what do I appreciate about Andres? I appreciate that he pushes me to be the best I can be. He doesn't let me slack and is always the first to point out when I can do something better. He stretches me to try new things. I am not sure if I would have ever moved out of my parents' house if he hadn't encouraged me as much as he did. Then the third thing, I'm not sure. Well, I know the thing I want us to work on is our communication. So many times, I don't feel heard. I want to learn how to share my feelings, wants, and desires with him in a way he can hear it. I guess the third thing I appreciate or admire about him is that, when he has a goal in mind, he is very focused on achieving it...no matter what it takes.

It feels good to get my card written out.

I hope he doesn't get upset with the things I wrote. I mean, our communication isn't bad; it's just that I don't always.... Lisa, stop second guessing yourself! You shared your heart. You are being honest and truthful. That's what you are learning right now in counseling; so just stop.

It's amazing what a self-pep talk can do. I add a few little hearts and such to make it special, fold it, and stick it in my purse. I plan on delivering it tomorrow during my lunch break. I'm excited thinking about making him feel special when he comes out of work to see the note on his car.

As I'm putting my pens away, I hear the front door open. *Perfect timing,* I thought.

"Welcome home, Honey," I greeted Andres.

"Hey."

"What do you need to do to get ready for Bobby's welcome home party? I already have the cake ready."

"I just walked in the door. Give me a sec."

"Ok. It's just that the party is going to start with Mestre Mota and

Bobby doing a demonstration. I really want to see that."

"I know. Let me just use the restroom and grab my things," Andres grumbled.

"Ok. I'll drive if you want."

"Yea, that would be good."

"Ok. I'll meet you out in the car," I replied, heading out the door to move things along.

We got there with a few minutes to spare. The smells were amazing. There is a fun buzz in the air. Every year Mestre Mota sends one of the students from the school over to Ouriçangas, Brazil for this experience. The small, traditional Brazilian town is about ninety-five miles north of Salvador. During his training, Bobby had shown interest in learning more about Brazilian culture. He trained really hard and put in extra work around the school. He was selected to go on this year long exchange program, helping at the schools, learning the culture, and teaching informal English classes. He also got to train in Capoeira a few times when he went into the bigger city of Alagoinhas. What a cool experience!

"Hi, Bobby! Welcome home!" I said, greeting the guest of honor with a hug.

"It is good to be back. I hear you and Andres got engaged while I was down south. Congrats!"

"Thanks. Yes, we are excited. Another Capoeira romance!" I teased. "More importantly, tell me about Ouriçangas."

"It was a life-changing experience. The people were so kind. And the food was AMAZING! One of my favorite parts was playing with the town's samba reggae drumming group. It's the sound originally created by the group Olodum. That music captures the heart of Brazil. It's all they play at carnival. Paul Simon helped to spread it on his song, 'The Obvious Child.' You'll hear a recording of me playing with the group from Ouriçangas in my presentation."

Wow! What an amazing experience. Hearing this brief snippet brings a flood of memories back from my visit there. Olodum actually played on our ship when we first docked in Salvador. I remember wanting to go back and spend more time in Brazil. I never imagined it would ever be a reality. Who knows? There may be a possibility of at least a week or two visit back to this vibrant country.

"Bobby's trip to Brazil was really cool," I commented to Andres on our drive home. "Do you have any desire to visit Ouriçangas? Even if it is just for a week or two?"

"That would be fun. I would want to study more Capoeira than he did; and I'm not so sure about the drumming group, but the rest of it sounds fun," Andres answered.

Finally, something we can agree on. This is a good sign. I'm glad we have Capoeira and the love of Brazil in common. At least there is one area of our relationship where there is a sense of peace.

"Hey, Rose, I am going to run out for lunch," I notified my co-worker. I know I have a brief window to sneak over and place my counseling assignment note on Andres' car. I feel so giddy right now. I always get butterflies in my stomach when I am doing something mischievous. Working together on building our relationship brings me so much joy. I sense my dreams coming true right before my very eyes.

As I pull into the parking lot, I see his car. I park several spots away so he doesn't notice me. I get out. The James Bond theme song is playing in my head. I picture myself in a black cat suit as I maneuver to secretly deposit the note filled with hope, love, and possibilities under the windshield wiper of his car.

As soon as it is placed, I run back to my vehicle undetected; almost peeing my pants. My playful dorkiness makes me chuckle. I can just imagine him feeling loved when he walks out to see the note on his car. The anticipation of the love I will feel when I receive the note from him brings a smile to my face. I wonder what he really appreciates about me. What about me stands out to him? This idea of going to counseling together has been really good!

While I'm cooking dinner, I anticipate Andres coming home. I feel like the Cheshire cat, all sorts of romantic scenarios are playing in my head. Maybe he will rush into the kitchen, hug and passionately kiss me, thanking me for the sweet note, and agree he is excited to work on our communication as well. Or, maybe he will come through the door with a bouquet of flowers behind his back, revealing them, saying, "These beautiful flowers are for my beautiful lady." My mind is really running away with things.

Then I hear Brenda's voice in my head saying, "Don't get carried away with unspoken expectations."

I quickly reel my thoughts back to reality. I take a deep breath and stop the Hallmark movies playing in my mind when I hear the front door unlock. To be completely fair, Andres has no idea about any of the scenarios that are part of my desires. I am too afraid to share them with him because, well, they are like Hallmark movies. They are pretty cheesy. Maybe someday when I am more comfortable, I'll be able to share my feelings.

"So, how was your day?" I asked with great anticipation.

"It was ok."

"Just ok? Did anything good happen?" I prodded.

"No, just same old same old."

"Oh. So, you didn't receive anything special?" I continue to interrogate, disappointment building.

"Are you referring to your note?"

"Um, yes. I was so excited to surprise you with it at work. I was starting to get worried it either blew away or somebody took it off your car."

"Oh, yea. No one took it. Thanks for doing that. When did you drop it off? I didn't see you stop by."

"I was sneaky! In my mind, I heard the James Bond theme song, and

I was picturing myself in a black cat suit," being vulnerable, sharing my dorky humor with him.

"What are you talking about? What do you mean a black cat suit?"

"I wasn't actually in a cat suit. It was just the scenario I was playing in my mind because I was trying to be stealthy, making it a surprise for you," I explain as his wave of judgment crashes over me.

"Oh, ok. Well, it would have been nice if you actually stopped in and said hello. And I don't know why you want us to work on our communication; I think we have pretty good communication. I guess it is something we can always get better at, but I think communication is one thing we do pretty well."

I never thought of going inside to see him. First of all, I didn't have a whole lot of time. My plan was to surprise him. Ok, mental note to self: he would rather me come in versus just leave a surprise for him. I'll keep that in mind for next time, and do things differently. The part that hurts is his rejection of my request to work on our communication. In seconds, he dismissed one of my deepest wants, needs, and desires.

The rest of the week went on as normal: work, Capoeira, and some wedding planning in small intervals so as not to spark any major fights. However, every night I went to bed without receiving my note from Andres. I became discouraged. When the feelings of being unloved and uncherished would creep in, I would remind myself of the set assignment and expectations. He has until our appointment on Saturday with Brenda to complete the assignment. So maybe he'll do it tomorrow. I continue to encourage myself by thinking back to our engagement. I know he is capable of planning great surprises...and yes, he does love me.

The sun rose on Saturday morning; still there was nothing. No note. No list of three things he appreciates about me, and nothing he wants to work on. I am crushed. I put thought and effort into his note. He even had a reminder when he received his...and he still forgot. Am I that forgettable?

"I'm going to cook some breakfast before we go to Brenda's. Would you like some?" I said in a deflated voice.

"Yea, that would be great."

I head into the kitchen, giving him time to redeem himself and write my note.

"Is breakfast almost ready?" he comes bounding into the kitchen with a hop in his step, yet empty handed.

"Yes. Here you go." I reply coldly.

"What's wrong? You seem grumpy today."

I know my M.O. is to be passive aggressive, expecting him to read my mind. This is the exact situation Brenda and I had talked about. I need to let him know my feelings and ask for what I want.

"I am hurt because I didn't get my note," I softly confessed.

"What note?"

Frustrated and unsuccessfully trying to hold back tears, I explain, "The assignment Brenda gave us to share the three things we appreciate about each other and the one thing we want to work on."

"Oh, that note," he chuckled at my attempt to share my feelings without getting emotional. "Oh, Baby, you know I appreciate you."

With the hurt turning to anger, I reply, "No, I don't. And I really don't feel appreciated now. We need to leave in five minutes, and you totally forgot."

"Well, let me get a piece of paper and write it out."

By this point, I am so irritated, I don't want the note. I don't want to have to remind my fiancé to love me and appreciate me. It is confusing because I am working on letting my desires be known versus having unspoken expectations. It's crushing when even the spoken expectations are completely forgotten and ignored.

Andres walks towards me with a ripped piece of scrap paper with a few words written on it. "I appreciate when you cook for me. I appreciate when we train together. I appreciate you for being my fiancé. I want to work on not fighting so much."

The note crushed me. I am fighting back the tears. This is almost worse than not getting one at all. Maybe it's that I had bigger expectations for this assignment. I was expecting some real thought and effort to be placed into the note. I took this assignment as a representation of our relationship. I guess I set my expectations too high. I feel so far from being loved and cherished.

Lisa, no relationship is perfect. They all require give and take. So, extend him some grace. I'm sure he realizes how much this hurt you. He is doing the best he can right now. We both have a lot going on. I am probably just overreacting anyway; it was just a stupid note.

"Why are you crying?" Andres questioned.

"I'm not crying," I lied, trying to hold the tears from dropping from my eyes.

"Yes, you are. This is really no reason to cry. It is just a note. You don't really need a note to tell you what I think about you. You know I love you. If I didn't, why would I want to marry you?" he reasoned.

"It's just…" I hesitated, not wanting to say anything to upset him before our car ride to counseling. "I had a different view of this assignment. It hurts that you didn't even remember it until I reminded you." I didn't even go into the fact the things he appreciates about me are all things I do for him, and nothing truly special about me.

"You are totally overreacting. It is just a stupid note. You know I love you. Like I said, if I didn't love you, why would I have asked you to marry me?"

Maybe he is right. It probably is just a stupid note. And I am really beginning to hate the fact that I seem to show my emotion through tears. I dry my eyes and shove the feelings of not being heard deep down inside. Going down, those feelings are like shards of glass, cutting into my tender heart. I take a deep breath, and choose to feel numb instead of the pain.

"Hello, you two!" Brenda welcomed us. "So, how did the assignment go?"

The silence is a giveaway; our story won't be used in the plot of a Hallmark movie. I take a deep breath, trying my best to stay in the place of numbness so my tears won't start to flow. Trying to be positive, I share how much fun I had writing the note for Andres and going on my reconnaissance mission to place it on his car.

She turns to Andres, "So, how was it for you to write a note to Lisa?"

"Well, I spent all week thinking about it, but I ran out of time to actually write it. I've had a busy week at school and work. I managed to give her the note this morning. So, I finished the assignment."

Is that what really happened? It didn't seem like he was thinking about it all week. Wait; that is a bold face lie. In our conversation at home, he'd totally forgotten about this whole assignment until I reminded him.

I am a ball of emotions right now: angry, hurt, betrayed, unloved, lied to. I should say something. Counseling is a place for us to learn how to have open and honest communication. On the other hand, I don't want to say anything that would make Andres angry. I have this feeling I need to protect the relationship we are building...after all, we are engaged to be married.

Chapter 13
A Change in Plans

Why does this have to be so difficult? This stupid wedding is nothing but painful. We have fought over EVERYTHING...well, except the colors of the wedding.

We have fought over the location; if it is a buffet or sit down; a band or a DJ; the number of people in the wedding party; who is on the guest list...I hate this. I've been walking on eggshells for the past six months. Although I want to be excited about planning for this day, every discussion we have turns into a battle where I feel I'm in the middle. I have given up sharing my opinion whenever it doesn't match Andres'. When our vision is not the same, he accuses me of wanting what my parents want.

I am so done with this tug-of-war. I just want this wedding to be over because once we are married, *then things will change,* I thought in my naiveté.

"We are getting close to having everything finalized for the wedding. The only thing outstanding is ordering the invitations. I think we have already agreed on the ones we want. We just need to figure out what they should say," I said with hope of this wedding being done. "Here is the traditional wording for wedding invitations," I continue.

I show Andres the wording, "Mr. & Mrs. Byrne request your company to the wedding of Lisa and Andres…"

He flipped out. "How come your parents' names are on there and my mom isn't mentioned? My mom has been more supportive for us than your parents have."

Oh. My. Gosh! I want to crawl into a hole and die. It is the typical way the wedding invitations are worded. And, yes, we have been fighting with my parents about every aspect of the wedding. The ONLY thing you haven't fought with them about is the fact they are paying for it. Without the bat of an eye, they have written checks for every deposit. And they have acquiesced to EVERYTHING "we" have wanted. I am so absolutely done. D.O.N. E….DONE!!!!

"I can't do this. I just can't do this anymore. This is supposed to be a joyous time. However, it has been nothing but heartache, pain, and fighting. I am dreading our wedding!" I exploded.

The sad part about this breakdown is I have been so focused on the wedding. I gave no thought to the idea that the wedding was just a taste of what our marriage would be.

"So, what are you saying? You don't want to get married?" Andres questioned with a hint of panic in his voice.

"No, it isn't that I don't want to go through with the wedding," I backpedaled. "I am so sick and tired of fighting and arguing and disagreeing about EVERYTHING!!!"

"You just don't like conflict. And if your parents just realize this is OUR wedding, not theirs, then everything would be better. They have been very unreasonable during this whole thing. It's all because they don't like me and they are trying to do anything possible to drive a wedge between us. Don't you see that?"

Actually, I don't see that. I realize my parents didn't like him at the beginning. After we became engaged, I saw them trying to build a relationship with him…with us. Even though Andres and I don't see it the same, I am bound and determined to make this relationship work. I gave Andres my word I would marry him. I don't want to add to the litany of rejections he has experienced in his life.

They say the definition of insanity is doing the same thing and expecting a different outcome. Well, every time we go to plan this wedding, it ends up in fighting and heartache. There has to be a different way. My frustration is interrupted by the phone.

"Hi, Lisa," Linda's familiar voice chimed.

"Hello," I said deflated and frustrated.

"You don't sound good."

"I'm not. We just got into another fight over this stupid wedding. I don't even want to do the wedding any more. I am so over it!"

"Are you and Andres ok? Is it that you don't want to get married, or you are over the wedding?"

Deep down, I'm not sure if I still want to marry him. I know I don't want the rest of my life to be a fight with my parents. I realize when you get married, it is important to create a new life with your spouse. That new life shouldn't include completely alienating your family. However, in my mind, once I said "yes" to the engagement, the wedding is a done deal. I don't want to be "that girl" that leaves the man standing at the altar. Also, so much money has already been spent on this wedding. Not to mention, we are in this stupid lease together. How would that work out? And the bigger reality looms; I don't want to be alone.

My swirling thoughts are quieted when I hear Linda's voice, "Lisa. Lisa?! Are you still there?"

"Um, yes, I am still here."

"I'm worried about you guys."

"No, we're ok," I lied. "It's just this wedding is becoming a pressure cooker and I think I just reached my boiling point. I can't take it anymore."

"You two are still planning on getting married, right?" she questioned.

"Yes, we are still planning on getting married; but I think the big wedding is off." My heart breaks as I say these words out loud.

I so badly want to have the pretty wedding with family and friends there to celebrate with us. I want my dad to walk me down the aisle and have my friends surrounding me on the dance floor. That's what the "marriage chapter" in my life is supposed to look like. Why does Andres have to be so stubborn?

"Are you going to go to the courthouse to get married?"

That thought makes my stomach turn again. That definitely isn't a part of the marriage protocol in my mind. I want the pretty pictures to show to our children: not a picture of the two of us leaning over a counter in the county courthouse, signing a marriage certificate with Mildred the

County Clerk as the only witness.

"No. I am not going to get married at the courthouse," I declared, too exhausted to explain myself.

"Well, why don't you see what it would cost to do a small, intimate wedding? ...Just us and your close friends Holly and Joe who can be your Maid of Honor and Best Man. You can invite your parents. You can still wear your dress. We can get a small cake and some pretty flowers. I can even see about finding a photographer. Despite the fact that it won't be the wedding you've been planning, it will still be a beautiful celebration."

Honestly, that scenario is a breath of fresh air. I actually feel heard. It's the first time in a long time I feel like any part of my needs or desires have been acknowledged. Even though it isn't the wedding I dreamed of, it is a compromise I can live with. I am so grateful for Linda. Maybe with her help, this wedding and marriage can actually work.

In only three months, Linda and I did it. We were able to plan and organize the mini-wedding! I feel bad my parents have been completely excluded from any of the planning. The only thing they are invited to is the actual ceremony. I'm not sure if they will even show up. I really want them there. However, I wouldn't blame them if they don't come. The way it all played out is a slap in the face to them.

Since Andres and I have been living together, our wedding day is proving to be pretty anticlimactic. Packing up our bags, grabbing our wedding garb that's hanging in the same closet; we leave our apartment together to go get married.

The car ride is quiet as we drive out of the city and make our way to the quaint bed and breakfast where we are scheduled to tie the knot. Emotionally, I am spent. Instead of being excited about saying "I do," I am running through the scenarios of how things will pan out with my parents. Will they even come? If they do, will Andres be decent to them?

I didn't ask my dad to walk me down the aisle. That makes me sad. I can't imagine how much that hurts him. No other family members of mine will be there. This wedding is going to be a disappointment. I am such a disappointment.

I'm grateful Andres is in his own world and hasn't asked any questions about me or my mood. If he asks and I tell him the truth, it will start a fight. If he asks and I tell him nothing is wrong, that will start a fight, too.

The courtyard where the ceremony is going to take place is lined with vibrant flowers. I smile when I see my parents are two of the eight people in attendance. The crowd will hit double digits if we count the photographer and the minister. This should be one of the most joyous days of my life: committing to be united to this man in marriage. Instead, I am numb. I guess it is better than being a hot mess of tears.

When the music began to play out of the CD player, I walked down the aisle by myself. The ceremony lasted all of 15 minutes. After we said "I do," we cut the cake; then everyone left. Andres and I went back to the honeymoon suite.

It is all over. I am exhausted. That isn't at all what I had imagined my wedding day to be.

Chapter 14
A Life Changing Opportunity

Now that the wedding is over, I expect life to get better. The fighting has pretty much subsided. I admit; I miss my parents. We don't see them much. I use the lie, "It's because we are busy with work, Capoeira, and life." However, I know the wedding caused extensive damage to the relationship. We've started practicing Capoeira basically every night of the week. I'm excited how we both are moving up the ranks. I was even asked to instruct a class last week.

Tonight as class is ending and people are preparing to leave, Mestre Mota stops us. "Andres, Lisa. Please join me for dinner tonight. I know you are hungry after tonight's practice."

It's always exciting when we get an opportunity like this. He cooked his signature Feijoada dish. As we were eating, the conversation took a VERY interesting turn.

"I am really pleased with the training you two have been doing lately. You both are very committed to learning the art of Capoeira as well as Brazilian culture. We usually send one young man over to Ouriçangas for the cultural exchange. Recently, the village has expressed interest in having a young couple from America come and stay. I would like to send the two of you."

WHAT?!?!?! Oh my gosh! Are you kidding me? The opportunity to go to Brazil for a year on a cultural exchange. That is AMAZING. Like, who gets to do that?

"You want to send Lisa and me over to your home village in Brazil for a year?" Andres questioned, confirming what we heard.

"Yes. I think you two would be a great representation of an American couple, and it would be a reward for all the work you have put in here over the past several months. Your lodging will be covered and you will receive a small stipend. During the day, you will be required to help out at the schools and teach an English class once a week. You will also be a part of the town's samba reggae drumming group. Along with learning the culture, the drumming group will give you the opportunity to travel to other parts of Brazil and experience it from the perspective of the locals."

"Yes, that sounds amazing. We would love to do it. Thank you for the opportunity," Andres confirmed on the spot.

"Lisa, I want you to make sure you can get the time off from your job. I don't want this experience to hinder your career," Mestre Mota advised.

"Oh, don't worry. If she needs to, she can always get another job. This experience is too good to pass up," Andres confirmed without any hesitation or input from me.

I will admit, I agree with him. This experience is a once-in-a-lifetime opportunity. However, the fact he just offered for me to give up my job without even asking troubled me. That feeling quickly went away when the memories of the warm tropical air, the beat of the Brazilian drums, and the hustle and bustle of the Mercado Modelo began to flood my mind.

My thoughts were interrupted by Mestre Mota's response. "Ok. Well, the plan is for you to head over in May of next year. You have about nine months to get things in order. Lisa, I am still concerned about your job, so please see if your company will give you the time off. As I said before, I don't want this trip to set you back in your career."

We finish dinner with the common Brazilian dessert, mousse de maracujá. The creamy passion fruit mousse left a sweet taste in our mouths. I am going to take that as a sign that our lives are about to change forever.

"I need to call your mom. She is going to be so excited for us!" I exclaimed.

"Yea, give her a call. I know when it comes time to sell our stuff and move out of the apartment, she will be able to help us."

Oh wait. Sell our stuff? What? I like our stuff. And I don't even want to get into it about the couch again. I still like the couch I picked out. Why am I so tied to this stuff? Come on, Lisa, don't let this ruin the mood. You can deal with your insecurities about getting rid of the stuff later.

"I am sure she will be more than willing to help. She always is. For now, just hearing the news, she is going to be so excited for us!"

"Yea, she is going to go crazy. You call her. I'm not in the mood to answer all the questions she is going to have."

"That is kind of rude, but ok," I said, calling her.

"Hey, Linda, guess what?" I said with great excitement in my voice.

"Is everything okay? It's kind of late."

"Yes, everything is fine. Sorry for calling so late. We have some great news that can't wait! Try and guess what it is!"

"Ummm, is it something for the both of you?"

"YES! But we aren't pregnant, so don't go down that road."

"Is it something to do with your jobs?"

"No. You're never gonna guess! We are going to live in Brazil for a year!" I exploded.

"WHAT?!?! Where? When do you leave? That is great! I am so happy for you two. Is it through the Capoeira school?" the questions came out like a flood.

"Yes. We went to dinner tonight with Mestre Mota, and he offered us the opportunity to go on the cultural exchange to his hometown north of Salvador, Brazil."

"What are you going to do about your job?" she asked.

"Well, I am going to talk with my boss Dereck tomorrow and see if the company offers any type of program where they will hold my job for me. It is a long shot, but worth asking."

"And if they don't hold her job for her, she is just going to leave," Andres chimed in from the background.

Why does that bother me so much?

Maybe it's because quitting your job to gallivant around the world isn't responsible; and it definitely isn't a part of the "traditional plan." It might also be that having a job brings a certain level of security.

Come on, Lisa, let go; live a little!

"Well, I know it's all going to turn out for the best for you two. That is such exciting news! Just let me know how I can help. And let me know as soon as you talk to your boss about your job."

Linda is always so kind and helpful. "Thanks! We will let you know once we have any more information," I promised.

The next morning as I wake up, I roll over and playfully poke Andres. "Are we really going to Brazil for a year?"

"Uh, yea. It's almost unbelievable," he answered, his voice groggy. "I'm glad I have been taking Portuguese in school. You know you will need to learn Portuguese. Mestre Mota has said very few people speak English in Ouriçangas."

"I know. That is one of the things on the long list that needs to be addressed to prepare for this trip," I responded. His comment seemed condescending. I am able to brush it off since I know Andres isn't a morning person. "I am going to speak with Dereck today to see what options I have about taking a leave of absence from my job."

"That's good. Remember to make it clear you are going on this trip whether he gives you the leave or not."

With his words, the pit in my stomach reappears instantly. I hate conflict. Also, I am just a marketing assistant. They can so easily fill my spot with someone else. I hate it when Andres places these ultimatums on me. First of all, threatening to do anything isn't really my style. Second of all, I don't think I really contribute anything that special to my workgroup where I can demand they hold my position while I gallivant around the globe.

Instead of sharing these feelings and possibly starting a fight, I stuff them down and cover it up with my meek response, "Ok, I will."

I pop in Paul Simon's *Rhythm of the Saints* album on my way into work.

Hearing Olodum, the Brazilian drumming group, performing on this album stirs my excitement about our trip to Brazil. My confidence to talk with Dereck today is growing.

Usually, I am one of the first people in the office; today is no exception. My cubicle is positioned where I see the coming and goings of all of my coworkers, so I am able to see the moment Dereck gets in. It's hard to focus on my work knowing in nine short months, I will be living in the southern hemisphere!

I notice Dereck walk in. I'll give him a few minutes to get settled.

Lisa, take a deep breath. The worst thing he can say is no... ...Which will then cause a whole 'nother chain of events to happen that I don't want to think about. Ok, girl, let's go!

As I make my way towards his office, the butterflies in my stomach are going crazy.

"Dereck, do you have a minute?" I asked, standing in the doorway of his office.

"Sure, come on in. How are you doing this morning, Lisa?" He is always jovial and encouraging.

"I am great. I want to let you know, Andres and I have been given the opportunity to live in Brazil for a year on a cultural exchange. The program goes from May to May."

"That sounds like a wonderful opportunity; especially for a young married couple. I remember when Patrice and I were first married; we had the opportunity to travel to Puerto Rico for three weeks. It is not on the same scale as what you are doing, but traveling together is a great way to learn about each other and grow as a couple. So how can I help you?"

"Well," I said, nervous to ask, "does Edge Cable offer any programs that would allow me to take a sabbatical and have my job waiting for me when I return?"

"I think we do. Let me check with HR today and see what's available. Lisa, you are a valuable asset to this team; I don't want to lose you. I will do whatever I can to keep your spot open here in this department."

Oh. My. Gosh. This is all falling into place! I'm excited about the possibility of a sabbatical program. And even more excited I won't have to lay down any ultimatums or quit my job.

His comment about how valuable I am to the team didn't even register.

"That would be great!" I responded. "Thank you."

"No problem. We will make sure it works out," he reassured me. "I'll let you know when I hear back from HR."

I can't believe this! I float back to my cubicle with excitement. I hesitate in calling Andres. First of all, I am pretty sure he is still sleeping. Second, I don't want to say anything to him until I know more. If I tell him it is looking good and then it falls through, it will send him through the roof.

My parents are the next people I need to tell. I don't know how they will take it. Will they see it as an amazing opportunity to grow and experience the world? Or will they see it as an irresponsible choice to leave reality and go live in a foreign country for a year? Even though I am a married adult, living on my own, I still don't like to disappoint my parents. Unfortunately, I have done my fair share of that recently. I think I'll wait until I hear back from Dereck about my job. It sounds less irresponsible if I have a job waiting for me when I got home.

Around 10:30 a.m., Dereck calls me down to his office. His voice doesn't give any hint as to the direction this conversation is going to go, which makes me nervous.

"Hi, Lisa. Come on in and shut the door."

Oh boy. Here we go.

"Well, I spoke with HR, and we do offer a sabbatical program with the company. You will be able to take one year of unpaid leave from the company. The only catch is they can't guarantee to hold your position open. Upon your return, you will be given preferential status for any open position equivalent with the pay and rank as your current position," he explained.

"Now I am pretty sure I can keep your spot open and have the other marketing assistants cover your work while you are gone. The truth is, I want you back in my department, not somewhere else in the company. However, I need to make the reality of the sabbatical program clear. If HR comes in and forces me to fill your position, I'll have to do it. Either way, though, you will have a job with the company when you return."

"Thank you, Dereck. I really appreciate your checking into that so quickly. What paperwork do I need to fill out and when do I need to have it submitted?" I calmly inquired. Inside, I am exploding with excitement.

"You are welcome. Lisa, you are already a great asset to this company. International travel like this will only make you more valuable. We have time on the paperwork. I will get it to you once I receive it from HR."

Dereck again told me how much he appreciates me. For whatever reason, his words don't sink in. I carry the belief that knowing and following the rules is the key to success. It's a foreign concept to believe I am valued and cherished for who I am. I have always felt I need to perform in order to prove my worth.

Going down the hall, I bypass my desk and continue to the small conference room. I want to call Andres and tell him the good news without my co-workers knowing just yet.

"Good morning, Andres. I have some great news! I just got done talking with Dereck, and I can apply for a sabbatical which means I will have a job waiting for me when we get back. It may not be the one I have now, but it will be a job."

"That's great, Babe. See: I told you there was nothing to stress about. And even if they don't give you a sabbatical, there are plenty of other jobs out there. This just makes it easier for you."

Why does he keep telling me if the company doesn't give me the approved leave, I have to quit? Doesn't he realize that whole idea is petrifying to me? I guess I'm bad at communicating because he doesn't seem to hear me. Either way, it's now a moot point; I'm just going to let it go.

"Well, I've gotta get back to work. I just wanted to share the good news with you. Love you."

"Love you, too. Will you be home in time to cook a light dinner before we go to Capoeira tonight?" he asked.

"Um, yea, I should be."

It's so difficult to concentrate! While working on my current projects, I find myself heading over to the internet to search out information about Salvador. I can't believe we have been given this opportunity.

I hope my parents will be excited for us. I don't know why they wouldn't be. They are big supporters of international travel. Having been to many countries themselves, and sending both me and my sister abroad, I know they embrace the concept of it. I know they are still trying to build a relationship with Andres, even though he doesn't see or respond to their efforts.

I have a job waiting for me when I get back. *Lisa, STOP TORTURING YOURSELF!* I hear Brenda's voice chime in, "The reality is you want your parent's approval. If you don't get it, you can still go on this adventure and have a marvelous time."

I take a deep breath, get back to the marketing plan for our new product bundle, and wait for lunchtime.

At noon, I grab my lunch and head into the little conference room to make my call. "Hey, Momma. How are you doing?"

"Lisa! It's so good to hear from you! We are good. How are you doing?"

Inserting as much excitement in my voice as possible, I reply, "Well, I'm actually doing great! I have some exciting news to tell you." I laid the bait, using the technique of suspense to hopefully work in my favor.

"Oh, you do? Please, do tell!" she played along.

"Well, Mestre Mota has chosen Andres and me to do the next cultural exchange to Ouriçangas. That is his home town in Bahia, Brazil!"

"Lisa, that is exciting news! So, when are you going? How long? Three weeks? A month?"

Well, at least she is excited and on board for now. I decide to vomit all of the information on her, hoping the rapid-fire approach would smother any thoughts of disapproval. "It's a one-year exchange program. We'll be leaving in May. They supply all of our housing and a small stipend when we are there. We will be doing some work in the schools and teaching English/American culture classes. And, oh yea, I almost forgot, I've already spoken with my boss Dereck; I can take a sabbatical from my job and have something waiting for me when we get home."

I can sense the shell shock from the other end of the phone. Even though this is a once-in-a-lifetime opportunity, I know a year in another country isn't "part of the plan." I just want my parents to be happy for me and proud of me.

"You will have the opportunity to go to Brazil for a year, have your housing taken care of, and receive a small stipend? And you will still have your job when you get back?" she asked, trying to make sense of the information I just dumped on her.

"Yep. Isn't that cool! Oh, and we will be a part of the town's samba reggae drumming group as well. That will allow us the opportunity to do some traveling around Bahia and experience the true culture of the area!"

"That sounds amazing. I am so excited for both of you. Why don't the two of you come over for dinner this weekend and you can share all of the details."

"Thank you for the invite," I responded, excitement mixing with dread. "I think it will work. Let me check with Andres to make sure we don't have something on our schedule that I don't know about."

"Ok, just let us know what works. We would love to have you both over and hear about this amazing opportunity."

"Thanks, Momma. I love you."

I do. I really do love my parents. It makes me sad Andres can't see my parents are really trying to build a relationship with us...with him. It makes me sad a simple invitation to dinner with them is shrouded in dread. When I mention it to Andres, there will be at least one snide comment and pushback; at most a full-on fight. What have I gotten myself into?

Chapter 15
The First Step

I'm fiddling around in the kitchen as Andres gets home. "Hey, Babe. Whatcha makin?"

"I was just going to make a couple of smoothies for us before we head down to practice. I know we need something, but nothing too heavy. I'll cook when we get home."

"Sounds good," he said, heading back to change.

"I spoke with my mom today," I yelled, continuing the conversation as he heads back to the bedroom. "I told her about our trip to Brazil. She is really excited for us."

"Well, good for her, because we are going whether she likes it or not," he responded as he emerges from down the hall to come give me a hug.

Ouch, that hurt. Does he always have to pit us against them?

"Well, they invited us to dinner this Saturday to hear all the details and celebrate with us."

"Really? We have to have dinner with them this Saturday?"

This is exactly what I hate. My parents aren't something to endure. Part of having a big family is building relationships, knowing people aren't perfect. "Well, I guess we don't HAVE to, but I think it's really nice they invited us over and are interested in hearing more about our trip."

"I don't know. I'll think about it."

Well, at least he is thinking about it. It wasn't a flat out "no!"

On our usual route to the Capoeira school, Andres asks, "Have you ever been there?" pointing to The Passion Palace, a huge adult store that was lit up in purple and pink lights.

"Um, no, I haven't," I replied, almost offended he would ask.

"I think we should go and check it out," he prodded.

"I think not. By the way, we are on our way to class, and I don't want to be late."

"Not right this second," he conceded. "Let's stop by afterward and check it out."

"Um, no. Those places are gross, and I don't want to be seen walking into one."

"Stop it. You are such a prude. No one is noticing who is walking in or out of that place. We should just go check it out. I am really curious to see what it's like on the inside," he pressed.

Why can't my no be no? And I am not a prude; I just don't want to go into a sex shop. Intimacy is something private between a couple, not something to be shared, watched, and perverted.

"I'll make you a deal. We can go over to your parents' house for dinner on Saturday night if we go to The Passion Palace tonight after class."

Really? Did he just bribe me like that? I know if we turn down my parent's dinner invitation, it will cause more damage in the relationship. And how bad can The Passion Palace really be? I just won't touch anything or make eye contact with anyone in there. I can't believe I am agreeing to this.

"So, you promise to go to dinner at my folk's house Saturday night if we go to The Passion Palace tonight; just this one time?"

"Yes, I promise," he said, agreeing to the commitment to go to dinner on Saturday night. However, he has no intention of this being our only visit to The Passion Palace.

After class, Randy asked if we wanted to stay and practice some more. Andres quickly declined. I am hoping the guilt and anxiety raging on the inside of me isn't showing on my face. I can't believe I agreed to go to that place. We quickly leave the school and head to The Palace. Ultimately, this is the first step down a very slippery slope into a deep pit.

As we pull up, I convince Andres to park on the back side of the building, in the dark, so no one can recognize our car. I put on the hat I had in my workout bag, hoping to hide my identity.

"Are you ready?" he said, an inordinate amount of excitement in his voice.

"No. This whole thing is creeping me out."

"Oh, come on. You are going to be just fine. It will be fun," trying to convince me to change my mind.

"No, seriously; I am really freaked out. Please stay right by me. I am not sure what kind of people will be in there, and I want you to protect me."

Protect me. That's what I want; for my heart, mind, and body to be protected. Just the thought of porn brought back memories of the date rape I endured in high school.

Come on, Lisa; stuff those feelings back where they were before. Don't let them come out now. Andres, I am asking for what I need. Please, please hear me!!!

"Oh, stop it. You are going to be just fine," he dismissed. "You want to know the type of people who go into places like this? Us. We are the type of people who go into places like this. If anyone sees us in there, they can't pass judgment because, well, they are in there, too. Stop being such a baby and let's go. You're ruining all the fun."

I swallow down the pain, shame, guilt, and anxiety, pull my hat down a little lower, and head into The Palace.

"Welcome into The Passion Palace!" a jovial voice greeted us. It came from a tall, lanky guy with jet-black hair, a spiked dog collar around his neck, black lipstick, and multiple face piercings.

"Thanks, man," Andres replied.

"Can I help you find anything?"

"No, we're just looking."

"Great. Movies and magazines are over there; toys are in that area; you can find lotions and potions over here. The apparel is over to your right. And back in the corner is our dominatrix section," he explained.

My head is spinning. I can't believe all of this stuff. I have to admit it doesn't seem as creepy as I had expected. Nevertheless, I still don't want to be here.

Andres heads off to the magazine section. I quickly follow, staying as close to him as I can. When we get there, he hands me a mag and whispers to me, "Here, take a look at this one."

Oh, my. I can't believe I am standing here looking at a porno mag. I don't want to stick out and draw any attention to myself. And I don't want to cause a scene between me and Andres so I start thumbing through the magazine. The pictures are just too much. Watching Andres, I am grateful he is still close. Knowing that I need to look interested in this magazine, I decide to try reading the articles.

I start reading this story about a young couple traveling on a small airplane up in Montana late at night. They happened to be the only people on the plane and were in a huge fight. The pilot and the flight attendant were "very friendly" to their passengers. The flight ended at a remote airport. The magazine graphically described how they all made out...together.

I find the story intriguing and disgusting at the same time. I notice I am physically aroused reading about their encounter, but repulsed by the fact these two couples were swapping partners. This is so against anything I've been taught. Marriage is a close, monogamous relationship between a husband and wife.

I quickly jump into the next story when Andres interrupts me. "Hey, Babe, are you ready to go home?"

"Um, yes," I said, flustered and thrilled that our visit to The Passion Palace is coming to an end.

"Do you like what you were reading?"

"It was interesting," I replied.

"What do you mean interesting? Did you like it?" he prodded.

"I don't know." Honestly, I am so confused. I don't want it because I don't want to own a porno magazine; although the story intrigued me. This couple was fighting; the fighting stopped when they started doing sexual things with these other people. The woman in the young couple felt so ignored by her husband, she ended up getting her needs met by this other man. Somehow, this brought her and her husband closer together. It doesn't make sense, but I can relate to the young wife...well at least at the beginning of the story. I could never imagine doing anything sexually in front of someone else, let alone with a man other than my husband.

In my hesitation, he grabs the magazine from my hand. "Here, I'll get that for you. It looks like you were enjoying yourself 'reading the articles'," he teased. He adds the magazine I was reading to a movie he had picked out. "Do you want to go look at the toys?"

"NO!" I replied adamantly.

"Okay. Maybe next time," he said walking up to the front counter.

WAIT?!? No, there won't be a next time. This was a one-time thing. I am not coming back here again. Our deal was we would come in here tonight. I know in my heart this isn't going to be the last time.

We just took our first step down a road leading far away from anything I know. The one thing I do know, it isn't good. I can feel a door has been opened that can't be shut. Along with feeling dirty, feelings of being inadequate are growing. I don't look anything like those women in the magazine. Compared to them, how can I ever be attractive to my husband?

My thoughts are quickly interrupted when I watch Andres take out his credit card.

WAIT! You can't purchase it on a credit card. The Passion Palace will show on our statement. The people at the bank will know. If we get audited, our accountant will know.

A new wave of shame and guilt came crashing over me. What did I agree to?

Chapter 16
A Unique Homecoming

"I've got some good news!" I exclaimed, walking in the door from work. "Oh, yea? What is it?" Andres asked with mild interest.

"I found a Portuguese class at the local community college. It's on Tuesday and Thursday mornings. I've already spoken with Dereck and he is going to let me come in late on those days. He said I don't need to make up the time as long as I get my work done," I shared.

"That is nice, but who is going to pay for it? You know we don't have the money for you to go to school."

"Well, that's the other cool part. It falls under continuing education with the company. All we need to pay is the $100 application fee.

"That is good because you will need to learn the language before we go over there if you want to be able to speak with anyone."

"I am aware of that, hence the reason I found this course." I said in a snotty tone. Trying to remain positive, I add, "I can't believe how supportive Dereck is about this trip. We are really lucky."

"It's not luck. It's good he is being so supportive. If not, you would just leave."

Not that crap again. Really? Instead of looking at all of the great things Dereck is doing for me, Andres still has to threaten me about leaving my job. The one I love; the one that is currently paying the majority of our bills. I know it isn't worth bringing my feelings up about this; he won't listen. Most likely, it will start a fight. It's a moot point. Because of Dereck's support, I won't have to leave my job.

The ringing of the phone interrupts my quiet Saturday morning. I pick it up and hear Linda's voice. "Hi, Sweetie. How are you doing? Are you getting excited about your trip?"

"Good morning, Linda. I am getting REALLY excited! I can't believe we are only three months away from leaving. Everything is falling into place. The main thing hanging in the balance right now is the fact our lease ends three weeks before we leave for Brazil. I checked with the leasing office. The cost to extend our lease for an extra month is a small fortune; one we can't really afford with trying to save up for the trip."

"Well, you and Andres are more than welcome to stay here with me for those three weeks," she offered.

"Thank you. I appreciate your offer. The problem is, if we stay with you, I would be looking at a minimum 45 minutes to an hour commute each way to work for those last two and a half weeks. With everything else we need to get done, I can't afford that kind of commute time. It's also a lot further from the Capoeira school."

"Have you thought about asking your folks if you could stay with them? They have been supportive of this trip from the beginning."

Just the thought rattles me. I can't even imagine Andres and I living in my parents' house for any amount of time. If my parents agree to it, I know they'll be gracious. The question is, could Andres be civil to them for three weeks? He has a hard time holding it together for dinner with them. And there is no way he can bring the porn stash we have collected into their house.

"Sweetie? Are you still there?"

"Yea, I'm still here. The thought of asking my parents if we could stay with them never crossed my mind; and well, your suggestion just sent my mind reeling. Do you think Andres could actually live with my parents for almost a month? You should know; he's your son."

"Well, if he stays busy with work and Capoeira, and you don't spend a whole lot of time actually at the house, I think you guys could do it. It would help out financially. It might even be a good way for you two to work on the relationship with your parents."

"You do have a point there. I'll run it by Andres and see what he thinks. We are actually having dinner with my folks tomorrow night. Thank you for being so supportive of us."

"I love you two so much!"

"We love you, too."

"Well, go talk to Andres and then reach out to your parents to see if you can stay with them. Oh, and ask Andres to call me. I don't know when the best time is to call and visit with him."

"Ok. I'll tell him to call you...and I'll let you know what happens with my parents."

That phone call didn't go anything like I had expected.

Staying with my parents would be great in many ways. Location wise, it's convenient for my work, our training, and my Portuguese class. It will save us a lot of money by not having to extend our lease for another month. It would also be nice being out of the apartment three weeks before we leave.

The thought of being close to my parents again makes me happy; I really miss them. Maybe Andres will get a new understanding of the fact my parents want to work on building a relationship with him. It's frustrating because he always thinks it's everyone else's issue. Maybe this will be what we need to put our relationship with my parents on a new trajectory. Now the hard part; I need to get Andres and my folks to agree.

"Hey, Babe, are you up?" I whisper in Andres' ear as I curl up behind him in bed.

"Yea, I am now."

"That was your mom on the phone. She had an interesting suggestion about where we can stay for the three weeks before we leave."

"I hope it isn't staying with her. First of all, it is so far away from everything we are doing; second, I'm not sure if I can actually live with her again...even if it's only for three weeks."

"That is rude, but no, it wasn't to live with her. She suggested asking my parents." I hold my breath, waiting for his reaction. Not expecting it to be very favorable considering his reaction to the possibility of living with his mom.

"Staying with your parents? Well, I guess if they will let us, that will work."

I am shocked. That was his answer? That easy? "Ok then. I'll ask my parents." I don't want to put any other stipulations on it for fear he will change his mind.

The next morning, I anxiously dial my parents' number. "Good morning, Momma. How are you today?"

"Well, hello, Lisa. I'm good. It's great to hear from you. Is everything ok? Are we still on for dinner tonight?"

"Yes, things are going well. Only three more months until we are headed to Brazil. I can't believe it! And yes, we are still on for dinner," I said, making small talk, building up the courage to ask my mom what seems to be a bombshell of a question.

"That is so exciting. How are the preparations coming along?"

"Good; really good actually. I am learning a lot in my Portuguese class. Andres and I have already started selling some of our stuff and packing up the things we won't need for the next few months. Actually, that is why I am calling." I don't know if I am the only one feeling the anxiety on the call, but I continue. "We are going to have a three-week window from when our lease at the apartment runs out and when we leave for Brazil. We can extend our lease, the downside being, it's really expensive. Will it be a possibility for us to stay with you and dad for that short time?"

I hold my breath.

"Well, I don't know. I'll have to talk to your father about that."

Well, at least it wasn't a flat out "NO!"

"I was planning on calling you as well. I wanted to tell you before tonight so there are no big surprises. Your dad and I want to extend the offer to allow you to use your bedroom here as storage for your things while you are gone."

WHAT? Wow, even after all of the stress and turmoil we put them through, they are still being so kind. It's amazing they offered to store our stuff at their house. That reassures me my parents do love us; well, at least me. Hopefully, if we can stay there, they will get a chance to know Andres better and be on the way to building a better relationship.

"Really? We can keep our stuff at your house while we're in Brazil? That's so generous. Thank you."

"Now I am thinking of just boxes. I am not sure about all of your furniture. Your dad and I talked about keeping the stuff in your room and maybe a few things in the basement. We just don't want boxes all over the house for the next year," she explained.

"I totally understand. Anything will help. We are planning on selling most of our furniture, so that shouldn't be an issue. Thank you." I'm excited, a little bit guilty, and definitely relieved we have a place to keep our stuff...for free. And if they came up with that offer on their own, the possibility of us staying with them might actually work.

"You are welcome. We love you so much, Lisa. I'll talk with your dad and let you know about the other thing. We will see you tonight at six o'clock for dinner."

I hang up the phone, completely stunned. After all we have put my parents through, they are willing to help us out. I really hope Andres sees the kindness my parents are extending to us and realizes this is what it's like to be a part of the big, loving family he talks about. I also want him to get the realization that this type of relationship requires some giving on his part, not just taking.

Thinking about my mom's reaction to speak with my dad about our request is inspiring. They really walk out the original design for husband and wife, walking through life together. I've never seen their discussion process; however, I know when the final decision is made, they are united in whatever it may be. I have never seen one throw anything back in the other's face. There is a loving playfulness between them that is so precious. I really hope someday Andres and I can have that kind of relationship. Our marriage feels so far from that right now.

Encouraged by the possibility of staying with my parents, I pack up more boxes and list the spare bedroom furniture on Craig's list.

Off in my own little world, listening to my Portuguese language tapes, Andres interrupts me. "How much longer are you going to be packing? You know we're not leaving for three months."

"I know. I was thinking: if I can get the stuff we're not going to use packed up, it will make it easier in the end."

The other thing I don't feel comfortable telling him is the process of packing and moving is still hard for me. I had lived in the same house from the time I was in kindergarten until I moved out into my first little one-bedroom apartment. And this is the third move in as many years. I don't say anything to him because I don't want my feelings discounted again. He will make fun of me and say I am being irrational and then question us going on the trip. It's not that I don't want to go on the trip; I just like the feeling of being secure. Every move feels like an upheaval of that security. It may be an irrational feeling—definitely one I can't ignore. However, right now, I don't feel comfortable sharing it with him.

"What do you have in mind for today, since packing isn't on your list?" I joked.

"I was thinking we can just go for a drive."

"Where?"

"I don't know. I want to get out and just drive."

That sounds pretty lame to me, and a waste of time. However, I know if he wants to go for a drive, he is going to go for a drive, despite the fact there is so much to do. My choice is to go with him or be left here alone to do all this work myself.

"Ok," I concede. "Let me just change and we can head out. And don't forget, we have dinner plans tonight with my parents at six o'clock."

We jump in the car and head off on our adventure to nowhere. Since we are just "going for a drive," I'm not really paying attention to the route he begins to take. Within a few minutes, we are pulling into the carwash.

"Really?!"

I hate doing the carwash thing with him. He's so particular about his cars. Although I admit it is nice to have a clean car, the process is painstaking. If you don't use the right towel or if you don't dry the car in a certain way, it becomes a huge issue. I try to just let him do it. Inevitably, he asks why I am not helping. It is a conundrum!

"Hey, Lisa, can you dry off the wheels?"

"Sure," I said with dread. "Which towel do you want me to use?" inquiring ahead of time to avoid getting yelled at if I pick the wrong one.

"Grab two yellow ones. Get one of them wet and wipe the wheels down first and then dry them with the other one," he instructed.

This is so stupid...even more stupid than a drive to nowhere. I grab the towels and try to hide my tantrum as I stomp off to get one towel wet.

Lisa, get it together, I say in my head, trying to encourage myself to get into a better frame of mind. *Andres is always happier when his car is clean. Helping him do this will ultimately make the day better. And just appease him by doing it his way. You are capable of cleaning a car, but remember what Brenda has taught you: it's ok to do it his way. As a couple, it's about working together, and not always needing to be right. Pick your battles.*

I take a deep breath and chuckle at myself and my inner dialogue. I wring out the wet yellow towel and head back to complete my wheel drying duty.

When we get done, I have to admit the car looks beautiful. Andres has a lift in his attitude as we finally head out on our journey to nowhere.

Watching the city scenery go by, I get lost in my own thoughts.

Is this what couples do? Just hang out like this? Why is it we always do the things Andres wants to do; rarely doing the things I suggest? The bigger question is, what is it that I want to do? I don't know. What do I really like to do? What are my hobbies? I love to craft and sew, which are things we can't really do together. And when I do jump into a crafting project, he only lasts so long on his own before he interrupts me and wants my attention. What do we really have in common? I want to talk with him about this. However, from past experiences, opening a discussion about me spending more time doing the things I like or spending time with my girlfriends or mom never ends well. It's like my desire to grow myself is a direct attack against him. So instead of the togetherness and oneness I see in my parents, we are actually at odds and battling against each other.

"You sure are quiet over there. What are you thinking about?" he interrupted.

"Oh, nothing really."

Yea, nothing I am going to tell you for fear of how you will react. Maybe I'll bring it up next weekend when we see Brenda. Why is it that even though we are together, I still feel so alone?

I know I have to come up with some sort of answer or he will badger it out of me.

"It has to be something. You haven't said a word."

"Just thinking about our trip to Brazil. Wondering what it will be like to be in a place that doesn't speak English," I lied. "I mean, I'm doing ok in my Portuguese class, but far from being fluent." Whew, that was close. I think that answer was good enough to appease him.

"You are going to do just fine. Mestre Mota said even though the people there don't speak English, they are very welcoming. And remember, Bobby didn't know the language at all when he went, and he survived," he encouraged. "Don't worry about it. You are totally stressing yourself out over something you really don't need to."

We drove around town, and he showed me some of the houses where he grew up and shared stories of his childhood. His mom raised him pretty much by herself. As he points out the seventh residence, I begin to understand why he doesn't get worked up about moving—it's just part of life.

As we drive down his memory lane, I realize how much I don't know or understand the man I married. I am coming to the realization I had married the idea of a perfect marriage versus getting to know who I was committing the rest of my life to. The sad part is I can't back out now.

As we make our way back over to our end of town, Andres suggests, "Wanna go to The Palace?"

"The Palace? You mean The Passion Palace?" I clarified.

"Yea. The stuff we got last time is fun. Let's go and see what we can find."

I really don't want to go...again. Who am I kidding? I didn't want to go the first time. I have to admit some of the stories in the magazine were arousing, despite the fact they were disturbing as well. I want to be pursued by my husband. I don't need magazines to get things going. Honestly, all he has to do to spice things up for us is come up behind me and start hugging and kissing me. Despite what I've told him, he's never tried it. Why do we need to watch other people? I remember Brenda encouraging me to speak up and make my wants and desires known.

"I thought the last time we went was just to check it out. I don't want to go again," I said.

"Oh, come on. Don't you enjoy the stories in your magazine?"

"I will admit they are interesting, but I don't want to go there again; and I don't need any more magazines."

"Interesting? Oh no, your reaction is a lot more than interesting," he chided. "I see you getting turned on when you read your stories; and you have to admit, the sex is much better after watching the movies."

Physically, there is something. The reality is it makes me feel gross. Sex is something that should be between the couple; not camera men and other people. And while there is some fascination in looking at some of the pictures, it also makes me go into this place of comparison and insecurity. I don't look anything like the women in these magazines or movies. They are so much skinnier and taller than me; and their boobs are WAY bigger than mine. Seeing my husband get so excited and worked up over those other women hurts and makes me feel inadequate. It is a battle between my emotions and my physical body.

I throw out the excuse, "I don't think we will have the time. We have to be over at my parents' house by six o'clock."

"We can stop by quickly. The movie we have is getting old. You can get a new magazine as well. Just twenty minutes," he pleaded.

I know it doesn't matter whether I agree or not; our next stop is going to be The Palace. It feels even stranger being there just hours before we meet up with my parents for dinner. I REALLY don't want those two worlds to collide. It will crush my parents if they ever found out.

Walking in this time is different. It's broad daylight; I can't hide in the shadows. I am still paranoid about who might see me walking in. One of our family friends lives a half a mile away; I would be so embarrassed if she saw me. The good news; there are less people so we can park close to the front door.

True to his word, we were in and out in about twenty minutes with a new movie and a new magazine. I cringed again when he pulled out the debit card to pay for this filth. As I worry about the impact of the physical proof of us buying porn, I am clueless to the emotional and spiritual ramifications of this purchase.

Ding dong. It feels strange ringing the doorbell at the residence I called home for twenty years of my life; however, it would be even more obnoxious to walk in like nothing had changed.

My mom's sweet smile greets us as my dad comes around the corner from the kitchen. They both have aprons on. Many times, they cook together when guests are coming over. Their love and warmth hit me the moment I walk in the door. I hope Andres feels it, too.

My mom gives me a big hug and a kiss; then turns with open arms to Andres. I receive a big hug from my dad. Then he turns and offers his hand to Andres, welcoming him into their home. It almost brings tears to my eyes, and gives me hope the relationship between all of us can actually be restored.

"Can I get you something to drink?" my dad asked. "Andres, I have some Corona beer. Lisa told me that was your favorite."

I want to pull Andres aside and say to him, *See!!! This is what it is like to be a part of my family. They love well and want to have a relationship with us. They care about you enough to ask about your drink of choice and then make sure that they have it waiting for you.*

"Yes, please, Mr. Byrne," Andres politely answered.

"Great! Come on in!" my mom said cheerfully. "We will get you both drinks. And for dinner, we made one of Lisa's all-time favorites, Chicken Cordon Bleu."

Wow. My parents put a lot of effort into dinner tonight. Making my favorite meal. Making sure to have Andres' favorite beer. Even having us over for dinner in the first place. I am so happy and content right now seeing the three people I love so dearly actually coming together.

Over dinner, my parents asked a lot of questions about Brazil. It was fun sharing our plans with them. They shared some of their overseas adventures with us as well.

As the meal is wrapping up, I chime in, "Mom and Dad, I want to thank you for being so kind and extending the offer to store our stuff while we're in Brazil. That will be a big help not having to get a storage unit."

"We are happy to do that for you two," my mom responded. "You are a young couple just starting out. This is a great opportunity to see the world and create memories together; and if we can help by storing your boxes, we are happy to." As my mom spoke, I look over towards my dad, he gives me a smile and a nod showing he's in agreement.

Mom continues on, "And your dad and I spoke about it, and you two are welcome to stay here for those three weeks before you leave on your trip. We don't want you to incur the extra cost of a full month at your apartment or deal with the stress of moving out right up to the day you leave."

I am shocked. I mean I know my parents are loving and generous, but this was such a long shot...and one that actually makes me a little bit nervous.

"Thank you! We really appreciate it," answering for the both of us.

"Yes, thank you," Andres chimed in.

Once we are driving away, I turn to Andres, "That's really cool my parents will let us stay with them for those three weeks."

"Yea, that's pretty cool. You know the best part about it? I actually get to go to the second floor of your parents' house and have sex with you in your old bedroom."

"Really? That's what you're looking forward to in this whole thing?" I questioned with disgust.

"Just being honest. It's always been off limits. Now that you are my wife, I get to do you in your old bedroom."

My two worlds collide again in a way I didn't expect. What I was sensing as a step towards reconciliation is being turned into an act of dominance. It hurts because I am the one used as a pawn in this game of chess.

Chapter 17
Wheels Up

The last three months have sailed by. I can't believe the only things left to pack are our clothes, toiletries, and the growing box of porn.

"Can't we just get rid of this stuff? I don't want to bring any porn into my parents' house," I asked.

"It is no big deal. We'll just pack it up and make a special marking on the box so we remember which one it is. They aren't going to be scouring through our stuff. It will be fine," he reassured me. "Besides, there are some good movies in there."

I'm not so sure about "good." I know it is a losing battle, so I let it go. I'll throw out the magazines and pack up the rest. I cover the top with a couple of towels, trying to hide the contents if someone did happen to open the box. I mark the outside "Master Bedroom," then write PP for Passion Palace in the corner to discreetly mark what is in the box.

Even though I'm not able to throw it all away, at least it's boxed up and we'll be free of the porn for a year.

We load up the last of our things and head over to my parent's house. It's strange coming back home with my husband. There are new rules in an old place. I feel like I am going to get caught having Andres in my bedroom. The comment Andres made about getting to have sex with me in my parent's house replays in my head. It's like I'm a conquest; and that is a way for him to beat my parents in the battle.

Things were going well for the first few days. No major arguments or awkward moments. Andres and I were still busy with wrapping things up at work and doing as much Capoeira as possible.

After practice tonight, we head home and devour some heated up left-overs.

"Hey, Lisa, let's go play with that Portuguese program on the computer,"

Andres said.

"You two go do that. I'll take care of your dishes," my mom chimed in.

That's strange. Even though I find the Portuguese computer program to be helpful, Andres has never been a big fan of it. We sit down at the computer at the end of the kitchen and fire it up. "Bem-vindo ao Português iniciante," the computer blared.

"Oh, man, that was loud. Turn it down!" I said, not wanting to be too much of a bother to my parents. My dad is in the other room watching TV.

"Yea, that was kind of loud." Andres and I laughed.

We worked through a few lessons in the Portuguese language program when we hear the TV turn off. Mom and Dad come into the kitchen with Mom announcing, "Good night, you two. Sleep well. I am glad things worked out for you to stay here. It's great having you."

She reaches out and gives us both hugs. I hug and kiss my dad, and they head up to bed.

Andres turns to me with a mischievous grin on his face that worries me. "What is that look for?" I asked.

With that, he opens a browser window and types in "sexy Brazilian women." I am mortified. I can still hear my parents getting ready for bed upstairs. There is a window in their bathroom that looks over onto the computer area.

"No!" I whisper, a look of unbelief and horror on my face. "Don't. Not in my parent's home, and NOT on their computer!"

"Don't worry: I turned the sound off so they won't hear anything."

"But they can look through the window. Besides, it's just disrespectful. And it will show in the browser history."

"Oh, come on. Quit being such a stick in the mud. They aren't computer savvy enough to even know about the browser history. Regardless, we will clear it and the cache so they will never know."

It has nothing to do with their computer skills. It's the principle. Here we are in their house, on their computer, and he is surfing porn sites.

"Come on, just sit here with me and look."

I feel stuck. I don't want to make a big scene. I also don't want to look at this stuff. And for sure don't want to look at it on my parent's computer! I sit there quietly because I don't want to disrupt my parents after all they're doing for us. I reason with myself that "this" would be over soon; *this* three weeks of living with my parents, and hopefully, *this* fascination and perversion of porn that has infiltrated our lives.

It's finally the big day! May 17. Off on our big adventure! I can't believe it! Besides the fact we will be landing in tropical Salvador, Brazil in a mere twenty-one hours, I am really grateful we were able to complete the three-week stay with my parents without any major issues. I don't think the relationship with them and Andres got any better. At least things didn't get any worse. Now I can let that worry go and focus on this great new chapter!

My parents drop us off at the airport with our two big backpacks. We give hugs and kisses and get into the mode of speaking Portuguese with a hearty "Tchau" as we head into the terminal.

International adventures are so much fun. There is an excitement of stepping into the unknown and living outside of your comfort zone. For Andres, this is his first time out of the country. I'm a little concerned because when he feels out of control, he gets agitated and mean. I hate it when he gets like this.

****

"Hello, this is your Captain speaking. We have reached our cruising altitude of 32,000 feet and are well on our way to Miami International Airport. We should be arriving on time at 11:20AM local time. Please sit back, relax, and enjoy your flight."

Hearing we are officially off on our adventure, I take a big sigh of relief. I look over and Andres is sleeping. It's so peaceful hearing the drone of the engines. I drift off into my place of daydreaming.

So, this is what it is like when my parents would leave my sister and me to go on their international travels? The two of them against the world! Open to meeting new people and seeing new things.

On most of their international trips, they would book their first and last night hotel, and a rental car. They had a basic route planned, but were completely open to change. They didn't want to be controlled by a strict itinerary. They always had such amazing stories from their trips: finding unknown castles; dining at local street side cafes; and meeting locals as well as other wanderlust couples.

That's what I want in my marriage...and here Andres and I are on an airplane to Brazil. The world is at our feet. In projecting the love I experienced in my parent's relationship onto ours, I have to ignore the manipulation to make the dream come into focus. I also have to dismiss my unheard feelings and his anger. However, I believe if I love him enough, the hurt from his past can be healed and we can have the life we have talked about having.

After making our connecting flights, a new excitement is rising out of the exhaustion as we finally touch down at Salvador International Airport. I can't believe it; we are finally here! We have logged over 5,600 miles. I lean over and give Andres a kiss to share my excitement. He brushes me off. I swallow my hurt and give him a pass. Traveling for close to twenty-one hours can make anyone cranky.

We make our way through immigration and customs. Finally, we are free to roam about the country! Mestre Mota's friend Pedro is there to pick us up at the airport.

"Olá! Bem vindo ao Brasil" exclaimed Pedro, testing our Portuguese skills.

"Olá!" Andres replied back.

"Welcome to Brazil!" Pedro reiterated in English to make sure we understood him. "We are so glad to have you here. Ouriçangas is about a 2½ hour drive. If you are hungry and not too tired, I was thinking we can get something to eat for lunch here in Salvador. I can show you around a little bit before we head back."

Andres looks towards me. I give him a huge grin and a nod. "Yes, that sounds great!" Andres answered for the two of us.

"Great! Let's get your bags and head out!" Pedro replied.

As we step outside, the warm, humid air hits our skin; the smell of the ocean assaults our nostrils. The excitement growing inside me overtook any feeling of exhaustion I had. I can't believe we're really living out this opportunity.

Pedro drives us into the heart of Salvador. Our first stop is the cultural center of the city called Pelourinho. Colorful colonial style buildings with wrought iron balconies and ornate doors line the streets. At the end of the street is the Igreja e Convento de São Francisco. From the outside, it looks plain. However, the white facade with the tall green doors houses one of the most ornate churches I have ever seen. The inside is glowing from the gilded walls and ceilings. I remember its breathtaking beauty from my previous visit.

"I know I promised to get you some lunch, but are you two okay with eating ice cream first?" Pedro inquired.

We both chuckle. "Sure! That's fine with us!"

"Great. There is a famous ice cream shop just down the street and the place I want to take you for lunch is in a different neighborhood."

"That's cool," Andres confirmed.

"Pedro, thank you for putting this together and taking us around. This is a wonderful welcome to Brazil," I chimed in.

As we leave Igreja e Convento de São Francisco, Pedro directs us to the famous Le Glacier Laporte Ice Cream. "The man who owns this ice cream parlor makes all of his ice cream chemical free. One of his famous flavors is called caraíba. It is made from the traditional Acerola cherry which is a berry grown here in Brazil. It's very high in vitamin C, so this is actually healthy ice cream! The owner takes the acerola cherry and mixes it with lemon and ginger to preserve the color and nutrients of the fruit."

I'm geeking out on all of the history and information Pedro is sharing. When I look over at Andres, I can tell he is starting to lose it. I know he is hungry and tired, a combination that never ends well with him. Adding to it, gilded churches and historic buildings aren't his thing. He gets annoyed when too many facts are divulged about something he doesn't care about. I can see his struggle to hold it together. He knows being rude to Pedro would be a huge embarrassment to Mestre Mota. I am grateful he is succeeding, but I don't know how long it will last.

"That ice cream sounds amazing! How far away is it?" I chimed in, thinking less talking and more walking. I know getting something in Andres' stomach, even if it's healthy ice cream, will be the key to keeping this afternoon from deteriorating rapidly.

"It's right there," Pedro said, pointing up the block. "And look, the line isn't too long."

I know marriage means taking the good with the bad; however, I have to say Andres' temper is something I really don't like. When he blows, it's scary and embarrassing. I find myself scrambling to do whatever I can to keep him from losing it in the first place. It also hurts that he is more concerned about honoring and pleasing Mestre Mota than he is about doing that for me. I hope this will change in the future.

After surviving the line and getting our cold Brazilian treat, I pipe up, "Pedro you are right, this ice cream is delicious!" I try filling the awkwardly charged silence created by Andres' mood.

"Good! I am glad you like it. The next stop is just a little north of here, Santo Antônio Alem do Carmo. I think you'll really like it, too. You will see some of the most amazing views of the bay, and we will get some moqueca. It is a seafood stew that is a 'must have' while you are here in Brazil. I think there is something else you will find very exciting when we get to this neighborhood; you'll see."

Pedro is an amazing tour guide. I really appreciate all of the interesting information he is sharing about his country and the city of Salvador. This brings back great memories of my traveling and experiencing the world during college. I love how travel pulls me out of my comfort zone. Being flexible is the key to embracing all of the great experiences that come with exploring abroad. Going with the flow is not how I would describe the Andres I know. The fact he is actually doing this trip and holding it together makes me really proud of him. Maybe this will be the turning point for our relationship.

The neighborhood Pedro brought us to was cute and very hip. Brightly colored buildings of blue, pink, and yellow line the cobblestone streets. Little outdoor cafes and local artist's studios are everywhere. As we ventured along, we both perk up when we heard the familiar twang of the berimbau. We turn the corner to see a group of around fifteen guys in a jogo. Their Capoeira skills are pretty amazing. As soon as we noticed them, Pedro got a big smile on his face.

"Isn't it exciting to watch people of that caliber practice right there on the street? That is the 'something else' I was talking about. We can come back and watch after lunch. I am really hungry. I am sure you two must be starving!"

Pedro led us to this cute little cafe for lunch. He was right; the view of the bay is amazing. The food is delicious as well. After our meal, we go back to watch the jogo for a little longer. It's exciting to see this martial art we have been practicing play out in real life on the streets of its homeland. I take a deep breath and relax, knowing Andres is enjoying himself.

"Well, we should get heading to Ouriçangas," Pedro said.

Leaving the city, Pedro leads our adventure through the lush countryside. There are palm trees, small creeks, and bogs everywhere. It's so different from home. Pedro is talking Portuguese to Andres to get an idea of his comprehension. I'm in the back seat, drifting off into my own little world. I'm so excited for Andres and I to be away in this place, just the two of us. It will give us time to really bond and build our relationship.

The 2½ hour drive went very quickly. I am pulled from my daydreaming when I heard Pedro announce, "Chegámos finalmente!" We are finally here. I can't believe it!

Pedro pulls up to the town's main government building. He takes us directly to the mayor's office.

"Hello, Mr. Mayor. Andres and Lisa are here."

"Hello! Come in!" He welcomes us into his office. "Please take a seat."

The conversation is short and sweet. He says he is very glad to have us in his town, and that Mestre Mota has spoken very highly of us and mentioned we have skills in building websites. This led him to ask if we could build an English site for the town during our stay. They would like to get more exposure for their drumming group and highlight the soybean and oilseed farms in the area.

"Yes, I would be happy to do that while we're here," I responded since out of the two of us, I am the one with the web-building skills.

"Great! Thank you. We have a computer for you. Just let Pedro know what software you will need to complete the task," the mayor offered. "Pedro, please show them their desk. Andres and Lisa, I will see you tomorrow night at the welcome party."

"Thank you," we both said in unison.

Pedro guides us down the hall and into The Department of Education office on the right. He shows us to a desk that is tucked back in the corner. The desk is accompanied by one computer and two chairs. The chairs are really close together.

The thought briefly crosses my mind, *Maybe Andres and I might get 'too close' over the next year.*

Either way, all I know is I am going to make the most out of this opportunity. I'm excited I can give back to this little town by building them a website.

Pedro proceeds to introduce us to the other people in this office. Márcia is the Director of Education; then, the other office workers, José, Ana, and Carlos. Neither Andres or I fully caught their job title or function; however, we do understand we will be sharing an office with them for the next twelve months.

"So, this is where you will need to report for work every weekday at 8:30 a.m. unless you are told otherwise. You have the computer there. What other software do you need?"

"I will need Photoshop and then the credentials to get into the web server. I can do everything else from there."

"Sounds good. I will work on getting that software and getting it installed."

"Now, let's take you to the local Pousada where you will be staying for the next couple of nights. You will love Antônia. Remember, she will be a good resource for helping you understand the language and some of the other things that go on in the town."

We leave the office and go a few blocks down the street to this quaint building. Pedro knocks on the door. This adorable little woman with salt and pepper hair piled on her head appears when the door opens.

"Olá," she said in a timid voice that matches her stature.

"Antônia, this is Andres and Lisa. Andres and Lisa, this is Antônia. She will take good care of you as you get adjusted to life here in the village. We will work on getting a couple of bikes so you two can get around town. You are in good hands. I need to get back to work myself. You have my number on the card I gave you. Don't hesitate to call if you need anything."

Chapter 18
Assignments

As soon as Pedro left, Antônia came out of her shell. She is excited to share with us about her town and her country.

In a combination of her broken English and simple Portuguese, she says, "I have prepared a traditional Brazilian meal for you. It will be ready in one hour. In your room is traditional Brazilian clothing. Wear that tonight for your first dinner in Ouriçangas."

Despite the language barrier, I notice a twinkle in her eye when she mentions the traditional clothes. My guess of Brazilian costumes awaiting us is confirmed when we get to our room. I can tell our relationship with Antônia is going to be a very special part of our time in Brazil.

I take the lead in responding. "Antônia, thank you so much for thinking of us. We will give them a try and see how they look." I give Andres a reassuring look it is going to be ok.

The traditional garb was laid out on our bed. This is so thoughtful! I am all about dressing up and having fun. Andres, on the other hand, thinks this type of stuff is extra. I know this is taking him WAY out of his comfort zone. I can see his struggle. He doesn't want to dishonor Mestre Mota by saying no; he also doesn't want to dress up and look foolish.

I put on the beautiful white lace dress. As I pull up the large crinoline slip underneath, the skirt flares out and makes my hips look huge. Seeing all she went through for us makes me chuckle, and reminds me of dressing up for cultural days in elementary school.

"This is stupid," Andres complained as he puts on his outfit consisting of baggy pants, an elaborate belt, a scarf for his neck, and a wide brimmed black bolero hat.

"Lighten up. It is for one night. You look adorable by the way."

"I feel like an idiot. No pictures," he stated.

"Come on. You look so...authentic!" I teased. I am honestly surprised. This is so out of his character to do something like this. It gives me hope that maybe he can change and lighten up, laugh a little at himself, and just be silly sometimes.

We head back to the dining area to make our grand entrance. Antônia is there with a huge grin on her face. We can hear her snicker at the sight of what she had lovingly created.

"Lisa, I have one more thing for you."

With that she pulls out a long white lace scarf and begins to wrap it around my head. I feel so special. She really wants to share her life culture with us.

As the headdress grows around my head, I can sense Andres getting more and more agitated. I hate that. This is such a special time and Antônia went the extra mile to make it memorable. He is missing it because he is too busy "feeling stupid" to receive the love she is showing us. I am determined to not let his attitude ruin this moment for me.

She puts the finishing touches on my headdress and took a step back. "You look beautiful!" she smiles and chuckles. "You both look very Brazilian! I need a picture."

I can see Andres' eyes roll.

"Come on, Andres. One picture, then you can take off the hat and the scarf if you don't feel comfortable," I said, trying to ease his worsening mood.

Antônia actually snuck in a few photos before Andres took off his Brazilian wardrobe. I want to keep my outfit on because there is something about the beautiful white lace that makes me feel special and pretty.

Dinner is amazing! Everything Antônia puts on the table is delicious. She made Pão De Queijo (Brazilian Cheese Bread), Feijoada (Black Bean and Pork Stew), Brazilian Style Rice, Acarajé (Black-eyed Pea Fritters), Limonada Suíça (Brazilian Lemonade), and Brigadeiro (Brazilian Chocolate Fudge Balls) for dessert. The combination of flavors is unique to our pallet, nevertheless tasty. Antônia is an amazing cook.

When she heads into the kitchen, I turn to Andres and say, "Wasn't this meal worth humoring Antônia by wearing Brazilian attire?"

He gives me an annoyed look. "We could have enjoyed this food very easily without needing to get dressed up."

He is such a party pooper.

We both got a great night's sleep. Who couldn't after close to twenty-one hours of traveling and a day packed with introductions and surprises? I wake up and almost have to pinch myself to make sure this trip to Brazil isn't a dream. Pedro is coming to pick us up at 9:30 this morning to show us more of the town.

Antônia has a light breakfast spread waiting for us. She prepared a pound cake and crepes; some filled with cheese and some with fruit. Everything is delicious.

"Good morning to the two of you!" Pedro said. "Are you ready to go? This morning you will meet the principals of the elementary and high school. This afternoon I'll take you back to the office and you can get started on the work we have for you there. Lisa, Photoshop should be loaded onto the computer by the time you get back this afternoon."

Visiting the schools is a blast. The kids are curious about us and want to play. We found out we'll be in the schools at least one day per week, so we will have plenty of time for interacting with the kids. I am glad Andres is excited about the idea of playing with the kids. It's nice when I see him with a smile on his face, enjoying life. It begins to make up for the times he gets agitated.

When we get back to the office, I start working on the site map of the new website. I'm going through the newspapers and magazines Pedro gave us to learn about this cute town. As I'm digging into the hard copy information, Andres is searching the internet for information as well.

"Hey, Lisa, look at this."

"Look at what? Did you find something interesting about Ouriçangas?" I inquired.

"Not about Ouriçangas, but it is interesting."

I look over and see a naked woman on the screen. REALLY?!?!? This is our first day in the office, and we are on a government computer. I can't believe he is looking at that. "Close that right now!" I commanded.

"Don't worry. We are back here in the corner. Nobody is going to see," he tried to reassure me.

"That's not the point. We shouldn't be viewing that on this computer. What if someone finds out!"

The wave of shame I thought was packed up in that specially marked box at my parent's house suddenly comes crashing over me again. I thought we would be without this porn thing for twelve months. I guess I am wrong. What is wrong with him that he finds this even remotely ok?

Realizing I can't make him stop looking, and fighting with him would just draw attention to us, I decide to bury my head in the information Pedro gave me and focus my work. I will be mortified if anyone finds out.

I am so glad to see the clock reach 5:00 p.m. I am ready to leave the office and get as far away from that computer as possible. Andres doesn't understand the reason for my anger. He is trying to convince me it is no big deal and that no one would ever find out. I personally don't want to take that chance.

The big welcome party starts at 6:30 p.m. I am exhausted from our first day at work; the jet lag is setting in. Not to mention I'm annoyed that Andres has been searching porn all afternoon at work. Antônia is so sweet in welcoming us back home. She has some Coxinha, Brazilian chicken croquettes waiting for us. After our snack, I inform everyone I want to go up and take a short nap before the big party tonight. I'm hoping that a little rest will help me feel rejuvenated and adjust my attitude.

Andres follows me back to our room wanting to fool around. First of all, I'm tired. Even more than that, I am annoyed with him. The last thing I want is for him to touch me. He is so worked up because he has been looking at naked women all afternoon. Just the thought of that makes me shudder. I am mad he did this on our work computer.

The deeper pain comes from the enjoyment he gets from looking at other women. It cuts deep into my heart. What's wrong with me that I am not enough to turn him on? All he wants is for me to take care of his physical needs. He's oblivious to the fact that I'm drowning in the insecurities of not being enough for my husband.

As I try to rest, he keeps prodding and poking at me until I break down and give him the attention he's looking for. I don't want him touching me, so it's very much a one-way transaction...and he seems more than ok with that. I feel used and completely dismissed. I know as his wife, I am supposed to serve him. However, shouldn't I be respected and cherished in return?

Quickly I dismiss the question for two reasons. First of all, it's really painful to even think about. Second of all, I don't have much time before I have to start getting ready for the party.

After a twenty-minute power snooze, I get up, wash my face, and begin to put on some fresh make-up. The concealer is doing a great job in covering up the black circles under my eyes. Too bad there is no remedy for the pain I am feeling in my heart.

Lisa, take a deep breath and ignore those feelings. There is nothing you can do about them right now, not to mention you have a party to go to tonight where you are one of the guests of honor. Showing up with a tearstained face and running mascara will cause people to ask questions. Those questions will cause you to lie or divulge the true source of the pain. Neither option is good.

I finish getting ready and head out to the front room with a smile on my face. After all, we are getting ready to go to the welcome party being held for us. Just focus on the positive and hope the rest will change.

This town knows how to put on a party! All of the food is delicious. There is a constant stream of people introducing themselves. Remembering all of their names as well as my Portuguese is keeping my mind busy. I'm sure over the next year I will come to know many of them better and the language will become easier as well. This party is just what I need. I'm excited to be part of this adorable town. I'm looking forward to building friendships, expanding my mind, and leaving them with the gift of an English website. It will be nice if my marriage could be strengthened during this experience as well.

Chapter 19
Building New Relationships

Tonight is our first meeting with the town's drumming group. Their name, Ritmo, means *rhythm* in Portuguese.

Growing up, I loved playing in the high school jazz band. My favorite was when different melodies and rhythms fit together to create a song. Music is one of the things I love about Capoeira as well. It goes one step beyond other martial arts by adding the rhythm of the song to the physical movement. I expect the music of the drumming group to be similar to some of the music we play at the school back home.

The fear of looking stupid keeps Andres from getting excited. Despite his great ear for music, he never played an instrument. Now that I think about it, he does everything he can to not play any of the instruments when we practice Capoeira.

"I don't know why we have to be in Ritmo," he grumbled.

"Why?!?! Because it is a part of the cultural exchange. And according to Mestre Mota, this will give us the opportunity to travel around the state and experience things here in Brazil we wouldn't otherwise," I answered.

"But it's stupid we need to actually play. I don't know anything about music," he continued to complain.

Trying to offer encouragement, I say, "What do you mean? First of all, you have a great understanding of music and rhythm. All of the music you listen to in your car. I've seen you air drum—you understand the music—you just don't know the technical terms and breakdown of the beats. Second, when you take a turn playing the instruments at Capoeira practice, you do just fine."

"Listening is different from playing. And as for playing in the jogo, I try avoiding that like the plague. That's just not my thing," he rebutted.

This is frustrating and annoying. It's like he is trying to make it difficult and no fun for either of us.

"I've noticed you would rather be in the inner circle fighting versus playing the instruments. Keep in mind: being a part of Ritmo is designed to benefit us. All you have to do is give it your best. They will understand you and I are new to this," I explain to him.

"It's different for you. You've played instruments before. You understand the timing of music—I never did that," he returns.

With that last statement, I can hear the voice of an insecure little boy ringing out. It breaks my heart. He is a great guy; too bad he doesn't seem to know it. It doesn't matter if he is good at drumming or not. People will still like him; and I will still love him. If I can just get him to realize that; imagine how amazing life will be.

"Here: would you like me to teach you about the time signatures of music? Samba is written in 2/4 time." I start writing it out, trying to explain. He looks at me like I am completely crazy.

"No, that doesn't make any sense to me. The way you are explaining it is just making it more confusing. So, stop."

And now he won't even take my help. I don't get why he doesn't see me as his #1 supporter. That's what a wife is supposed to be. Maybe I am not doing it right. I wish I could make him feel better about himself.

After this conversation with him, I am anxious about tonight. I can sense Andres is getting agitated about the whole thing, which usually ends up in some kind of explosion. I hope he can hold it together. Today, I'll do my best to encourage him without mentioning drumming practice.

After dinner, we hear a honk coming from outside. It's Marcos, our ride to practice.

"Hi! Are you ready? Here, you two will need these," as he hands each of us a pair of drumsticks.

"Thanks!" I said. "I am both excited and nervous for tonight."

"Don't worry. You don't have to be perfect. Just come on in and have fun," Marcos encouraged.

Andres remains silent and pouting.

We pull up to the high school and make our way into the gymnasium. I recognize many faces from the welcome dinner. After putting their things down, each of them disappears into the storage room and comes out with various drums of all shapes and sizes.

Marcos grabs two of the drums and begins giving us a basic drumming lesson. It starts with some simple beats. He is emphasizing the importance of which hand is used for each hit. This is part of the performance that goes along with the music. This is fun. I'm enjoying the challenge of this new experience...immensely. Andres? Well, not so much.

"Dum-da-dum-dum, like that." Marcos instructed.

Andres' drum responds "dum-dum-da-dum."

"No, not quite. Almost. Long, short, long, long."

"That is what I played! I don't get this. I'll just sit out and watch. Lisa, stay here with me."

Why does he have to put me in this difficult place? I want to play. In the past, if I didn't bail out with him, he got angry. If I followed his lead, we never went back.

One thing I hate is how frustrated he gets when he is challenged. Anger overtakes him and he just gives up. It's like he tells himself he is worthless because he didn't succeed on the first try. If he feels he failed at an activity, he doesn't want me to experience the joy of doing it; or even worse, succeeding at it. That's when he asks me, or expects me to quit with him. Ultimately, I know he won't quit Ritmo because of his commitment to Mestre Mota.

The reality of that thought stings.

Because of his commitment to Mestre Mota, I know I won't have to give up the experience of drumming.

What does Mestre Mota have that I don't? Why will he suck it up and do something he doesn't want to do for his martial arts teacher, but wouldn't do it for his wife?

This isn't the first time he has done this. *Lisa, don't dwell on it,* I tell myself, in hopes of making the sting go away. Maybe he will learn that sticking something out, even if it is hard, can end up being a good thing.

We make it through our first night of practice. Andres actually started figuring out the basic beat. Watching the rest of the group practice and hearing the rhythms really helped. When we get home, I notice him tapping out the beat on the table.

"Hey, that's it! You got it!"

"Probably not. I am sure I have messed something up with it."

"Do it again. It sounds right to me."

He taps it out.

"That is so close. Wait a touch longer after the second beat," I said.

"Never mind; I give up. I am just not cut out for drumming. I'm going to bed."

Why does he always have to be such a downer? Practice was so much fun tonight except for his little tantrum. At least it was a passive aggressive, pouty tantrum and not a big blowup. I wish I knew what to do to change him. How can I get it through his thick skull that it is ok to mess up? His standard of being perfect isn't good for anyone involved.

Chapter 20
Candomblé

It's Friday afternoon. We're finishing up work when Pedro appears in our little corner of the office.

"Olá! How are you two doing today?"

"Hi, Pedro. We're good. Andres and I are finishing up things here. We had a great week at the elementary school harvesting their gardens."

"That is great! I hope you got a chance to taste the fruit of your labor. I came by to invite you to a Candomblé ceremony this weekend. Are you familiar with it?"

"A little. Mestre Mota mentioned it before. It is the native religion of Salvador, right?" Andres chimed in.

"Well, not native. Its roots are actually from Africa. During the slave trade, the 4.9 million slaves from Western Africa brought their native religion with them. The Portuguese slave owners were adamant about converting the slaves to Catholicism. To appease their masters, many of the slaves would appear to follow the Catholic religion while using the images and statues of the Catholic saints to represent their orixas, or lesser deities that ultimately serve their main god Oludumaré."

This little history lesson from Pedro is quite intriguing. Being raised in the Catholic Church, I wasn't allowed to explore other religions. Knowing they existed was about the extent of my knowledge. It's fascinating that by the conviction of their faith, the slaves still found a way to worship their gods, despite their oppression. After over twenty years of going to church and Catholic elementary school, my religion was more a series of rules. I have no true understanding, relationship, or conviction for the God I am apparently supposed to be serving.

"When and where is this ceremony?" I ask.

"It is tomorrow night at 7 p.m. at the local *terreiros*, or what you would call church. I'll pick you up at 6:30 p.m. Since you two aren't followers of the religion, you aren't allowed to participate in the ceremony, but you're welcome to observe it."

I look to Andres to get a read on what he thinks about the offer. I'm sure he'll be interested in the cultural experience. However I'm not sure how he feels about the religious aspect. He had no real church experience growing up. I am not even sure if he has ever been to a church service. We never really discussed spirituality except for him being adamantly against getting married in the Catholic Church. With a semi-interested look on his face, he nodded his head.

"Yes, Pedro. We would love to go. Thank you for asking. What should we wear?" I asked.

"Modest clothing—and something white if you have it. Again, you will just be observing, not participating. Just to let you know, there will be some dancing, chanting, and singing. They will be calling in the protector gods. There will also be incense burning and some plates of food. I am just letting you know because for some, the smell gets pretty intense. The food is just for the participants; so make sure you get something to eat before I pick you up. I want you to have a good experience."

"We appreciate both the invitation as well as all of the information. We'll be ready to go tomorrow night at 6:30."

"Sounds good! See you then."

I turn to Andres. "That sounds interesting and kind of scary."

"I bet it is going to be more of a show than anything. I think religion is just a crutch for people who aren't strong enough to deal with life on their own. At least it will give us something to do tomorrow night."

His ungrateful attitude really bothers me. Pedro didn't have to invite us. I knew very little about this part of Brazilian culture. Even though it was mentioned as a local religion when I visited in college, I didn't have the opportunity to experience a ceremony. Oh, well. I'll let Andres be Andres and just be thankful he agreed to go.

Pedro and his wife are right on time. "Olá! Are you guys ready?"

"Yes, I think so. I am a little anxious about what we might see or experience at this thing tonight," I admitted.

"Oh, it is going to be good. I think you will find it interesting. And by the way, you might see someone go into a trance."

"Um, what do you mean by that?"

"It's nothing to worry about. It's when one of the gods enters into one of the practitioners. If this happens, don't do anything. And if you feel yourself being pulled into a trance, just go with it. We can't control the gods. But I promise; we won't let anything happen to you."

I am no longer anxious; now I'm scared. The church experience I had growing up didn't include dancing, chanting, and trances. God is God and He doesn't possess anyone and make them dance. Maybe this isn't such a great idea. I'm getting that pit in my stomach that tells me I am entering into something I have no business being around.

We pull up to this small, cinder-block building on the outskirts of town. It's dimly lit, mainly by candles. The smell of sandalwood is heavy in the air, with whiffs of a mixture of musty and floral smells. Pedro ushers us to a rickety wooden bench along the side wall. We are in the section for observers, only separated from the participants by a thin white string. The participants are dressed in all white, the women wearing headdresses similar to the outfit Antônia dressed me in the first night we got into town.

As the ceremony starts, the participants begin chanting and dancing. Despite the fact that this isn't like any church service I've attended, I'm beginning to relax a bit. I find myself moving to the chanting and the drumming. I can't understand a word they are saying because the whole service is in the ritual language of Yoruba—not even Portuguese.

About twenty minutes into the service, the woman sitting close to me begins to make these guttural sounds and twitching movements. With that, she jumps up and starts spinning around. People are clearing the way for her, giving her all the room she needs to move. I'm scared.

Assuming this woman is going into a trance, I definitely don't want to go into one. It looks like it hurts. She is moving so fast and out of control.

I start searching my memory to find the words of a prayer, any prayer. *Our Father, who art in heaven...* I begin to recite in my head, seeking and longing for comfort and protection from this eerie experience. As I continue, I notice this prayer is helping to ease the fear.

I look over at Andres. He is intrigued and entertained—not scared at all.

After dancing and spinning for about twenty-five minutes, the woman in the trance falls to the ground like a rag-doll. It looks like it hurt. As she starts coming to, they sit her down on the rickety bench right next to me. I don't want to be anywhere near her. I don't want the residue of whatever possessed her to jump on me! This service can't get over fast enough. This was a really bad idea.

After about an hour and a half, the service came to a close. As we walk out, they hand each of us a little candy. I politely take it, thinking, *Like I am going to eat that? Heck no. It is going in the trash as soon as Pedro and his wife drive away.*

Once we get in the car, Pedro inquires, "So, what do you think? Did you enjoy it?"

"It was...interesting," I tried to answer with a response that won't offend.

"That was WILD! I can't believe how fast that woman was spinning and dancing and that she didn't hit anything or hurt herself. She is going to feel sore tomorrow!" Andres chimed in with great enthusiasm.

"Yes, one of the gods possessed her. That's what made tonight so special. She should be just fine since she wasn't doing any of that under her own power."

WHAT?!?!?! None of that was under her own power? She was a puppet for these gods. This is CRAZY!!! Church has always been more of an obligation for me. I know I haven't been in a long time, but at least the church I go to, one that talks about Jesus as our Lord and Savior, doesn't possess people, dance them into exhaustion, and throw them on the floor.

As we pull up in front of our house, I say, "Thank you, Pedro, for inviting us. That was definitely a unique experience."

"You are welcome. I am glad we could share more of Brazil with you."

That is a part of Brazil I think I could have done without, I thought to myself.

Chapter 21
Living on Our Own

Life in Ouriçangas is going well. Since we're the first couple on this exchange program, they want to make sure we have enough privacy; so they moved us into a house of our own for a few months. It's exciting to have our own little retreat. It also brings a new level of isolation. Despite the language barrier, when we stayed with Antônia, we spent hours practicing Portuguese and sharing about each other's culture. There was joy and laughter.

Now that it's just the two of us in our own place, the atmosphere is different. We pull up to the dark little house and stash our bikes on the side. Inside we have all of the necessities. The only thing lacking is the feeling of home. The conversations between Andres and I consist of complaining; not very uplifting or encouraging—and always in English.

"What are you making for dinner?" Andres asked.

"That is a good question. I am going to try to make Moqueca, that fish stew Antônia made for us the third night we were here. She gave me the recipe."

"Good. I hope you remember it. I'm hungry and I don't want dinner to be nasty."

I want to say, *If you don't want dinner to be nasty, then cook it yourself.* Instead, the thought comes out, "I'll do my best. This kitchen is different from what I am used to back home. The good news is you're hungry. They say hunger is the best spice!"

"Whatever. How long will it take?"

"It should be about an hour. Why don't you grab a snack for now?"

"Really? An hour? Can't you make anything quicker?"

"Stop, you'll be fine. Just eat some chips or something."

I blame his attitude on being hangry. Usually, once he gets some food in his stomach, he's better.

There is a growing animosity between us over the porn that just won't seem to go away. Every day we are in the office, he visits sex sites. He keeps telling me we won't get caught. Personally, I don't want to take the chance. Regardless, he doesn't listen to me. It reminds me of our first trip into The Passion Palace. I know he's not going to take no for an answer.

As he is going through our stash of snacks, he perks up, "What do you think of Juliana from Ritmo?"

"What do you mean? She seems really nice. She has always been kind to me, but I don't really know her that well."

"Have you ever noticed her when she is drumming; the way she moves? She is really sexy."

Huh? I am so confused. My husband is trying to tell me how sexy he thinks this other woman is. That hurts. Then I remember how turned on he would get when we first started watching porn. "Why are you telling me this?"

"What do you mean, 'Why am I telling you this?' I have seen you look at her like that. She has a beautiful body and how she moves is intriguing."

WHAT?!?!?! Now this is pushing too far. The porn is one thing. Now you are objectifying this gal in Ritmo? That is too much. The whole thing just got way creepy!

"Look at her like what? She is a pretty gal, and it's entertaining to watch her drum. I enjoy watching her excitement and enthusiasm for creating music."

"I think it is because you find her sexy."

Oh, my! I can't believe he's even saying this. I mean, I appreciate how pretty she is, but I don't find her sexy. I'm not attracted to females. He is definitely watching too much porn!

"What makes you say that? I don't look at her or think of her like that. And, I hope you aren't thinking of her like that either. We are guests in this village. The fact you are even mentioning this is just wrong."

"Oh, come on. You know you have thought of it."

"Um, no. I haven't."

This whole conversation is wrong. It feels like a cat and mouse game. I hate it when he tells me what I am thinking. After he says something like that, I question myself—was I thinking that? Or anything close? I mean, I have noticed her physique before. Maybe it's because I was an art major in college. I took several figure drawing classes which gave me a different appreciation for the human body. I am intrigued by how the different parts are put together and how the body moves. I never had sexual thoughts when we were studying the human figure.

I'm confused and quite honestly disgusted he is even remotely thinking this way about this woman.

And what about me? I'm your wife. I have never heard you call me sexy.

The conversation over dinner held an awkwardness, but nothing else was said about Juliana. We don't have a TV in our place, so there is nothing to distract us.

After dinner, Andres starts up again. "So, tell me again the story you liked from the first magazine you got from The Palace."

I am annoyed. First of all, I didn't get the magazine- I didn't even want it. He got it for me. Second of all, I am still hurt and annoyed by the conversation before dinner. I sense he is horny and wants to have sex. I want nothing to do with him.

"No," I replied.

"What do you mean, 'No'? It will be fun. I like watching you get excited when you tell the story."

This conversation is annoying because it almost sounds like he cares about me and my excitement, although he never really cares about what makes me happy. I can feel the manipulation; however, I would never call it that. If I did, it would require me to acknowledge my own husband is trying to control me—and that is too much for me to admit.

I also don't like to confess that when it comes to porn, once I turn off my thoughts and convictions, my body dramatically reacts physically to what I am seeing. I am conflicted because I really don't like it...at all. However, my body's reaction makes me look like a liar. Then there is the part of me that just wants to please my husband and keep peace in my home. Honestly, it is all so confusing.

My thoughts are interrupted. "Come on; tell me about how the flight attendant started 'serving' the passengers."

I give up. I surrender. I know what he wants; and there is no stopping him until he gets it. This is pretty much the pattern that has been established in our relationship. My feelings, desires, or boundaries don't matter. He will keep pressing until he gets his way. Trying to make it easier for me, I convince myself to focus on the physical part that is enjoyable and ignore the mental and emotional part of me that is crying out with screams of distress.

The sex last night was pretty wild. Many scenarios and people were fantasized about. I was the flight attendant, the woman at the store, the stripper...but me, Lisa, Andres' wife wasn't sexy enough, pretty enough, or anything enough to pleasure him. I was able to override my thoughts and emotions last night. This morning, though, they are so loud I can't seem to shut them up. This isn't what I had anticipated marriage to be. I feel horrible.

Come on, Lisa, brush it off. You are on a year sabbatical from life, in a beautiful town in Brazil. You have many things to be grateful for. Stop feeling sorry for yourself.

I know I have to give myself a pep talk to get ready for the day. We're in the office today, so I know I will be in a constant battle with Andres over the computer. First of all, I need the computer to work on the website we're supposed to be building. Second, I am still mortified the people in the office will find out the smut coming through the network to our computer. I keep trying to tell Andres there are no language barriers when it comes to pictures of naked women.

I take my shower trying to clear my mind and wash off the dirty residue from the night before. I notice all of the delicious food we've been eating is starting to impact my waistline; this doesn't help me feel any better about myself.

Lisa, stop thinking about it. You only have the opportunity to experience Brazil like this once. You have always been a little chunky; that's how you are built.

I quickly finish my shower and cover up with a towel so I don't have to see my body any more. The battle in my mind over not being enough is already at a code red; my inner demons don't need any more ammunition. I need to focus on burying the feelings and emotions from last night. I only have a short time to get myself together and put on my happy face before we need to report to work.

The daily chorus of "Bom Dia" rings out as we walk into the office. I am still trying to convince myself it's a good morning. Andres and I head over to our little corner of the office; he jumps on the computer.

"I need the computer for a few hours today," I said. "I am to the point in building the website that I need to be online."

"Ok, you can have it in a little bit."

On the inside, I am rolling my eyes and shaking my head, hoping it doesn't show on the outside. I organize the information I have so I can be ultra-efficient once I get control over the mouse.

"Hey, Lisa, come look at this site. I signed us up."

I step behind him to see what he is talking about. FunAdultFriends.com is asking 2-looking-4-fun to fill out their profile. The pit in my stomach is enough to make me want to vomit. I don't want to ask who "2-looking-4-fun" is because I already know the answer; and it's one I don't want to hear.

I am so confused and hurt right now. I've been trying to tell him my true feelings about the porn and fantasizing about other people. He just won't listen to me. Like he didn't listen to me when I told him I didn't want to go to The Passion Palace. The dismissal of my feelings really hurts. To avoid that pain, I've stopped sharing my feelings with him. I'm finding myself even going as far as trying to agree with him to avoid the rejection that comes with not being heard or acknowledged.

On top of all of this, I am so isolated down here. There is no one I can talk to. I can't call anyone back home because Andres and I are always together; not to mention the cost of an international call. I can't email Linda because Andres and I are sharing an email account. He would blow a gasket if he saw me talking about this with his mother. My feelings are so overwhelming. I don't know how to process the emotions, or navigate this situation; so I just stuff them. Put a smile on my face and jump into my passive-aggressive ways, hoping Andres will catch the hint.

"FunAdultFriends.com? Really? Why did you even sign us up for that? First of all, we are over 5,600 miles away. Second, I don't want to meet up with anyone else in person. Fantasizing is one thing; meeting up with someone else is a whole different ballgame."

"That's the beauty of it. We are over 5,600 miles away, so we can just talk about it while there is no way we can actually meet up with these people."

I am totally flabbergasted. Not only is this site perverted, now he is being completely deceptive, too. I have to get away from all of this. "I'll be back, I've got to go to the restroom."

What has my life turned into? Maybe he is right. Maybe we are safe because we are in a completely different hemisphere. It's just talk, no action; so at least that part is good. However, I can't trust it will stay here. Just like the promise to "go to The Passion Palace once" was a lie, I have a feeling this profile won't go away when we get back to the States.

As I'm wrestling with that, the next disturbing thought enters my head, *What is he going to put on our profile?*

I don't want a picture of my face, and I really don't want a picture of my body. This is so wrong. I don't know how to get out of it. I still hate the fact that even though my mind and heart are screaming, there is something in my physical body that is stimulated by this.

This is all so overwhelming—I can't deal with this. My solution right now is to just ignore it. I need to use the computer to work on the website. Taking over the mouse will stop this train wreck; at least for now. I still can't believe this is happening.

"Hey, Andres, I need to use the computer to work on the website," I announce coldly as I come back into the office.

"Ok. Give me just one more minute. I am just finishing up our profile."

I want to ask what he wrote. At the same time, though, I don't want to know what it says. I just want to take the keyboard and mouse away from him to make him stop. It's devastating that as his wife, he won't take "no" for an answer.

As the weeks pass, "2-looking-4-fun" started getting some hits. At least he used some discretion and posted a picture of us from the back.

He is always the first one to the computer to check the inbox. "Hey, babe, come take a look. We heard back from 'couple_for_fun'."

I HATE THIS!

"Why are you talking to another couple? I told you: I don't really want to meet up with anyone, and I ABSOLUTELY do not want to meet up with another couple."

He gives me his usual response. "We are 5,600 miles away. We aren't meeting up with anyone. We are just chatting. Lighten up."

I don't want to lighten up. This is really starting to consume him and has already completely taken over our sex life. It is never just the two of us in bed anymore.

Chapter 22
Homeward Bound

I can't believe we're heading home in two weeks. I feel a great sense of accomplishment with the website launching next week. Andres finally caught on to the drumming, and we were able to travel to many other small towns, back to Salvador, and even as far as Rio de Janeiro. We have built some great relationships and made some great memories.

One thing I'm extremely grateful for is we never got caught with the porn Andres was viewing on the computer. At least I'm assuming they didn't find out. No one ever said anything.

I'm a little concerned about what it will be like once we get back home. We have chatted with many different people on FunAdultFriends.com. It's safe while we're here in Brazil because we're so far away. Once we get back to the States, I have a feeling things are going to continue to progress even though I don't want them to. I really don't want to live out this fantasy of his. I don't know how to deal with it, so I am going to ignore it for now and enjoy our final days here in Brazil.

"The going-away party tonight was a lot of fun. I can't believe how many friends we have made over the past year. Do you remember when they had our welcome party? We knew NOBODY!" I said.

"Yea, I guess it was cool. The mayor still bugs me. I think he's up to no good," Andres complained.

Really? They gave us a beautiful going-away party in our honor, and you have to complain about the mayor?

"Be nice. I get it; the mayor is a little different. First of all, you don't really know him. And second of all, we are leaving in a week," I reacted.

"Whatever. The guy is a creep. So, when we get back home, we are staying with your parents until we find an apartment, right?"

"Yes, we are welcome until we find a place. My mom said we can stay for a month or two if necessary. They don't want us to be rushed in finding a new apartment."

"Oh, don't worry; we won't be there for a month or two. I PROMISE. We are going to be looking for a new place the first day we get back."

Really? Is he already hating my parents again? The first day back we will be dealing with jet lag, visiting friends, readjusting...but you are going to dive right into the stressful task of looking for a new apartment? UGH! His immediacy drives me crazy! It's one thing if we HAD to. However, we have the gift of being able to take our time.

"Well, just in case we are either too tired that first day back, or nothing good is available, we have a place to stay, free of charge."

"Oh, don't worry; we will find something."

Just let it go. It isn't worth arguing or getting upset.

I have resigned to the fact that this is the way he is. Not really the "give and take" I expected in a marriage. I hate conflict; and since he is going to do whatever he wants to do anyway, it isn't worth the fight.

"Ladies and gentlemen, we will begin making our final approach into Kansas City International Airport shortly. The skies are clear and it is a mild 66°. We will be landing at 11:42 a.m. central time. Please remain seated until we make our way to the jet way and the captain has turned off the seatbelt signs. Thank you for flying with us today."

I can't believe our twelve-month sabbatical from life is over. In some ways, it feels like we have been gone for forever. In other ways, it was the blink of an eye. Either way, it was an amazing experience.

My thoughts are interrupted by Andres poking me and nodding to the flight attendant. "Look at her. She's hot. I betcha the flight attendant in your story was blond, just like her."

"What are you talking about?"

"That flight attendant that just walked by; I bet she would be great at 'servicing' us. Do you think she is a part of the 'Mile High Club'?"

Really? This perversion crap? Again?!?

"Andres, stop. First of all, these people around us speak English, so it isn't like in Ouriçangas where people can't understand what you are talking about. Second, I don't want to go there right now." *I really don't want to go there ever. I know I have been losing the war; I am hoping to at least win this battle.*

"Oh, come on. You know you thought about it."

"No, I didn't think about it. I was thinking about the experiences we've had over the last year, and what a blessing it was to live in Ouriçangas, meet the people we met, and to visit the other parts of Brazil we were able to visit. I am not always thinking about sex."

"You're being lame. Look at her when she walks back. She just looks fun," he continued.

I shift my weight and turn away from him, making it very clear I'm not entertaining his conversation. A wave of anxiety washes over me, realizing the 5,600-mile buffer of safety is rapidly disappearing.

As we come up the escalator into the baggage claim area, my parents are waiting for us. It's so good to see their faces! I am still amazed they treat us the way they do after the fiasco of the wedding.

"Welcome home, you two! We are so glad you made it back safely." My mom has a huge hug for each of us. My dad gives me a big hug and shakes Andres' hand, welcoming us home.

"We have your favorite dinner of Chicken Cordon Bleu as your welcome home meal for tonight."

My mom has a gift of hospitality. She always thinks of little ways to show people love. A smile spreads across my tired face. "Mom, you are the best. Thank you. And to both of you, thank you for coming to pick us up AND for letting us stay at your house again while we look for a new apartment."

"Yea, we are going to start looking for a new apartment this afternoon," Andres chimes in.

"Oh, you don't need to rush to find a new place today. International travel can be tiring. Just take today to rest and see some of your friends. Andres, I am sure your mom is very excited to see you two. There is no rush in moving out," my mom said.

"It is no big deal. We need to get back into our own place as soon as possible."

What is his issue about this? I am tired; and whether we start looking today or tomorrow, it isn't going to make a difference on our move-in date. Although this man is driving me crazy, I don't have the energy to argue. Apparently, I will need to preserve all the energy I have to go apartment hunting this afternoon.

"What's one of your favorite parts of the trip?" my mom inquired.

"I loved playing with Ritmo, the town's drumming group. It was really fun to play and we got to be a part of many festivals and celebrations. We also made some really good friends in Ritmo," I chimed in. "Andres, what would you say was your favorite part?"

"I liked being a part of the Capoeira jogo in the village and when we went to Salvador."

It feels good to be a part of a welcoming English conversation. I didn't realize how exhausting it is to constantly be conversing in a second language. It also feels good to have Andres and my parents talking. It sounds stupid to be excited about something that should be so normal; however, I am celebrating the little steps towards the complete reconciliation I am hoping for.

Pleasant conversation continued for the entire ride home. As soon as we got to the house, we grabbed our big bags and hauled them in.

Our family tradition upon return of an overseas trip is to spend time hearing stories of the great adventure. It also includes the giving of the special gifts brought home from the foreign destination. I can sense my mom trying to foster this tradition with us.

"Are you two hungry? I can make you both a sandwich and you can tell us more about your trip. Also, I am happy to do your laundry for you.

Just unpack it and bring it to the utility room. I'll get it taken care of," my mom said out of her true servant's heart.

"Yea, a sandwich would be good," Andres said.

"Yes, please, Momma! Thank you!" I chimed in. "And while you are making them, we have some special presents for you and Dad."

I dig out the Brazilian ceramic figurine, the hammock chair, and the coffee we brought for them. We shared more stories while we ate.

As soon as Andres finished his sandwich, he turned to me, "Hurry up and finish eating. We need to go look at apartments."

"Really? Do we have to leave right this second? We just got home and I am tired. Can we please start looking tomorrow?"

"No, we need to get started today. I don't know how long it will take to find a place."

"Waiting one day isn't going to make that big of a difference."

"Yes, it will. If you don't want to go, that is fine. But I am going to find an apartment this afternoon."

I hate it when he gives ultimatums. It's so stupid. If I could trust him to find a place that would include some of my likes, it might be ok. If I want to have any chance of getting some of my preferences in an apartment, I know I had better go with him.

We finish up our lunch and head out. I still can't believe we landed this morning from a twenty-one-hour flight and this afternoon we are apartment shopping.

We head towards the neighborhood of our last apartment to start the hunt. It was in the hip part of the city and close to the Capoeira School and our friends. As we drive, I start getting anxious because of one particular place that's between my parent's house and our final destination: The Passion Palace. I hope he doesn't remember—or at least that his mind is so focused on apartment hunting he won't want to go there. I hold my breath as he drives towards that horrid place. After we passed the entrance, I let out my breath with a quiet sigh of relief.

There is no vacancy in our old building, but there is a place a few blocks away. It's not as cute as our old place, and it's at garden level which brings up safety concerns for me. Besides, being in the basement makes it feel like a dungeon, which doesn't seem to matter to Andres because he is hell-bent on getting the lease signed today. At least this place is in our budget.

He got his way. Moving day is in two days. I am exhausted.

"Hey, did you call your mom to let her know we got back safely?" I asked.

"No. You can give her a call later," he said.

"I am sure she is wondering and worried why she hasn't heard from us yet."

"She'll be fine. I wanted to get out and look for an apartment, and I know when I call, she will want to talk."

My heart breaks with how rude he is to his mother.

"Now that we have the lease signed, we can visit her," I suggested.

"That sounds good. I know she will be excited to see us."

He makes a left-hand turn, leading us away from his mom's house.

"I thought you said we are going to see your mother. Why did you turn left?"

"I'm going to stop by The Passion Palace. We haven't been there in a long time, and we need some new stuff."

"Um, we're staying at my parent's house for the next few nights."

"It's fine. We can sneak it in and just take it up to your room. They'll never know."

I guess I got the answer to my question. This porn thing isn't going to stop. I have a feeling the FunAdultFriends.com thing isn't going to stop either. I'm tired, discouraged, ashamed, and trapped right now; I really don't know what to do.

Chapter 23
Welcome to the Dungeon

It's moving day...again. I'm still not functioning at 100% because of jetlag. At least we don't need to pack anything up. We just need to move boxes.

I'm not going to ask Holly and Joe for help because Andres burned the bridge with them as friends. Whenever we asked them for help, they were right there. The one time they asked us to help them, Andres insisted it was more important we attended a Capoeira class versus help them.

Randy is kind enough to help. Fortunately, we don't have too much stuff. At least one benefit of moving into a garden level apartment is there are no stairs to contend with.

"Is that it?"

"Yep, that is the last of it," Randy reported.

"You are amazing. Thank you for your help today. I don't think Andres and I could have done it ourselves," I said.

"No problem. I'm glad I could help," Randy replied.

"Once we get settled, we will have you and Marie over for dinner."

"That sounds good. I know Marie would like that as well. You know she doesn't have a whole lot of friends, and she always enjoys when we hang out with you guys," Randy said.

"She is a very sweet lady. I'll work with Andres to make sure we get something on the calendar."

"Hey, man, thanks for your help today. Once we get settled, we will have you and Marie over for dinner," Andres offered, joining the conversation.

"We have already talked about that. Good minds think alike!" I confirmed.

"Sounds good. We'll see you down at the school," Andres said as Randy left.

"Have you called your mom? I know she wants to come by and see the place today."

"No, not yet," Andres grumbled. "Maybe she can come down, bring us lunch, and help us unpack."

That sounds so rude. Invite someone to your new place, ask them to bring lunch, and then expect them to help unpack.

On my way to being completely offended, I hear Brenda's voice in my head. "If you want something, ask. Don't expect people to be able to read your mind. It is up to them to say yes or no; and then for you to respect their answer."

That sounds like a simple concept. Why do I have such a hard time with it? I have so much of my self-worth tied up in the fear of asking for what I want. It's like if I need or want something from someone else, it means I am not enough. And then, when I finally ask, if they say yes, there is guilt and shame for putting them out. If they say no, then there is something wrong or bad with me. Ugh. This is too much to think about right now.

"I am sure she will be happy to come over. I'll keep working on unpacking the kitchen because it's really a one-person job since this is a 'one butt' kitchen!"

Andres reached out to his mom. Sure enough, she was excited to see the place and help with unpacking. She agreed to pick up burgers on the way over as well.

I have to say, this place is starting to come together. I know we aren't going to be here forever, so I can deal with the darkness. As for the safety part; well, I just need to be a little braver.

I will admit: Andres is a machine when it comes to unpacking. In three days, we are completely unpacked. One of the first things he made sure was set up was the computer. Go figure. And he has already updated our profile on FunAdultFriends.com. He keeps asking me to sit with him and look at profiles. It is so strange shopping for people to engage with sexually.

"What do you think of this couple?"

"First of all, I told you: I am not interested in another couple. I don't want to be with any other man." My subconscious fears of trusting men with my body makes me cringe at the thought. "Second of all, it's getting late, and I need to get some sleep. Tomorrow is my first day back in the office. I'm going to bed. And you should probably get some sleep as well because you have your job interview tomorrow."

"Ok. Well, you go to bed. I'll be there in a little bit." He leans over and gives me a peck of a goodnight kiss, distracted by his computer search.

I go into the bedroom feeling alone. My stomach is in knots and I'm angry and hurt. I want my husband to come in and hold me, protect me, and tell me I am safe. On the other hand, though, I don't want Andres to even touch me because he's not listening to me when I tell him I don't want to be a part of this swinging lifestyle or the porn. He doesn't seem to care about me or my feelings, making me feel even more vulnerable and alone.

Stuffing these feelings, I get ready for bed, putting on my least sexy pajamas—not that it matters. I curl up in a ball on my side of the bed. I silently cry myself to sleep, hoping Andres is considerate enough to not wake me up, expecting any sexual favors when he finally makes his way to bed.

Beep - Beep- Beep. I can't believe it is already 6:00 a.m. Even though I fell asleep quickly, I definitely didn't get a restful night's sleep. Not good for my first day back to work. Andres' interview isn't until later. I am trying to be quiet getting ready, so as not to wake him.

I move into the bathroom and stand in front of the mirror. Who is that woman staring back at me? Her face is very pale except for her eyes; they are red and puffy. She looks like a wreck. I hope a hot shower will wash away the pain and shame, or at least the evidence of it.

The pulsating water is doing a great job of waking me up. Surprisingly, most of the puffiness in my eyes went away. I'm able to cover the rest with makeup. I really wish we had looked a little further for a place to live. Literally, this apartment has three small windows; all of them partially underground. It would be easier to wake up if I actually saw some sunshine.

Lisa, stop being so pessimistic. This isn't your forever home. It's fulfilling its purpose for now, I tell myself, trying to salvage a positive mindset for the day.

It's going to be strange heading back to my old office; back to a familiar place, except as a different person. I'm excited everyone here speaks English and I won't have to be worried about getting caught on FunAdultFriends.com. It's also nice I get some time away from Andres. Looking back, that was one part of our trip to Brazil that was really difficult. We were literally together twenty-four hours a day, seven days a week.

The building looks the same as it did when I left. I take a big deep breath and start walking in like I had many times before. I sense a big shift is about to take place.

As per usual, I am one of the first people in the office. My cubicle is there waiting for me. I'm so grateful I was able to take a sabbatical and they kept my position open for me. I log in and start dealing with the 34,232 emails in my inbox. Fortunately, many of them can just be deleted. There is also one marketing campaign for me to get started on waiting for me on my desk. I guess Dereck was banking on the fact my habits of being an early riser wouldn't change during my time in Brazil.

The morning is filled with joy as I receive a warm welcome from my co-workers. Kristi made her famous cinnamon rolls as a welcome back treat. I feel so loved.

"Welcome back, Lisa!" Dereck's voice boomed, making me jump. "It is so nice to have you back. I know you have some things to do to get caught up. Regardless, I would like to speak with you in my office at 10:30. I have something I need to discuss with you."

"Um, ok. Do I need to prepare or bring anything with me?"

"No. Just yourself."

"Ok, I'll come down to your office at 10:30."

What does he have to discuss with me? Am I in trouble? I just got back. Now I am nervous. Why do I always think I am in trouble? I call Andres to let him know something is up. I hope to get some reassurance that he is there for me, no matter what Dereck has to say.

"Good morning, Sweetie. Are you up?" I said.

"Yea, I'm up. How is it being back in the office?" Andres asked.

"Good, I think. People are happy to have me back and Kristi made her delicious cinnamon rolls. I am nervous though; Dereck set a meeting for me to talk with him at 10:30 this morning."

"What are you nervous about? You haven't been there to do anything wrong."

"I know, but I hope they aren't going to take away the sabbatical or something."

"You are crazy. Dereck was happy to have you back, right?"

"Yes."

"Ok, so stop tripping. It is going to be fine. I have to go get ready for my interview. Let me know what he says. I am sure you are just freaking out about nothing...like you always do."

"Thanks for the encouragement...I think. Good luck on your interview."

"Thanks."

Am I freaking out about nothing...like I always do? Was that a backhanded word of encouragement? I guess the real question is, "What is wrong with me? Why do I always freak out about things?" I need to be more self-assured and stop with these feelings of insecurity; just be who I am. I am not sure if I know who I really am, though. Growing up, I got really good at being who my parents wanted me to be. It was easy to do when all the people I needed to please had the same expectations. Now, the people around me have conflicting expectations of me, so I don't know who to be. I just want to make everyone around me happy and proud of me. I want to do whatever it takes to be loved and accepted by all of the people in my life.

I am sure Dereck is just going to ask me about my trip. I hope that's all. UGH...make these reeling thoughts in my mind STOP!! Put it out of your mind for the next ninety...actually eighty-six minutes. There is nothing you can do about it, so stop stressing over it.

I dive back into my horrifying inbox and make some great headway. The number of unread emails is now into the low four-digits...and I am able to actually stay occupied until my meeting. It's finally time. Deep breath, and down the hall I go!

Knock-knock. "Hello, Dereck. Are you ready for our meeting?"

"Yes. Come on in and shut the door."

I follow his instructions and hand him a box of brigadeiro, Brazilian fudge I brought back from our trip. "This is a little sweet treat for you and Patrice. I want to thank you again for your help in setting up my sabbatical as well as keeping my position available for me."

"You are welcome. You have always been a great asset here in the department; and after your study abroad, you are even more valuable. There are two things I want to speak with you about today. First of all, in my conversations with HR about your time off, as part of the company wide diversity initiative, they would like you to do a presentation about your time in Brazil at a Lunch-and-Learn for the company. You are welcome to share about whatever aspect you would like; just keep in mind it has to be in line with the theme of diversity."

"Wow, I would love to! Would there be a way to project a PowerPoint? It would be great to share some of my photos."

"We can make that happen. I am glad you are happy to share your experience. As for the second thing, you know the Marketing Manager position came open right before you left?"

"Yes. Brad took that other position in Operations."

"You're right. Have you ever thought about stepping into management?"

"I was thinking someday I would be in management, but I am one of the youngest people in this department; and I just came back from a year off. I heard Bill and Sarah both applied for it. They both have been with the company longer than me."

"Well, the position is still open, and I would really like for you to apply for it."

Very confused, I sit there and let it sink in. I am excited about the possibility of management; however, I feel so unqualified. Plus, I was just gone for twelve months, and my boss is asking me to apply for a promotion? How does that happen?

"Ok, I will get my resume together and submit it."

"Good. Please do, and submit it by the end of the day tomorrow. We need to move forward on making a decision for this position."

"Ok. I can do that; by the end of the day tomorrow," I confirmed, still a bit shell-shocked.

"Great. Thank you again for the goodies. And plan on the Lunch-and-Learn for the second Thursday of next month," he said while standing up and reaching out his hand.

"Sounds good. I'll mark it on my calendar. Would it be ok for Andres to come to the Lunch-and-Learn?" I asked as I stood up.

"Absolutely. We would love for him to join us," he replied, along with a firm handshake.

I walk back to my cubicle with great unbelief.

Who comes back from a twelve-month vacation and gets asked to put in for a promotion? I don't know why he asked me to do that. I really don't think I am that special. Besides, what are Bill and Sarah going to think? Both are older than me AND have been with the company longer than me. If I get the Marketing Manager position, they will report to me. I don't quite know how that is going to work.

I head straight to the conference room to have some privacy for my call to Andres.

"Well, I just got out of my meeting with Dereck."

"And...how did it go?"

"Well, first he said HR wants me to present at next month's Lunch-and-Learn diversity event and talk about our trip."

"That is cool. What else?"

"And then he asked me to apply for the Marketing Manager position."

"See, I told you there was nothing to worry about. You always expect the worst. I don't know why you do that."

"Well, I need to apply before the end of day tomorrow. I have to update my resume, so I might have to stay a little late tonight to get that done."

"It won't take you that long to update your resume. There is no reason for you to stay late. Don't start setting a precedent or Dereck will always expect you to stay late."

"What if it takes me extra time to get everything finished?"

"It isn't going to take you that long. You need to be home on time tonight."

I hate it when Andres gets like this; which is more often than not. It is like he tries to be supportive, although there are many strings attached. I can go after my dreams, as long as it doesn't impact him in any way, shape, or form.

"I have to get back to work. I'll see you tonight," I said.

"Ok, I'll see you at the regular time so we can go to Capoeira together tonight."

"Bye," I said without promising him anything.

Well, I better buckle down. I have a lot to get done in the next few hours.

Thinking about this promotion throughout the day, I'm getting excited. Unfortunately, I'm also worried that ultimately it will cause more of an issue at home. The job includes some travel. I don't know how Andres will deal with that. He has already made it clear he doesn't like me staying late. Maybe I can ask for a laptop and be able to work from home instead of having to stay late at the office.

I guess this is a case of me "freaking out about it like I always do" according to Andres. *Lisa, just ignore it and it will all work itself out.*

I can't believe it. I actually made it home on time...and got everything done. I'm exhausted, but excited as well. "Hi, Sweetie, I'm home."

"Hey. Hurry up and change. We need to get heading out to the school."

As I head to the bedroom to get changed, I call out, "So, how did your interview go?"

"It went good. I am pretty sure I have the job. They said I was the last one they're interviewing and they'll get back to me tomorrow."

"REALLY? That's great news! That was quick! Most job searches take forever! Tell me about the company and the position."

"It's with the Melman Honda Dealership. The position is entry level service advisor with the possibility of promotion. I'll get to work in the car industry, and they have decent benefits," he replied.

I am excited for him...for us!

"And when I was leaving my interview, there was this pretty blonde gal that came walking down the hall. She is a little bit taller than you and about twenty pounds thinner. She smiled at me. I can tell she is really nice; she could be a lot of fun."

All of the excitement that was building drained out of me quickly. First of all, he is on a job interview and thinking about having sex with the people there. And then to describe that other woman the way he did crushed me. I am carrying some extra weight I put on while we were in Brazil; I am already self-conscious about that. Hearing him mention she is much thinner than me feels like salt being poured over an open wound. Finally, is he really going to go into this new job and start soliciting his co-workers to fulfil his crazy sex fetishes?

I don't know what to say, so I don't say anything. I change and get ready to go to class.

When we get home, Andres is worked up. He must have been thinking about that gal from the interview all afternoon and evening. We go to bed and he turns on one of his porn videos. He wants me to fantasize with him about his possible new co-worker. I feel so belittled and degraded. Nevertheless, I do what I feel I have to do to please my husband.

The next few weeks fly by quickly with many great changes. I received my promotion to Marketing Manager, and Andres got the Service Advisor position with Melman Honda. It's amazing how quickly things are moving and changing for us. It's working out how it's supposed to. We're even talking about buying our first house!

See Lisa, keep focusing on the positive and maybe this marriage will turn out "happily ever after" like you always hoped and knew it would!

Chapter 24
When Fantasy Becomes Reality

"That gal I was telling you about from the dealership; her name is Shelby."

"Which gal?"

"The pretty blonde I was telling you about. I think she would be into 'playing'."

Oh, that gal from the dealership. I can't believe he is actually thinking about propositioning someone he works with; let alone the fact he has been working there for just a few weeks.

"Andres, I know we have been fantasizing about this for a while, but I don't think I want to actually go through with it. It's one thing to talk about it, yet another thing to do it—and I don't want to."

Honestly, I don't know where I found the courage to say how I felt about the situation. Despite the fact it wasn't a big, bold, "No, I WILL NOT do this," it was a stronger *NO* than I had stated before. Inside, I am bracing for Andres to go off on me.

"Oh, Baby, it'll be ok. It will add some fun to our life. I love you. I'm not going anywhere. You are my wife. You are the woman I am coming home to every night. This will just add a little bit of spice to things."

Nothing about adding another person into our sex life sounds or feels right. It doesn't even feel right to have the porn in our lives; I can't imagine how bringing an actual person into the mix will make it better. Although I hear him when he says I'm his wife, the fact he's interested in other women makes me feel so inadequate.

Why did he marry me if he needs someone else to make him happy? To top it all off, why isn't he hearing me? Is this the compromise part of marriage?

"Can't we just add our own fun and spice? I don't think it's a good idea to do anything with someone from your new job. I mean, what if your boss finds out? You work in a VERY small department; something like that will spread like wildfire—and would not be good."

"We DO have fun and spice in our marriage. You are sexy hot...this will just be a wild experience. The truth is, most couples want to experience either a threesome or a foursome; they just never do. If we try and don't like it, we don't have to do it again. And don't worry about the people at my work. Nobody will find out. Shelby is discrete. It will be our little secret."

He is such a sweet talker. Even though his arguments don't make sense, there is a part of me that wants to believe him. I have so many questions.

If I am so "sexy hot," why does he need other women who are prettier, skinnier, and sexier than me to get him aroused? If we don't like it, we don't have to do it again...well, I am telling you I don't like it, so why aren't you listening? How do you know if Shelby is discrete? Didn't you just meet her? And how do I know that you and Shelby won't take things further when I am not around?

Feelings of inadequacy, jealousy, and rejection attack my heart; I don't know how to make them stop. I am afraid to put my feelings into words for fear of Andres' reaction. He has been sweet until now, but he can flip in an instant. Then the voices in my head start mimicking Andres, "You are freaking out...like you always do." Maybe couples watch porn and add other partners more than I realize. Maybe I am just being a prude.

Andres took my silence as agreement with him. "I've been joking around with Shelby at work. Let's just have her over for dinner and we will see what happens."

This whole thing feels like a freight train I have no way of stopping. I don't mind having her over for dinner; it just seems sneaky. Does she have any idea of his ulterior motives? Will he continue to push the envelope? If she says "no," will he respect her? This concerns me because he isn't respecting my "no."

"Does she know what you have in mind with this dinner

invitation?" I asked.

"Our chats have been alluding to the idea of her watching the two of us. She doesn't want to participate," he said.

"So, you have actually told her that we...I am ok with this?"

"I told her that you know I am talking with her about this. She is really cool about it. She says she really isn't interested in doing anything with you."

"Good; and well, I don't want her doing anything with you." Jealousy is rising up inside of me, and I don't like it at all. "I don't feel comfortable with this, Andres. I know we have talked about having someone else join us, but I really don't want this to happen."

"Oh, come on. What's it going to hurt? She isn't going to do anything other than just sit there and watch. And I don't want to back out now. I have already convinced her to come over; she is looking forward to it."

He has already convinced her...and she is looking forward to it? What about me? I'm not looking forward to it. I am feeling self-conscious about my body; Andres has already clearly stated that she is taller and skinnier than me. Besides that, I don't want anyone else in our sex life.

"I don't know. I don't think it's a good idea."

"Well, I have already invited her over for dinner this Saturday night, and I don't want to back out."

"So, in this whole conversation, you are not asking me if I want to do this, you are TELLING me she is coming over for dinner and sex on Saturday night. You have arranged this with her before you arranged this with me." I am so infuriated and hurt.

"Don't even go there. You and I have talked about this and you have always been okay with it. Now I actually get things set up for us and you change your mind. If we cancel, it will make me look like a liar."

"We talked about it in general and fantasizing, but we never talked about having Shelby over to the house. You just set it up before asking me. I don't mind having her over for dinner, just not the sex stuff."

"Well, we will still have her over for dinner, and see what happens from there."

I am so angry right now. He invited her over without even asking me. I don't want her coming over for dinner because I can tell Andres isn't going to respect my boundaries at all...he may not respect her boundaries either.

The atmosphere at the house is tense. The dread of Saturday night is weighing heavily on me. I want Shelby to feel welcome in our home as a dinner guest. That's how I was raised. The issue is: I don't want to welcome her into our sex life. How do I navigate that?

Saturday finally arrives. My stomach is in knots thinking about tonight's dinner. I am making lasagna, garlic bread, and a salad. I want it to be simple and quick. Not trying to be rude, I just want to protect my heart and my marriage.

"It's just dinner tonight, right?" I try to confirm with Andres.

"Yes, dinner. And if we all are ok with it, something more. We will just see how it goes."

"I'm not sure if I am ok with anything more," I try to plead my case once more.

"Relax. It will be fine. Just wait and see how it goes," he tries to assure me.

Ding-dong.

"Andres, please grab the door," I yelled. I don't want to be the one responsible for letting her into the house.

I hate the battle going on inside me. I don't want her here. I don't have anything against her—actually I'm interested in making a new friend. Maybe the more accurate truth is I don't want Andres here. I hate that he is pushing this swinging thing, and I feel tonight is a point of no return. Once we take it from watching porn to actually having someone else here with us, it takes it to a new level. One I don't want to go to.

"Hi, Shelby. Come on in. You look really pretty tonight," Andres said.

I can already feel the jealousy stirring in me. I don't remember the last time Andres told me I looked pretty. I try to remind myself I am being petty.

Create a welcoming home, Lisa.

"Shelby, this is Lisa. Lisa, this is Shelby."

"Hello. It is nice to meet you. Welcome to our home. Can I get you something to drink? We have lemonade, beer, or Coke," I said.

"Hello. I would love a beer, please. Thanks for having me over."

It's awkward. We can all feel the big white elephant in the room. I am feeling so convicted.

What kind of woman would agree to this?

That question is addressed to both of us. She seems like a nice gal, and Andres was right; she is pretty. So why is she even bothering with any of this craziness? None of it makes any sense to me.

Dinner is nice. The basic, get-to-know-you conversation; nothing alluding to anything sexual. I begin to relax and enjoy her company. I'm even entertaining the thought of possibly having a new friend.

As we finish dinner, Andres speaks up, "Shelby, do you want to watch a movie?"

I HATE that question. That is Andres' foreplay line. When he asks me, it's referring to a porn movie. Even though I have told him multiple times I don't want to, I can't believe he is just plowing forward in making this thing happen. In seconds, my guard goes back up, my heart closes, and I am pissed.

I can tell that Shelby is thinking he's talking about a "regular" movie.

"Sure, we can start one. I may not be able to stay for all of it. What do you have?"

"Well, we have *Die Hard, Men in Black,* or *Friends Fore Play.*"

I can't believe this. My emotions are fluctuating from anger to shame to embarrassment to worthlessness. I can't believe he actually has a porno movie down here and offered that up as a possible movie option.

I can tell Shelby is kind of embarrassed as well. Let's say she's not jumping at the chance.

"Well, I don't really care," she said sheepishly.

"Ok, well then, let's watch the last one. Do you mind if Lisa and I fool around while we watch it? You are welcome to touch yourself or do whatever you want."

I can't believe his boldness. Clearly, she isn't into this; she just doesn't know how to say no. I'm not into this either. But when I told him, he didn't want to hear "no." I could make a big scene and walk out. Unfortunately, the fear of the repercussions of that reaction causes me to keep my mouth shut. I stuff my feelings and follow along.

As Andres originally mentioned, Shelby didn't want to participate. She is just sitting on the couch watching. I feel so self-conscious and embarrassed. Nothing about this is enjoyable. I just want it to end... which eventually it did. As we get dressed, Shelby awkwardly leaves.

After she is gone, Andres turns to me. "What did you think? That was really exciting!"

"It didn't seem like Shelby was very interested."

"That's why we need to find someone off of FunAdultFriends.com. They will be into the experience."

I begin to question if Shelby was ever interested in any of this or if Andres had coerced her into coming over. Maybe he had been talking about it and it sounded so absurd to her, she thought he was joking. Either way, I feel bad for her. It seems to me she didn't know how to bow out of this ridiculous situation that she didn't want any part of in the first place. I am right there with her.

Now that it's all over, the physical act of sex between me and my husband has been cheapened. I always expected it to be a special, playful time of intimacy between the two of us. It has been reduced to a performance for someone else's enjoyment.

Chapter 25
Opportunity for Escape

I'm grateful it's Monday morning so I can go to work and get away from Andres. My job is a place where I'm heard and appreciated.

I usually like the peace and quiet that comes with getting into the office early. Today, though, the silence is deafening. The flashbacks of Saturday night haunt me. The thought of it makes me feel like a commodity. I still worry about Shelby. Am I projecting my feelings onto her? Maybe she was into it—although I really don't think that's the case.

At this point, I not only feel cheap and used, I also feel horrible: my husband's actions could have made this woman experience something sexually she didn't want to. The thought makes me nauseous. I don't want to be a part of anything that remotely violates someone like that.

These feelings are getting to be too much. People will be coming into the office soon.

Stop, Lisa. Stop thinking about them. Put them aside. Shove them down. Do what you have to do to put a smile on your face. Ah yes; think about that new project that Dereck mentioned. The first meeting is at 9:00 a.m. Focus on that.

Last week as I was getting ready to leave, Dereck started telling me about a special project he wants me to manage. Edge Cable has a new initiative to be more visible in our mid-size cities. The brief insight he gave alluded to the possibility of working on a sponsored event in one of our Midwest markets. I have a feeling my career is getting ready to take off.

"Good morning, Lisa. Are you ready for our meeting?"

"Good morning, Dereck. Yes, sir, and very excited about this opportunity."

We head down to the third-floor conference room where some of the players for this project are already congregating. There is a tray of pastries and coffee sitting on the side table.

So, THIS is how the big dogs roll.

With that, the VP of Marketing and the VP of Operations walk into the room. Dereck wasn't kidding when he told me this will give me exposure to more people in the company. I'm excited and nervous at the same time.

As the meeting unfolds, they reveal Edge Cable has signed on to sponsor the 1st Annual Chalk Festival in Peoria, Illinois. I've been selected as the Marketing Manager to oversee our participation in this sponsorship. This opportunity will give me exposure to many people both inside and outside of the company. It will also be a very nice addition to my resume!

"Since the goal of this sponsorship is to increase our visibility in Peoria, it will require some travel out there to build relationships," Annabelle, the VP of Marketing stated.

"Not a problem. I will do whatever is necessary," I respond, trying not to let my overwhelming excitement embarrass me. I can't believe I get to travel for business! They are trusting me to write up and execute the full marketing plan for our involvement in this event. This is like real, grown-up stuff!

"Ok, great. Lisa, please have your marketing team work the plan and send it to me by the end of the week. We are looking to roll out our new bundled services in that area right around the time of the event; so keep that in mind as you develop the plan. If you have any questions or need anything from me, don't hesitate to reach out." Annabelle closed the meeting with confidence and very clear marching orders.

Dereck and I shake hands, say our good-byes, and head back up to the sixth floor. I appreciate that Dereck is not just my boss; he is also my mentor. I am excited about the idea of traveling for business. With it being my first time, I'm also kind of nervous and not quite sure what to expect.

When we get in the elevator, Dereck can sense I need some guidance.

"Lisa, let's meet in my office so we can figure out a plan," he said.

"That sounds like a great idea. Thank you. And thank you again for the opportunity to be your Marketing Manager."

"You are the best candidate for the job. I'm pleased you will be representing our department on this project."

We head into his office and close the door. "So, who do you want on your team to work on this project?"

"I would say Phil and Susan. They are the most creative and knowledgeable, and are good at managing their time, allowing them to take on some additional work."

"I do agree they are your top marketing assistants. Have you thought about—" the chiming of an incoming call interrupts Dereck in mid-sentence. "Hold on. Let me take this."

"Hello. Dereck Jones speaking...Hello, Baby." The tone of his voice and his body language totally changed. "Yea, that works. Thank you for doing that. Baby, I am in a meeting right now with Lisa, talking about the new project. Can I call you back in a little bit? Okay. Love you." He hung up the phone and said, "That was Patrice. Man, I don't know what I did to deserve her. She is beautiful, intelligent, and loving. Well, I am not going to question it, I'm just gonna tell God, 'Thank You!'"

"I was pretty sure it was Patrice. If it wasn't, it would be 'a whole-nother Oprah!'" I said with a smile on my face and a twinge of pain in my heart. I could sense the love and passion he has for his wife just through his voice. I hope that someday Andres will have that kind of love and passion for me.

Lisa, don't get sappy now...stuff it.

"Ok, so back to this project. You were about to offer another suggestion besides Phil and Susan," I said.

"Oh, yes. I agree. They are our top marketers. However, thinking about employee development, what about using Susan as the lead coordinator and having Phil, Kim, and Nancy all help with the brainstorming and campaign ideas. That way you can mentor Kim and Nancy. This will help with morale in the department and grow their skill sets."

"Wow, that's a great idea. I love how you focus on growing the people in your organization. I know I have been directly impacted by your philosophy."

"Now you are starting to get it. A successful leader is one who develops their staff to the point the department runs smoothly whether he or she is physically there or not. It is about building trust in the relationship and the necessary skills to help them be the best they can be. When the team can run the day-to-day things on their own, they have ownership in their work. Then, once you trust them to get the job done, you are free to go and build relationships and find other work for the department."

What an amazing conversation. I get the sense Dereck really believes in me. He trusts me and wants nothing more than for me to become the best version of me. Through this conversation, I have a whole new respect for this man. I feel empowered to be able to move forward successfully in my career.

"Oh, and one other thing; you will need to be there for the event. Mark that on your calendar now. Plan on flying in on Thursday, and being there through Sunday evening."

"Thank you for the opportunity. I'm really excited. I have family in Chicago. Would it be possible to either head out early or stay a few days after to visit them? I have heard of people doing that with business trips."

"Yes, that's fine. You will just need to pay for your expenses on those extra days. It's something we can definitely work out. You are already starting to understand how to find additional, ethical benefits from being in management. Good job!"

"Thanks again, Dereck, for ALL of your help. I'll start writing up the workflow for my team and get that back to you by the end of today."

"Great work, Lisa. I look forward to seeing what you come up with."

I am on cloud nine walking back to my office. I can't believe this is happening to me. I was just in a meeting with two of the VPs of this company. I'm working on this great new project. I get to travel for work,

AND I get to see family on the company's dime! It feels so good to have Dereck's support.

I can't wait to share the good news with Andres. As soon as I get back to my office, I give him a call.

"Hey, Andres, guess what? I just got out of that meeting about the new project I was telling you about and…I get to go on my first business trip! I mean the whole project is really cool. I will be managing the marketing campaign for the 1st Annual Chalk Festival in Peoria, Illinois! I also get to be there for the event as the official representative for Edge Cable!"

"What, you mean you are going to leave me here? How long are you going to be gone?"

His words crushed my excitement. "Dereck asked me to plan on being there for the event, which is four days. I was hoping to stay for a couple of days after to visit my cousin and her family."

"And now you are going to leave and go see family without me? That's just rude. If I knew this was a part of your promotion, I wouldn't have let you take it."

What? Rude? It is for my job. So much for being excited. And now you aren't even supportive of my new position?

"Well, the trip won't happen for a few months. I'll see what I can do to be gone for the shortest amount of time possible. And maybe you can fly out and join me to meet the family," I acquiesced. I really want to visit my cousin on my own. It has been a long time since we have spent time together. If I could gain his support by including him, I am willing to give up that desire. "Well, I have to get back to work so I am not late getting home."

"Do what you gotta do. Don't be late getting home. Don't give that company any more than the forty hours a week you signed up for."

Why can't my phone calls with Andres be like the one Dereck had with Patrice? Why is it that Andres is only happy for me to grow and expand as long as it doesn't impact him? It's like he's against anything that will allow me to flourish.

Stop thinking about it, Lisa. It is time to work on this new project...which is such a great opportunity!

Oh, my gosh! I totally lost track of time. I am late heading out of the office. Andres is going to be pissed. I better call him so he doesn't worry. I am grateful my call went to his voicemail.

"Hi, Babe. I am SO sorry. I completely lost track of time. I am running about thirty minutes late. I am ok. I'll be home as soon as I can. Love you." That's kind of a lie, because I am actually closer to forty-five minutes late; but thirty sounds better. Why can't he understand this new project means a lot to me and it could have a BIG impact on my career? Why does he have to be so controlling?

The whole drive home is filled with dread. I don't want to hear it when I walk in. I hate the stress of trying to hurry home so I am not late, while at the same time dreading the idea of getting to my final destination. It shouldn't be this way.

I park my car, take a deep breath, and head into the house. "Hi, Honey. I am sorry I am late."

"Hey. Come over here."

I put my stuff down, shocked he isn't angry or yelling at me about being late. He is sitting at the computer. As I walk up behind him, I realize why he isn't upset.

"Look at this couple. They look pretty hot, and aren't too far away. I am talking to Tony, the guy, right now. Janet, his wife, is still at work."

My heart drops. First of all, I really want all of this to stop. Second, I told him from the beginning I don't want to be with other couples or single men.

"I thought we had agreed we weren't going to engage with other couples—just single females."

"Lisa, you know single females in this lifestyle are called 'unicorns' because they are so hard to find. This is a nice couple. We don't have to go all the way with them. Relax. We are just talking with them right now."

No, YOU are talking with them right now. I don't want anything to do with this. When will this stop!

I walk away from the whole situation to go change my clothes. As I head into the bedroom, Andres follows me. He is obviously worked up from his time on the computer and tries to engage me while I am changing. "I'm not in the mood. I am tired and unwinding from a long day at work."

"Are you going to let work steal our fun?"

This isn't "our" fun, I thought.

"Here, let me help you relax," he said, kissing my neck.

This was out of character for him, and a quick change from where he just was. Even though I am tired and upset, maybe if I just relax and give in and take care of him, he won't push the thing with Tony and Janet.

I quickly find he hasn't changed; it was just manipulation to get things started. As we began to get intimate, he starts fantasizing about Tony and Janet.

"Can it just be us right now?" I asked.

He ignores my request. Emotionally, I'm checked out. Physically, I'm going through the motions, receiving no pleasure from any of it. I can't decide if he doesn't notice or doesn't care. Either way, I feel used.

"I'm gonna take a quick shower and go start dinner."

I can't lie next to him anymore. I just want to cry. However, I know if he sees any tears, it wouldn't be good. So I go into the bathroom, step into the shower, and let the tears stream down my face. I long for the shame and pain to be washed away by the hot water. This isn't what marriage is supposed to be...is it? I know they talk about compromise and doing whatever it takes to make it work. The problem is I feel like the only one compromising is me. This is not what I had expected or wanted.

The warm water is soothing. I wish I could stay in this cocoon of comfort forever. I'm saddened, knowing I have to go back to my relationship of being unheard, uncherished, and unloved. I still don't understand what is so wrong with me that my husband isn't sexually attracted to me. Maybe it's the few extra pounds I am carrying. Maybe it's because I don't look like a model. Maybe it's because I am nothing special. No matter what I am, I have made the commitment to be his wife. For me, divorce is not an option.

I turn the water off and prepare to emerge back into my reality. As I head into the kitchen to work on dinner, I notice Andres is back at the computer.

"Hey, Lisa, we don't have anything going on this Saturday night, do we?"

"No. Not that I know of. Why?'

"Well, we do now. Tony and Janet are coming over for drinks, and then we will see what else happens. I just confirmed with Tony."

My heart is crushed. What part of, "I don't want to be with other couples" doesn't he seem to understand? I don't want any part of this lifestyle anymore.

"Tony is really excited to meet you."

What?

That is crazy. I mean my own husband isn't physically interested in me...so why is this other married man even remotely curious about me? I mean, there is something wrong with me—I am ugly, or frumpy, or something. I can't seem to make sense out of any of this. It's emotionally too much. I can't think about it anymore; I just shove the feelings down and finish making dinner.

Chapter 26
He Loves Me, He Loves Me Not

All week I have been thinking about what Andres said.

"Tony is really excited to meet you."

What a strange comment. First, that any man, let alone one who is married, is excited to meet me. Second, Andres is completely ok with it. I mean, obviously I am not really anything special physically because my husband insists on looking elsewhere. It's also confusing because Tony's wife Janet is beautiful. So why is he looking elsewhere?

"Do you need me to cook anything for our guests tonight?" I ask.

"No, just drinks. Well, maybe some appetizers; nothing really heavy. I don't want to be full and bloated when they're here."

"Ok, I'll have chips, salsa, and guac for snacking."

"That sounds good. I am excited. Tonight is going to be fun."

I am not looking forward to tonight. I would love it if Andres put even half as much effort into our relationship as he does searching for other people to be with.

Coming to the conclusion that I can't have my desire, I begin to think about Tony. Is he really interested in meeting me? I mean, what if he really is? Maybe he will actually find me attractive. Not that I want any kind of relationship with him; after all, I am married. Physically though, would he care about me enough to meet my needs? That would be something I haven't experienced in a while.

Not being able to stop the hands of time, the knock I've been dreading all day finally happened. Andres was quick to open the door and welcome this other couple into our home.

"Hello, come on in. I am Andres and this is Lisa."

"Hello, I am Tony and this is my hot wife, Janet. Here, this is for you," handing over a six pack of beer and offering his hand to Andres.

Tony came over and hugged me. "Hello, Lisa. You are more beautiful in person than you are in your photos; and your photos, they're hot!"

His comments and his touch released a wide array of mixed emotions. I was never one for one-night-stands; and here we are, meeting these people for one reason and one reason only. I'm really not into this. However, I know if I don't go along with it, things won't end well between me and Andres. Then Tony released me from the hug, keeping his hand on my lower back holding me close to him.

I feel myself blush. I can't remember the last time I heard a compliment like the one he gave me. Even though it's awkward, and he could be lying, it still feels good. His kind words help me relax a little bit.

As couples, we made some small talk and set the ground rules for how far we would go with the other person's spouse. It was so strange to have this conversation. I'm pretty leery because I don't have many good experiences of my sexual boundaries being respected by Andres or even the guy that date raped me in high school. Tonight, it was like we are in contract negotiations...and agree upon them with a handshake.

And then it all starts. Tony and I head off into one corner; Andres and Janet go into another. At first, I am distracted, wanting to see how Andres was treating Janet. Then Tony gets my attention. He is very attractive and well built. He starts sweet talking me, asking what I like, and telling me what he likes about me. This is new for me. This is the attention I've been longing for from my husband. I very quickly get pulled into being with Tony.

As the night continues, everyone respects the ground rules that were set. At the end of the encounter, I actually feel better about myself than I have in a long time. Despite the fact this encounter makes me believe I might be an attractive, sexy woman, there is also a vein of shame and guilt knowing I was just physically with a man who isn't my husband. My husband knows about it; he actually arranged it. So does that make it ok? It doesn't feel ok. However, I did get something out of tonight that I've been longing for.

After they left, the debrief began between us.

"So, what do you think? I personally think tonight was just hot!" Andres blurted out.

"It was interesting. Tony and I had fun. I don't know much about Janet other than she is pretty."

"Yea, I heard you getting really excited over there with Tony."

With those words, a wave of guilt crashes over me. I was getting excited with Tony because he showed me the affection I desired. Even if he was faking it, he was faking it really well.

"I was enjoying it...a little bit, but he isn't better than you."

I didn't want to admit that I enjoyed any part of it. I also don't want Andres to think I enjoyed Tony more than him. Andres' jealousy can turn scary very quickly.

As he continues on, I realized he isn't worried about me enjoying myself with Tony because he really enjoyed the conquest of Janet. My mind starts churning out many tormenting questions. What if he was talking to Janet the way Tony was talking to me? Was he really caring about her physical needs over his own? What does she have that I don't have that turned him on so much?

My insecurity of not being enough is at an all-time high. This roller coaster of emotions is too much.

I need to get away. "I am going to go take a quick shower before we head to bed."

"Can I join you?" Andres said in a playful voice.

I really don't want him to. I need time alone. I want to wash away what just happened.

"No, I just want to take a quick shower by myself and then I'll meet you in bed." I really hoped he would be ok with that answer.

"Ok. Come meet me back in bed for round two!" he said, all excited. I'm surprised he's ok with it. He must be still running on a high from the experience with Tony and Janet.

I turn on the shower as hot as I can stand it. I want to keep the memories of how Tony talked and touched me because it felt good. At the same time, it is painful because it was from a man I can't have. The harsher reality is that my own husband can't and won't do that for me.

I know I can't dawdle too long in the shower; Andres is waiting for me. I let the water wash away any of the mixed emotions it could; I shove the rest down in my heart. I have to do something with them because they are so painful. If I even start to think about them, I know I will cry. My tears are one thing that Andres has no patience for at all.

I turn the water off, dry myself with a towel, put some lotion on my face to minimize the tear stains, and head back into the bedroom. Andres is waiting for me; not necessarily happy to see me, but happy for what I can do for him.

Chapter 27
When the Cat's Away

"I can't believe our trip to Illinois is in a couple of weeks. I am getting excited!"

That isn't a total lie. I am excited about going on my first business trip and seeing my cousin and her family. The fact Andres had a fit and is meeting me there halfway through the trip still bothers me. Fortunately, I am focusing on the positive.

"Who are you going to have dinner with the night before I get there?"

That's a strange question.

"I don't know. Maybe someone from the event committee or a counterpart from the Peoria office; most likely I'll eat by myself."

"Well, you better not be having dinner with any guys out there."

Huh? Now I am really confused. Where is this coming from? I have never been unfaithful to my husband...well, except for when we were swinging. Since he knew about it and was there...that doesn't count as cheating.

"Honey, I would never cheat on you—if that is what you are alluding to."

"Good. Well, when you are gone, I might just see about having Tony and Janet over for drinks."

Ouch. I know when says he would have them "over for drinks," he means to mess around. I am going out to Illinois on business, not to cat around. I haven't given him any reason not to trust me. Now, out of his own insecurities, he is threatening to have this couple over when I am gone. I kind of wish I never got this promotion so I wouldn't have to deal with this situation.

Lisa, take a deep breath. Get out of your emotions and talk with Andres. His past fears of abandonment are coming up. This is when you can step in and love him, support him, and fix the hurts of his past. Be the loving and caring wife you are supposed to be.

I walk over and sit down right in front of him, grab his hands and say, "I am not going to cheat on you. I am not going to leave you. I love you."

Something in him broke. Tears are welling up in his eyes. I can sense his pain. I really wish I could make all of his hurt go away.

What can I do to make him trust me? If he just lets me love him, I know I can make it all better for him. That is the lie I tell myself.

As quickly as the tears appear, they dry up.

"You better not cheat on me. I can't handle that."

I'm so confused with that statement. If he doesn't want me to cheat on him, why is he so adamant about bringing other people into our sex life? It's like he believes I will cheat on him so he can make it easier for himself by controlling the situation. He wants to call the shots. He wants the control.

"Are you serious about inviting Tony and Janet over while I am traveling?" I want to see if this is an idle threat. According to their profile, they won't do anything if both of us aren't there. However, I am more concerned with Andres' intentions.

"Probably not. They most likely wouldn't come over anyways. I just don't know what I am going to do. It is going to be boring without you."

Although that response doesn't make me feel any better, I can sense this is more of a pity party or guilt trip versus his actual plan.

"It is going to be one day and one night without me. Go to work; then take two classes of Capoeira. I'll have dinner in the fridge; all you have to do is heat it up. The next day, you'll go to work and then head to the airport. I'll be waiting for you when your flight lands at the other end. You will really be alone for about thirty-six hours. You can do that."

I feel like a mother to a child versus a wife to a husband. I get a hint of exactly how broken this man really is.

I know I can fix him if he would just let me.

I don't know where I got the idea it was my job to fix him.

The night before I left, I was hoping for a passionate evening of "goodbye" intimacy with my husband. When I tried to initiate this with him, he rolled over and said he was too tired. I can't believe it. He is having a total temper tantrum over a business trip. I don't get it. I roll over myself, feeling the sting of rejection. I curl tightly into a ball, longing to feel his arms wrap around me and hold me. Instead, I feel a coldness radiate off his back. This is really not what I had envisioned my marriage to be.

The alarm welcomes me into a new day and my first business trip. I feel like such a grown-up! I don't want to show too much excitement because Andres is still throwing his passive aggressive temper tantrum. His attitude is actually making me even happier that I am leaving him here.

There is a small part of me that is wondering if he is going to have someone over tonight; I choose to ignore that thought. I could drive myself crazy if I worry about him cheating on me every time I'm not with him. I would start treating him the way he is treating me about this trip... and I don't want a relationship like that.

The fact he isn't a morning person, on top of his silent treatment of disapproval, made the car ride very awkward.

"I'm excited for you to join me and meet my cousin," I lied.

"Yea. That will be fun," he droned.

"You will be headed back to the airport in roughly thirty-six hours. Why are you so upset about this?"

"I just don't like you leaving me."

"But I am not leaving you. This is a business trip. I will be busy with the final details of this event until you get there."

I don't know why I waste my breath. I've told him this before. It wasn't enough for him to believe me then...and it still isn't. Well, maybe if this business trip goes well, he will be better for the next one...baby steps.

"You told me that before. You are still leaving me. Tonight, I am going to see if Tony and Janet want to plan on coming over next weekend after we get back."

"Oh, ok." I am trying to deal with this man for the rest of the ride to the airport. Whatever about next weekend; maybe he will forget about it by then.

We finally pull up to passenger drop-off. He leans over to kiss me goodbye with a simple peck.

"Here you go. Have fun on your 'business trip'," he says with childlike bitterness.

So much for the romantic movie scene of the husband getting out of the car, passionately embracing his wife, and whispering sweet nothings of how wonderful it will be when he meets up with her in thirty-six hours...for a weekend of fun and adventure. I guess I've been watching too many chick-flicks and my expectations are set too high.

Honestly, I would be happy with him giving me a hug and helping me get my bag out of the car. Or even, "I am really proud of you. Knock'em dead. I know you are going to do great." I am not picky. Pretty much anything would have been better than what I got.

Whatever. I have to get going so I don't miss my flight.

"Bye, Sweetie. I'll see you in about thirty-six hours! Love you."

"Whatever. Yea, love you, too."

I am going to choose to not let this hurt me. I need to get my head on straight and get excited about this trip. I am comfortable with the flying thing. The first time renting a car has me a little nervous. I know I can figure it out, but I really wish I had my husband's support. He'll get there eventually. If he just sees that this is going to all work out ok, he will change.

I successfully find my flight and board with no issues. The man next to me is very friendly and tries talking to me although I don't really feel like talking. I share some simple pleasantries and then shut him down.

I am reflecting on the conversation I had with Andres on the way to the airport. I can't think too much about it or I will cry. If I'm honest, it really hurts. The fact my husband doesn't trust me, he can't be supportive of my new promotion, and the arrangements for him to join me for a weekend get-away still isn't enough leaves me discouraged.

And now, he is going to use this time home alone to set up more time with Tony and Janet. The thought of him inviting them over tonight returns. This really isn't what I expected marriage to be like. I can feel the tears welling up, so it is time to stuff all of these feelings deep down inside.

Lisa, keep on loving him; he'll come around, I try to encourage myself.

When we come into our final descent, I open my eyes and start pulling myself together. I have to pick up my rental car and get on the road to Peoria. My flight was perfectly scheduled for me to get to the office in time for an 11:00 a.m. meeting.

I'm honored Dereck trusts in me the way he does. I can't believe he put me in charge of this project and sent me on this business trip all by myself. I am barely old enough to get a rental car; and he is depending on me to travel on the company's behalf. This is crazy to me. I'm so excited about this project and how it is turning out.

Being so caught up in finding my way to the rental cars, I totally space calling Andres to let him know I landed safely. I step to the side of the concourse, pull out my phone, and call him.

"Hi, Honey. I just wanted to let you know I landed safely and I'm on my way to pick up my rental car."

"Nice of you to finally call. Your flight landed twenty minutes ago. Were you talking with some guy on the plane and you forgot about me?"

WHAT?!?! Is he being serious?

"Um, no, I wasn't talking with some guy on the plane."

Well, I had been, but I'm not going to admit that to him. It was totally innocent and I stopped talking with him at the beginning of the flight.

"It took me a while to get off the plane because I was closer to the back, and then I was walking down the concourse focusing on following the signs so I could find my way to the rental cars," I stammered.

"Yea, whatever. At least you got there safely. I've gotta go."

"Ok. Well, thank you. I'll see you tomorrow?" not understanding what I did wrong.

"Oh, yea, I'm coming. I'm not going to leave you in a big city like Chicago all by yourself. You never know who you will meet and run away with. Bye."

"Bye," I said to a blank phone. With my confidence rattled, I need to get my mind back on track and focus on the task at hand.

I can't believe him. Where are these accusations coming from? I have given him NO reason to even think I am cheating on him. Whatever. I can't think about that right now. I've got to find the Hertz counter.

I successfully acquire my white Ford Focus and find my way onto I-190 East, looking for the exit to I-55 South. These little wins send my confidence soaring once again. I really love to travel and explore new places and meet new people. And now I am doing it on someone else's dime...even though my final destination is the thriving metropolis of Peoria, Illinois, population 113,532.

As I drive, I think about the blessing it is to be given the responsibility of our department's part in this project. If this event goes well, we could potentially roll this out into some of our other smaller cities.

The two-and-a-half-hour drive went pretty quick. Before I know it, I'm exiting the highway and making my way to the Edge Cable offices.

"Hello, I'm Lisa from the Kansas City office. I have a meeting with Don," I said to the woman at the front reception desk.

"Oh, yes. He said he was expecting you. I'll let him know you are here." She proceeds to dial his extension. "Don, Lisa from Kansas City is here for you," she paused. "Ok, I'll let her know."

"Don is on his way down. Would you like a bottle of water while you wait?"

"Yes, please."

For some reason, this makes me feel special. I mean, it is just a bottle of water and a simple phone call to a coworker. However, this time it includes travel and the responsibility of this new project. The most satisfying part is Dereck has complete confidence in me to execute it with excellence.

A tall, skinny man with a head of curly hair walked out of the elevator. He came up to me with an outstretched hand.

"Hello, Lisa! It is nice to meet you in person after all of the conference calls we have been on. We are headed up to the fourth floor conference room. You can see samples of the promotional swag and print material for the event."

As I walk into the conference room, I can sense the excitement. Don introduces me to everyone. It's great to put faces to the names. We go through the agenda, confirming the time frames and locations of the deliveries and the schedule for our corporate tent.

"Lisa, once we are finished up here, I'll take you over to the venue so you can see it in person," Don said.

"Sounds good! I can't wait. You all have done a great job here on site bringing all of the marketing plans into reality. I appreciate all of your hard work," I said to the team.

"Great. Well, we all have our final 'to-dos', so let's end this meeting so the fun can begin," Don directed.

Everyone grabbed their things and filed out. Don and I picked up the marketing samples and straightened up the room.

He said, "Let's drop this stuff off at my office and we will get going. We can grab a bite to eat for lunch and then go to the site. I am sure you are starving from your travels this morning."

"That sounds great. Now that you mentioned it, I guess I am pretty hungry."

Don pulls up to a good old fashioned Midwest diner for lunch.

"I hope this is ok. It will give you a real taste of the Midwest—and their burgers are the best in Peoria."

"That sounds good to me. I am always up for a good burger!"

Over lunch, Don told me about his wife and son. I can tell he is very much a family man who loves his wife dearly. It makes my heart happy to hear how much he cherishes her. At the same time, trepidation is growing inside of me. If Andres knew I was having lunch with Don, even though it's an innocent business lunch, he would explode. I hope he will stop being so insecure about our relationship.

We finish lunch and head over to the event venue. It is filled with the hustle and bustle of people setting up tents, marking off sections on the street for the artists, and preparing for the food vendors. Don and I head over to our corporate tent located in the middle of all of the festivities.

"Don! The signage looks great! It really stands out. And the stage is in a great position. You have various local bands lined up to play throughout the festival, right?"

"Yes, ma'am."

"And the 'Get the Edge Bundle' bags are going to be handed out here at the tent?"

"Yes, we have a full roster of people from the company who have volunteered with their families to hand out bags. They will all be wearing Edge polo shirts. We also have stations where people can sign up for the bundled packages right here on site."

"Great job, Don. This is going to be a great win for the company."

"Oh, come with me. I want to introduce you to the event organizer, Liz. She has been an amazing resource for us."

We head in the direction of this little ball of energy. She is wearing a headset over her curly red hair which kept her hands free to direct people to where they need to go.

"Hi, Liz," Don said, getting her attention. "I want you to meet Lisa. She is from our corporate offices in Kansas City."

Liz reaches out her hand, "It is nice to meet you, Lisa. We really appreciate Edge's sponsorship of this event."

"I thank you for all you and your team have done. This looks great!" I replied back to this beautiful, vivacious woman.

"I don't want to be rude, but I need to direct the delivery of the Port-a-Potties; the crappy part of being the event coordinator!" she said with a laugh. "Don't hesitate to reach out if you need anything from me."

"Will do. Go take care of business," I said with a chuckle.

As Liz headed off to coordinate with the Port-a-Potty guy, I reflect on her confident, fun, caring, and take-charge attitude. She is the kind of person I would like to be friends with. She seems to know what she is doing and walks in that assurance. Too bad she lives almost 400 miles away from me.

"I am going to take photos and send them back to Dereck so he can see how things are shaping up."

"That sounds like a marvelous idea," Don agreed. "After you are done with that, we can head back to the office. We don't have any other meetings scheduled until the start of the event tomorrow at noon. You are welcome to use the conference rooms at the office if you would like."

"I think I am going to get checked in to my hotel. I can get the rest of my work done from there. Thanks for the offer."

When we return to the office, I jump into my rental car and find the hotel. I am on cloud nine right now. I can't believe how this whole event is coming together. I check in and head to my room. I give Andres a call. I want to share how great my afternoon went.

"Hey, Sweetie! How are you doing?"

"Fine. How did your thing go?"

It sounds like he is over whatever he was upset about, which is good.

"It went great! Everything is in place. We checked out the venue. The tent looks amazing, the stage is set, and all the giveaway bags came out perfect."

"Who is 'we'?" he accused.

"Um, Don. He is the Edge project lead here in Peoria," I replied, confused and defensive.

"How old is this Don guy?"

"I don't know. Maybe in his mid-40's. He reminds me of Bob Ross, the guy that paints the happy trees," trying to add some levity to a conversation that I can tell is quickly headed to a bad place.

"Well, has Don hit on you?"

"Uh, NO."

"I am sure he wants to sleep with you."

Ew. That thought never crossed my mind. It didn't seem to cross Don's mind either. Why is it that Andres is so preoccupied with the idea that I am going to either cheat on him or leave him while I am on this trip? He is being so unreasonable. I don't know how else I can assure him that I am not going anywhere or doing anything with anyone else.

Despite the fact I want to share with him the cool things that are happening, I don't like calling him because he acts like this. However, I will call him if for nothing more than to reassure him that he can trust me.

"He does not want to sleep with me. First of all, he is much older."

"Age doesn't matter. Older men are always wanting younger women," he interrupted.

"Stop it. This is crazy. First of all, he hasn't made ANY sexual advances towards me. Second, if he did, I wouldn't entertain any of them."

Why am I being accused of things I've never done and never plan to do? It hurts.

"Yea, whatever. I know he wants to screw you. Oh, and by the way: Tony and Janet aren't free next weekend, but I have been talking to this gal Becky. She is going to show our profile to her husband Andy and see if he is interested in getting together."

I am a complete sea of emotions right now. The empowered and excited feelings I had at the beginning of this call have changed to hurt and anger because my husband is basically accusing me of cheating—or at least not trusting me to be faithful. At the same time, he is soliciting us out for sex. Our profile being shown around makes me feel like a piece of meat. To top it off, Andres is making all of these plans without so much as asking me anything. This thing is getting way out of control.

"Andres, I don't think I want to get together with any couple next weekend."

"What are you talking about? You had a lot of fun with Tony. And Andy is good looking. Don't you trust me?"

"It isn't that I don't trust you. I just don't want to get together with another couple next weekend...any couple."

"You will really like Becky and Andy. She is spicy."

"What do you mean by, 'She is spicy?'"

"We have been chatting back and forth; and let's just say, she has a kinky mind."

That sends me through the roof. He is accusing me of cheating on him when nothing is happening and he is over there having sex conversations with some woman. I am so hurt and so done.

"It sounds like you have been having fun with her already."

"You were in her story, too."

That doesn't make me feel any better. In fact, it makes me feel even more violated since I have no idea what her kinky mind did to me.

"That isn't very reassuring. I need to go. I have to answer some emails and find some dinner before things close around here. I love you. Bye."

Right now, I don't feel a whole lot of love towards my husband. I think before I do anything else, I am going to take a hot shower. It will help clear my head.

As the hot water runs down my face, tears begin to flow. This is so not what I expected or wanted my marriage to be. Why can't he be happy for me with this business trip? I just want his support. Why is he accusing me of cheating on him? That is the furthest thing from the truth. And why does he need to keep looking elsewhere to find sex? What is wrong with me that I am not enough for him?

I've gotta stop thinking about it. It's so overwhelming.

After my shower, I check my emails. Dereck is asking for an update. I'm glad to let him know that everything is set and ready to go. I attach the photos I took earlier as confirmation. Upon checking in with all of my direct reports, things back in KC seem to be running smoothly. I smile to myself.

I remember one of the first pieces of advice Dereck gave me about being a manager.

"The sign of a good manager is having a department that runs the same whether they are physically there or not."

He taught me it's a combination of trust, proper training, and confidence in your employees to do their job. I know he laid much of the groundwork before I started, but I am proud of the fact that things are running smoothly without me there.

Now that my work tasks are complete, I should check our joint email account. I don't really want to see what's in there. That's the one connected to FunAdultFriends.com. In some ways, I want to know what Andres is up to at home; in other ways, ignorance is bliss. I would never log onto the site with my work computer anyways.

Just the thought of all of that drowns out the excitement I'm feeling with my work accomplishments. Instead of dealing with that, I close up my laptop and decide to explore Peoria. I need to get some dinner before I go to bed.

Don had suggested *Fred's Diner*. He was funny when he suggested it.

"Don't let the boring name fool you. It is some of the best diner food in the country!" he said.

I could use a little comfort food right about now. It's only ten minutes from the hotel. The plain cinderblock building covered in a mural of Americana can be spotted from two blocks away. I can feel the buzz and friendliness emanating as I park the car. This is exactly what I need right now—a happy culinary adventure.

"Hello, and welcome to Fred's Diner! Where are you from and where are you going?" a boisterous voice welcomed me as I walked in the door.

"Hello. I'm from Kansas City on business; working on the 1st Annual Chalk Festival that's happening this weekend."

"Well, welcome! Table for one?"

Table for one: that sounds strange and lonely. I'm not used to dining alone. I'm always with Andres—and before that, I was with my parents or a friend.

"Yes, please."

I don't really have a choice. Well, I guess I do have the option of ordering take out and eating in my hotel room, but I want to explore;

and that takes being pulled outside of my comfort zone. After all, I have been around the world and lived in a foreign country...I'm sure I can eat by myself at this little diner in the heart of the Midwest.

I sit down and browse through the menu. Don was right, they have great diner food. I settle on the patty melt.

As I wait for my food, I watch people come and go. I notice this couple about my age walk in. The woman's laughter caught my attention. Her husband is such a gentleman. He's holding the door for her, and quickly goes up to the hostess station to request a table. They obviously are locals because the hostess recognizes them right away, and doesn't greet them with the trademark question, "Where are you from and where are you going?"

I'm fascinated watching this couple interact. It's like they are in this beautiful dance: the dance of Ladies and Gentlemen acting like Ladies and Gentlemen. When the hostess seats them, he steps aside and lets his wife go first. As she steps in front of him to follow the hostess, he looks at her from head to toe with a tender yet excited look in his eyes. It is like I could hear his thoughts: "Man, she is sexy, smart, and funny...and she is going home with me. I am the luckiest man on earth."

My thoughts are interrupted by my waitress placing a huge plate of food in front of me.

"Here you go. Can I get you anything else?"

"No, I am good. Thank you."

"I saw you noticing Jed and Jennifer. Aren't they the cutest couple? It is like they are right out of a Hallmark movie. He absolutely adores her, and she is so good to him."

"Oh, boy, you caught me!" I blushed. "It's so refreshing to see two people so in love."

"I agree. And they have been together since they were in the second grade. Well, you enjoy. Let me know if you need anything else."

"I will. Thank you."

As I begin to eat, I start thinking about my marriage. I don't think

Andres has ever really looked at me like that. He has never opened a door for me. It isn't fair to judge him on not opening my door because that has never really meant much to me. After all, I am fully capable of opening my own doors. However, I can tell Jed was doing it not because she couldn't, but because he WANTED to. He wanted to treat her like a princess. The waitress said they have been together since the second grade. With a quick calculation in my mind, I marvel at the fact they have been together for about twenty years and are still acting like that.

My gaze found its way back to this adorable couple. They aren't the mushy, all over each other kind of couple; they are just happy and in love. When the waitress went to take their order, they were kind to her as well. One thing that really bugs me about Andres is that most of the time when we go out, he is rude to the wait staff. Well, maybe not "rude", just not friendly. And eventually, he ends up getting irritated with them.

Lisa, STOP THIS! Stop comparing your relationship to this couple. Andres has been through a lot, and you two are working through things. Just keep loving him, and eventually he will get to that place.

I enjoy the rest of my meal thinking about what it would be like to have Andres look at me the way Jed looked at Jennifer. It feels good.

Seeing it is already 7:45 p.m. jars me back to reality. My plan was to get to bed early so I am well rested for tomorrow. I also want to touch base with Andres again. Hopefully, this time he is in a better place. Hopefully he is done sexting with Becky.

I give him a ring when I get to my room.

"Hey, Baby, how's it going? I just got done with dinner and wanted to call and tell you 'I love you' before I head to bed."

"Oh, hey. I am good," he responded.

"Good. What are you doing? You sound very preoccupied."

"Oh, I am watching NCIS. Do you need something?"

"No, just calling to hear your voice."

"Okay, well here it is. It is getting to a good part in the show. I'll talk to you later."

"Okay, I'll see you tomorrow. Bye."

Ouch. I feel totally dismissed. It is too much for me to deal with right at this moment. I try to think back to some of what Brenda taught us.

Make sure he knows your needs. Don't just set expectations in your mind without communicating them to the other person. Maybe I wasn't clear enough that I wanted to talk with him or that I just needed a little bit of encouragement and love from him. Isn't the fact I called enough to say I want to talk with him? And I can see if he was truly in the middle of something, but his recorded TV show was more important than me. Maybe I am asking for too much. Just let it go. Don't make a big deal about it. You will see him tomorrow night.

Today is the big day! We have one final meeting at the Edge offices at 8:00 a.m. As I pull up to the office, I don't feel as confident as I did yesterday. It's a combination of being tired from the travel as well as my heart still hurting from the interaction I had with Andres last night.

Don greets me with a cheerful smile as I walk in.

"Good morning, Lisa. Can I get you a cup of coffee?"

As soon as I see him, I hear Andres in my head, "I am sure he wants to sleep with you." I shudder. It makes me feel violated even though Don never did anything to imply those were his desires.

Lisa, ignore that thought. Not every man is looking at you as a piece of meat. You are much more than that.

I was oblivious to the seed Andres had planted in my mind with that simple comment. That lie, coupled with my past experiences, began feeding a warped sense of identity in my mind.

Don is the same pleasant gentleman I experienced yesterday.

"Yes, please," I finally respond. "Actually, you can just point me in the right direction and I can get it myself." I don't want him to do anything special for me.

"I'll walk you to the break room. I need a cup of joe myself."

I don't want a cup of Joe, or Harry, or Tony, or Andy. Oh my gosh! I can't believe my mind just went there. Don was talking about a cup of coffee. But it is true: I really don't want any other men. I just want my husband to love me and cherish me.

"Lisa, are you ok? You kind of blanked out for a moment," Don said with concern.

"Oh, I'm sorry. I guess I need that cup of coffee more than I realize."

The meeting went great. Everything is in order for the event today.

"Here, Lisa. Make sure you wear your Edge volunteer shirt today," the woman in charge of the volunteers said, handing me my very own branded polo.

"Thanks," I said accepting the shirt. "Don, I'm going to slip into the restroom and put on my shirt, and then we should head over to the venue."

As soon as the words left my mouth, I start second guessing myself. Were my words sexually charged? I hate this place of insecurity. I find myself questioning my words and actions as well as the motives of others.

"No worries. Just come to my office when you are done, and we can head over to the venue," he answered, with no hint of offense.

I go to the restroom and put on my new shirt. When I see myself in the mirror, I notice the sadness in my eyes.

Lisa, stop it. You have an amazing opportunity today. Pull yourself together. Don't think about what Andres said about Don. You need to focus on this event today.

I take a deep breath, put on some fresh lipstick, and force a smile as I stuff the feelings of unworthiness below the surface so I can focus on today's event.

We head over to the event where everything is in place. The volunteers are right where they need to be. The stage is ready for the first band to set up. I call Dereck to give him an update.

"Hi, Dereck. I just want to let you know that things here look great! Did you get the photos I sent over last night?"

"Hi, Lisa. It is great to hear from you. I did get the photos. You've done a great job. Are we ready to take orders for our bundled services right there at the tent?"

"Yep. It's all set."

"Great. I knew I selected the right person for the job. Enjoy the event and the extra couple of days with your family. Just give me an update on the sales numbers at the end of the day."

What an accomplishment. I am grateful for my team back in KC as well as Don and his team. It's now time to wait for the festivities to begin. My plan is to hang here until around 6 p.m., then I will make the two-and-a-half-hour drive to pick Andres up from the airport. He will hang with me at the event tomorrow. Sunday morning we will head back to Chicago to be with my cousin. It seems like a lot of driving, but it's what I have to do to appease Andres. I really hope he will stop being so jealous.

I have a break in the action before the event starts, so I decide to call Andres.

"Hey, Babe, how are you doing?" I asked.

"Fine, I guess. It sucks. I have to go into work today and you are out there playing."

"Um, I am not playing. We are coordinating this event. It isn't like I am just hanging out."

"Oh, 'we' are coordinating this event. How is your boyfriend, Don? What are you coordinating with him? Some after-hour events?"

"Andres, stop. It's nothing like that. There is absolutely nothing going on between me and Don."

At this point, I really wish I hadn't made this call.

"Well, I have to get going. I need to greet the band and get them on stage. I'll see you tonight at the airport. Have a good day and a safe flight."

His flight is scheduled to get in at 8:47 p.m. Hopefully by then, he will be in a better mood. It is so frustrating how he doesn't trust me.

Speaking of trust, I wonder who he has been chatting with while I have been gone. He told me about Becky; I really hope he kept it online and didn't meet her without me. It hurts enough that he is sexting with her, but it would really hurt if he met her in person. That would be like cheating. Would it be cheating if I knew about it? The lines of what's okay and what isn't have become so blurred.

My thoughts are interrupted by Liz, the event coordinator.

"Hi, Lisa. Things look great. Is there anything you need from me?"

At that moment, a terrifying thought entered my mind. What if Andres suggests we proposition her tomorrow? A wave of nausea sweeps over me before I can shove that thought out of my mind.

"No. We are good," I said, coming back to reality, doing my best to dismiss that fear.

The rest of the day went without a hitch. Before I know it, it's time to hit the road to get Andres. The last thing I want to do is make him wait at the airport. That would for sure start the weekend off on a bad foot.

Chapter 28
The Art of Illusion

The app shows his flight is on time. As I wait in the overflow lot, my mind begins to wander and dream of what our life will become.

We both are doing well at our jobs and hope to move into a house soon; then babies. I am excited to be a parent. We will take those cheesy photos of us wearing matching jammies for Christmas. Most of all, we will be that happy, loving family Andres so longs for...and I want, too. I can give him that; and he can give that to me. If I can only get him to realize I do love him and I am not going anywhere. If I can only get him to understand that being part of a loving family requires give and take from everyone...but it is worth it.

My daydreaming is interrupted by his ringtone. "Hey, Babe, I landed and am off the plane. Where do I go?"

Ok, Lisa, get on your A-Game—if he starts out the trip getting lost in the airport, it is going to be a miserable night.

"You got this. Just look for the signs that say 'Baggage Claim'."

"But I didn't check baggage, so I don't need to go to baggage claim," he argued.

"I assumed you didn't check baggage. The passenger pick-up is right outside the baggage claim area."

It frustrates me when he asks for help, then proceeds to question the help I offer.

Deep breath, Lisa. Don't get bent out of shape and tip the apple cart.

I begin to make my way to passenger pick-up.

"Let me focus on what I am doing here to make sure I get to the right place; I don't want to keep you waiting. Just follow the signs to baggage claim for United Airlines and I will pick you up outside those doors. Call me when you get there."

I knew this is going to be a tricky exercise in timing. Besides getting lost, he doesn't do well with waiting either. I know I can't hang out in the passenger pick-up area, so the drive by has to be timed perfectly. I really wish he would just lighten up and relax a little. This is such a stressful way to live. I have to keep being strong and continue to love him; then he will change.

As I approach passenger pick-up, my phone rings.

"Hi, perfect timing. I am just pulling up. I'm in a white Ford Fusion."

"Ok, I am waiting outside."

"Which door?" I asked.

"I don't know. The door I came out of?" he snapped.

"Please take a look at the door; there is usually a number on it. That will make it easier for me to find you."

It's stupid I have to explain myself like this to him. When I ask a question, it either puts him out or makes him feel stupid. Why doesn't he see me as his #1 fan? Why doesn't he see us as a team?

Maybe that is the reason I have a hard time asking him for what I want or need. Wow! What an epiphany. Then I think about what it might take to get him to change. For the first time in my marriage, I am not so sure it's worth it.

"I'm outside door 208," he grumbled.

I hope he snaps out of this grumpy mood quickly. I have learned how to deal with this type of behavior, but I don't want to subject my coworkers and my family to it.

I pull up to door 208 and see his sourpuss face waiting for me. I stop, get out of the car, and exclaim, "Welcome to Chicago!" with my arms open wide, hoping for a Hallmark Movie couple's embrace.

"Hey," he flatly responded, leaned down, and gave me a simple peck on the lips.

This sucks. I don't really want him here in the first place, and this is exactly why. When he is not in control of things, or he is out of his element, he has a tendency to get really grumpy and takes it out on everyone around him...which ends up being fun for no one. And if you try to say something about it; well, it just makes the situation worse.

"Are you hungry?"

If he is, getting some food could be a quick fix to this situation.

"Yea, they only served peanuts on the plane. To top it off, the little old lady next to me wouldn't shut up."

"We can stop and get you something to eat. That will help."

I hate the black cloud he carries with him. I just need to be stronger and love it out of him. I just need to show him how things can be different and how we can create the amazing life we both really want to live.

We pick up burgers and fries for the long drive back to the hotel. As soon as we begin to eat, I can sense a shift in his mood.

Looking forward to tomorrow, I say, "I think you'll really enjoy the chalk festival. We got to see the artwork submissions. They are amazing. There is one that looks like monsters coming out of a manhole cover. It's a complete illusion."

"That's cool. We will have to go check them out together."

"Um, I can spend a little bit of time with you tomorrow, but I have to work the event. That was the deal we agreed on with you coming out Friday night."

"You have already spent so much time on this stupid event, and I don't want to spend the day alone."

I am beyond frustrated. I should have never agreed to have him come out here on this trip. Just like those monsters coming out of the manhole cover, my whole marriage is just an illusion of a loving relationship. He tells me what I want to hear and then does what he wants to do. I am too tired to argue with him. The rest of the drive to Peoria is quiet and tense.

When we arrive at the hotel, I announce, "I am going to go take a shower so I can get to bed. I have a busy day tomorrow."

"Ok, whatever," he replied

I turn the shower up to just below scalding and step into the stream of hot water. I was so excited about tomorrow until Andres got here. I don't want to have to battle with him all day tomorrow.

Deep breath, Lisa; it will all work out. If tomorrow runs as smoothly as today, it won't be an issue to spend some time with Andres.

I finish up my shower, dry off, and put on my PJs. As I turn the water off from brushing my teeth, I hear heavy panting coming from the main room. I open the door to find Andres laid out on the bed watching a porno.

"What are you doing?" I yelled.

"What does it look like I'm doing? Come join me."

"No. This room is booked through my work. I don't want a porn movie associated with my name. How am I going to explain this to Dereck?"

"Oh, stop it. I am sure he watches porn when he is traveling, too."

"No. I am not going to stop it. Turn that off. NOW!" I lost it. I can't believe he doesn't even care about my reputation at work.

"It doesn't matter if I turn it off now, it's already charged to the room," he said smugly. "Just relax. Everybody watches this stuff. Quit being so paranoid."

I'm crushed. I can't seem to get away from this perversion. And now it is going to show up on the bill I need to submit for my expense report. I don't even want to get into bed with him. Unfortunately, I am exhausted and I need to get to sleep. He better not even try to touch me.

As I wake up, I am relieved to realize Andres decided to use his better judgment and not ask me for anything last night. I have no idea how late he stayed up. I am still mortified his movie rental is going to show up on my tab.

Lisa, push it aside. You have a busy day ahead of you!

I get ready, and as planned, head to the event early to meet my team. Andres will grab an Uber over to the event and meet up with me later. There is a part of me that is glad to be leaving him at the hotel, knowing I don't have to deal with him. I'm also nervous, not sure what he will do while I am gone. What if he contacts someone through FunAdultFriends.com here in Peoria?

Lisa, STOP IT! I scold myself. *This is your husband. You should be able to trust your husband.*

With that, I walk out the door. As soon as it shuts, I put a smile on my face and step out into my world of success and confidence—being the Marketing Manager for Edge Communications, running a successful event.

My great morning is interrupted around 10:00 a.m. with Andres' ring tone.

"Good morning," I answer, a slight chill in my voice.

"Hey, Babe. I'm hungry and I think I missed breakfast."

"Yes, they stop serving breakfast at 9:30."

"Well, I'm hungry."

Really? Can't he do anything for himself? He is an adult, and he knows I am working.

"Well, why don't you grab an Uber over here like we planned? There are several food vendors here at the event. We can get a bite to eat for lunch."

"Ok, I guess that will work. Are you sure you can't come pick me up?"

"I told you, I am working. Call me when you get here."

Mental note to self: he is never allowed to join me on a business trip again…that is if I ever go on a business trip again. It may just be easier to not travel.

As soon as he arrives at the event venue, we head right to the food area. Fortunately, the lines aren't too long. He grabs a big turkey leg. I go for a gyro and a big basket of fries for us to split. It seems like both of us have relaxed a little bit and are able to enjoy the food and each other's company.

"Did you get a good night's sleep?" I asked.

"Yea. I finished watching the movie and went to sleep not long after that. You fell asleep faster than you usually do."

"I was tired…and hurt."

"Are you gonna bring that up again? Really? Let it go. Everybody watches porn. It's really no big deal."

Not that I have ever had any in-depth conversations about watching porn with anyone, but I don't think everybody watches it. Either way, I don't want to get into that discussion here.

As we're eating lunch, Liz walks up.

"Hello, Lisa. How is the food?"

"Hi, Liz. The gyro is delicious. Definitely keep these guys for next year. I would like to introduce you to my husband, Andres," I said placing my hand on his arm. "Andres, this is Liz. She is the one who has been in charge of putting this whole thing together."

"It is nice to meet you, Liz. Wow, gorgeous and capable," Andres said with a creepy inflection in his voice.

Liz was shocked by his comment. "Um, it's nice to meet you, too. You two enjoy the rest of your lunch. I need to go check on the artists to make sure they have everything they need," she said and quickly left.

"She would be really fun," Andres said with a perverted twinkle in his eyes.

"I can't believe you said that to her. She is my business contact. Please do not bring any of the swinging lifestyle into my business world."

"Oh, come on. You're no fun."

"I am serious. I don't want you to watch any more porn in the room the company is paying for, and I don't want you to proposition or even comment about any of my coworkers in a sexual manner."

"Ok, so what's in it for me?" he said.

"What do you mean, 'What's is in it for you?'"

"I mean, you asked me for something, so what are you going to do for me?"

Is this really a bargaining chip? Do I really need to do something for my husband in exchange for him to not be a pervert around my coworkers?

"OK, fine. We can get together with any couple of your choosing off of FunAdultFriends.com when we get home, as long as we don't know them in any other way—and you can set the boundaries. Just stop mixing your pleasure with my business."

A huge grin emerges on his face. "Deal."

I can't believe I just made that kind of deal with my husband. It feels more like I made a deal with the devil. This whole thing feels like such a compromise on my morals, if I even have them anymore.

Thankfully, Andres kept his end of the bargain. He kept all of his perverted thoughts to himself the rest of the day. I am so grateful he didn't say anything else to Liz or any of my other coworkers.

As I contemplate the deal I made with my husband, a new wave of fear washes over me. What if he tries to proposition my cousin and her husband? This perverted sexual desire has gone way too far; I have no idea how to stop it.

Chapter 29
The Windy City

It feels good to wake up after a successful event. We made all of our numbers. I was interviewed for the local news. Our mission for this event was accomplished. Now we get to head back up to Chicago and spend the next couple days playing in the city and hanging out with my cousin and her husband.

"I am excited for you to meet my cousin Izzy. I know she is going to love you," I said to Andres as we packed our bags.

"I don't know about that. No one else in your family loves me."

"Both Izzy and her husband Matt will love you. Just be yourself," I coax, trying to reassure him.

I'm trying my hardest to make this meeting a positive one, knowing he is nervous to meet more of my family. Trying to hold all of this together is exhausting. If things spiral out of control, it will be devastating. I wish I could trust Andres to be...normal.

We check out and make the two-and-a-half-hour drive to the Windy City. When we get close, I call Izzy. "Hi, Cuz! According to the map, we are about thirty minutes away, so that will put us at your place at around 2:00 p.m. Will you guys be home?"

"I am so excited you all are here! I can't wait to catch up with you and meet Andres! Yes, we will be home when you get here. Do you guys like Indian food? Matt's favorite restaurant isn't far from our place and they are known for their Chicken Tikka Masala. He really wants to take you there."

"Perfect. Yes, we do eat Indian food. We can't wait! See you soon," I said and hung up the phone.

"Indian food? I want Chicago-style pizza," Andres complained.

"They want to take us to Matt's favorite restaurant. It's a kind and welcoming gesture. It isn't so much about the food, but the fact he wants to share something that means a lot to him."

"Whatever. That isn't what I wanted."

This is exactly why I didn't want to have him join me. Contrary to his belief, life isn't always about him. I really want to smack him and say, "Suck it up, buttercup." But I know doing something like that would make his already wavering mood go south.

"Well, let's just go there tonight, and we can ask to go to a place with Chicago-style pizza tomorrow night," I try sweet-talking him into agreement.

"I guess I don't have a choice, so whatever."

"No matter where we have dinner, it will give us a chance to get to know each other."

"If it doesn't matter where we have dinner, then why can't we get Chicago pizza?"

Oh my gosh! He is acting like a spoiled child! I am about at the end of my rope. However, if I come unglued and go off on him, I know it will destroy the whole night. I want to point out to him that his demanding, childlike behavior is what makes people not want to be around him. He gets this way because he is nervous about making a good impression. What he doesn't realize is this kind of behavior makes him look like a complete jerk! When will he realize that life isn't always about him? I guess a better question is when will I stop enabling this behavior?

"Fine. If you want to tell Matt that you would rather get Chicago Pizza versus his favorite Indian restaurant, go right ahead. I am out of that decision. I'm just excited to spend time with my cousin and her husband."

"Good. I'm sure he knows of a great pizza place. Chicago is known for their pizza."

How did that happen...again? He has a way of manipulating me and my words to switch things around to get what he wants. Honestly, I don't care if we have pizza or curry; it's just rude to be someone's guest, and demand where to go to dinner. It's like he doesn't know the basic etiquette of interacting with people. He definitely doesn't understand what it means to give and take in a relationship. Let me rephrase that: he doesn't seem to know the "give" part of a relationship.

Now I am battling the downward spiral in my attitude. To keep me from getting upset and disappointed, I throw any of my expectations and desires for the next couple of days out the window.

We complete the rest of the ride without any conversation.

"537, yep, that is their house. Don't hit anything trying to parallel park. You kinda suck at it in your own car, and now you are in this crappy rental car," Andres finally spoke up.

Wow, what a vote of confidence. I hate driving him around. He is so critical. Too bad the rental car is in my name.

"Don't worry, I've got it. We may need to walk a few blocks so I can find a big enough spot unless I can get you to help me."

That's a novel concept, for a husband to help his wife. Just then I see a spot at the end of the block, one that is easy to back into.

"I am kind of nervous about meeting more of your family. What if your parents called ahead and told them what they think of me?"

There is a sense of genuine fear in his voice that breaks my heart.

"Oh, Honey, Izzy and Matt are going to love you. And I know my parents didn't call and say anything about you." My parents are really trying to mend and build a relationship with Andres, but this wasn't the time to mention that. "Come on; let's go have fun!"

After his confession, I am feeling a twinge of guilt because I was so upset with him earlier. When he gets anxious, he tries to control things. In light of this conversation, the fight about dinner plans makes more sense. I somehow seem to rationalize his rude behavior; even to the point of excusing it.

We hit it off immediately with Izzy and Matt. After loosening up, Andres makes the request for Chicago Style Pizza tomorrow night for dinner. I am shocked and impressed with the fact he seemed to listen to me.

See, Lisa, he is changing. You just have to be strong and patient.

Sunday afternoon was a blast. We visited the Lincoln Park Zoo and walked around Navy Pier. We did a lot of laughing. I am most grateful Andres didn't bring up anything about swinging or porn when we were with them. I am glad our shameful secret remained just that...a secret.

However, once we get to our hotel room, the Andres I know returns.

I am in the bathroom getting ready for bed and he calls from the main part of the room, "Which movie do you want to watch?" and proceeds to list off two different porn options.

My happy and hopeful mood from the day is crushed. Why can't I have that happy-go-lucky, playful husband I had this afternoon? What is wrong with me that when the two of us are alone together, he does this? Why does he need porn or other people to make him happy? Why am I not enough?

"Do we have to watch one of those movies? Aren't they expensive?" I try persuading him to change his mind.

"They aren't that expensive. If you don't want to watch it, that's fine. I'm going to."

"Whatever. I'm tired from the day. I'm going to go to sleep."

We are in the same hotel room, which means I will have to watch or at least listen to whichever one he chooses.

I was looking forward to some intimate time with the man I spent the day with. Now I find myself curled up on my side of the bed with my back to my husband, feeling very unloved, unheard, and rejected. I hope I can fall asleep before he gets too far into the movie; I really don't want to hear it.

"Come on, Babe, we are on vacation. Come play with me. We have to get ready for Becky and Andy next weekend," he said, not taking the hint I want no part of what he's suggesting.

"I'm too tired for tonight. And did you really set something up for next weekend with Becky and Andy? You didn't even ask me; I've never even seen their profile. It is like you are just going off and doing all that without me. I really don't feel comfortable with that," I responded, my back still to Andres. My insides are trembling; I am trying to hold the tears back as I lay my true feelings on the table.

"What? Don't you trust me?" he snapped back. "And, well, I will use Becky and Andy as your payment for our agreement from yesterday."

My stomach turns when he mentions our agreement from yesterday.

"Before yesterday's agreement, you promised me we would do this swinging thing together. You also said that at any time, either one of us could say 'stop' and we would stop. Well, I don't like that you were doing whatever you were doing with Becky while I was gone. I don't like that you are making plans with another couple without me being a part of it." It would be a lie to tell him I don't like the swinging thing at all, because as much as it hurt, it is meeting some of my needs. I'm scared. I am asking him for more than he wants to give.

"I would never steer you wrong. And by the way, you are the one who left me to go to Peoria. What else was I supposed to do while you were gone?"

I didn't leave him to go to Peoria; it was a business trip. There are plenty of other things he could have done while I was gone for one night other than have a digital or verbal sexual encounter with some random woman. Right now, I am so tired and hurt; whatever I say will land on deaf ears.

"Never mind; do what you need to do tonight. I'm tired."

With that, he softened his tone.

"Come on, Honey; let's not fight. I'm sorry I made the arrangements without you. I do think you are going to really like Andy." Then he starts rubbing my back. The porn is on low in the background. He is already excited and pulls me towards him. I really want no part of this tonight; however, I give in to please him.

When he is done, I turn over with my back to him again. He doesn't seem to notice or care about my needs. He apparently got what he wanted from me. I fall asleep, silently crying, feeling used, unheard, and uncherished.

The fact our secret never got out makes this trip a success. However, as we wait for our plane, Andres is taking a sexual inventory of the people walking by. It feels so violating. I try my best to tune him out. From our conversation last night, he doesn't have plans of stopping any time soon.

Chapter 30
Minus One

The next weekend came and we experienced Andy and Becky. The next few years were filled with various different couples, none of which became friends, just additional sexual partners. Intimacy, the aspect of being private and personal between a husband and wife, is anything but in our marriage. The series of one-night stands, hedonism, and superficial judgment of others is overwhelming and really crushing my heart. Telling Andres I don't want to do this anymore and him not listening crushes me even more.

"Hey, Babe, since we don't need to be anywhere tomorrow, let's see if we can find someone to come over and join us tonight. I've already contacted Chris and Sara as well as Andy and Becky. Both couples are busy. Come help me look for someone else."

He asked like he wanted me to help him pick out a movie. The thought of people looking at our profile, making the superficial choice, "hot or not," makes me cringe. To top it all off, I am currently cleaning toilets; and there is nothing about that task that makes me feel sexy.

"I want to get the cleaning finished. Just let me know when you find someone."

By this point, I'm glad when he does his searching without me. I'm really over it. I feel so empty and hopeless.

"Hey, Lisa, none of our couple friends are available, and there aren't any good new ones. Come, look. I found this single guy who is your type and seems interesting."

"A single guy? Are you really ok with that?"

"Yea, as long as he doesn't want to do anything with me. I want to watch him with you."

"Really? That wouldn't bother you...to share me like that?" asking the question, feeling more like his possession versus his wife. Although I can't quite put my finger on it, it feels like we are slipping further into this evil web of perversion.

"You've been with other men, so it's no big deal."

It's no big deal? It's a really big deal. My husband is totally fine with me being with another man...as long as he can watch.

That is so sick and twisted. It's like I am becoming the star in his personal porn flick.

"I'm gonna message him and see if he is available tonight."

I guess he took my silence as agreement.

I run the vacuum, hoping the loud hum will drown out my thoughts. Focusing on creating perfect lines in the carpet helps me hold back the tears.

"Good news! Frank is up to meeting tonight. He's actually a rep for an electronics company. He doesn't live here, but he said he makes it to Kansas City often. So, if things go well, this could turn into something really fun. We're going to meet him at his hotel room."

I don't know if it is going to this guy's hotel room, or the fact I am the only female with two guys that makes the idea of the meeting so cheap and transactional.

This isn't what I had signed up for, and I can't seem to find the door of escape. Divorce isn't an option. If it was, how would I make it on my own?

Who would believe me that any of this really happened? If they do find out, the next question would be, "Why did you let it happen?" And then the most painful thought flashed in my mind, *If you did leave him, who would want you? You are just a used piece of meat. Damaged goods.*

I realize focusing on the lines in the carpet isn't enough to stop the tears. If Andres sees them, he will blow up. Quickly, I put the cleaning supplies away and escape into the shower with my feelings of desperation, grateful for the running water that will camouflage my tears and drown out my sobs.

While I am in the shower, Andres hollers in, "You getting all gussied up for tonight?"

"Of course," is the only answer I can muster.

"Good. You are hot, and I know you are going to blow Frank's mind tonight, which is going to be fun to watch."

I don't respond. In my mind, that compliment actually reduces me to "just another porn star." This whole thing has snowballed so far from the first trip to The Passion Palace. What would life be like if we had stayed and practiced Capoeira instead of stepping into the world of smut and perversion? What could I have done differently to make my husband love me? I thought by doing what he wanted, he would cherish me. Unfortunately, he seems to cherish me less and less; and use me more and more.

I wish there is some way to get out of this, but God hates divorce. I don't know why I even care about what God hates or doesn't hate. I haven't been to church in years. I can't go there now because I am so dirty and broken. I would have to tell the priest about all of my sexual sin. To be honest, I don't want to tell that to anyone.

I am so alone and trapped, no way of escape. It feels like I am on a bullet train to destruction; it keeps going faster and faster, and I have no way of getting off.

Deep breath. Take a deep breath, Lisa.

As I exhale, I shove those feelings down into my heart which is already shattered. The pain of the rejection is already festering in the brokenness. I don't know how much more I can shove inside, but don't know what else to do. I hope I can siphon some feeling of caring and approval off of Frank tonight. I hope he finds me pretty or sexy. I hope he treats me ok.

My stomach is in knots. Even though meeting up with someone just for the transaction of sex was nothing new, there was something very different about this meeting.

I don't want Andres watching me with another man. I am afraid of his temper. Thinking back to when his jealousy would turn to anger, I shudder. His rage is scary. For tonight, I don't know how much I should enjoy the interaction with Frank. If I like it too much, Andres could get jealous and blow a fuse. On the other hand, if I don't like it enough, I'll get yelled at for not partaking.

Is this what marriage is supposed to be? In good times and bad? Through thick and thin? It doesn't feel right, but how would I bring any of this up to my friends? That is if I had any friends left. Would I just come out and ask, "Do you and your husband swing? If so, how much do you enjoy being with another man?" Or would I ask, "Is it asking too much for my husband to be interested in only me? Is fidelity an outdated concept?"

Who am I kidding? Even if I did have a friend to ask these questions, it would be a matter of Andres and me having the conversation and things changing between us...and I don't see that happening.

Getting ready for our meeting tonight, I look in the mirror. I don't recognize the woman staring back at me. To begin with, her beautiful creamy caramel hair has been bleached to a brassy blonde. More troubling is the sadness in her eyes...a sadness no makeup could cover. I wish I could do or say something to make things better for her. Despite the sadness, I see she possesses a natural beauty, strength, and hope...three characteristics I wish I had.

The conversation with myself is interrupted by Andres coming into the bathroom. "I am so excited about tonight; I almost can't stand it."

Feeling like I have no other choice, I play into the game. "It is going to be wild." I continue to put on my make-up and pretend to be excited.

"I think you should wear your short pink skirt and your tall boots," Andres directed. Then he started going into a graphic description of what would eventually happen to those clothes.

He always liked that look. I think it looks like a hooker's outfit. I am trying to ignore him while at the same time groan and interject into his verbal fantasy at the right time. He really doesn't get that I am not interested in this at all.

The walk to Frank's hotel room was reminiscent of the walk into The Palace for the first time. I am paranoid everyone can tell what we're about to do. We slip in the side door.

"What is the room number?" I ask. It's already embarrassing enough being a booty call; I don't want to knock on the wrong door.

"He is in room 217, or should I say 'Lucky 217!'" he confirmed with a great excitement that made my stomach retch.

We get to the room and every part of me wants to turn and run away. I know that's not an option. Andres knocks on the door. It quickly opens and we are greeted by the same face that was on his profile—so at least he is honest about that, which is a good thing.

"Hey, man, I'm Andres and this is Lisa."

"Hey, come on in. Wow, Lisa, I thought you were hot in your pics. You are more beautiful in person!" Then he turns to Andres, "Man, are you sure about this? If I had a woman that was this hot, I wouldn't share her with anyone."

He offered us each a beer and about five minutes of small talk before things started to heat up. It is so strange. As usual, my body reacts to his physical touch the way it's designed. I am able to detach my feelings and emotions of what is going on and let my body take over.

Surprisingly, Andres is really enjoying the show. I'm grateful because my biggest fear is he would get upset and turn it into a scene. At the same time, I'm crushed because it doesn't bother him at all to "loan me out" like a piece of property.

Frank said he wouldn't share me. I wonder if anything could ever work out between me and Frank? If it did, would he stay true to his word?

As the activities come to an end, I am torn. Glad it's over, but not looking forward to going home with my husband, knowing he will want to relive it. I am emotionally and physically tired. Frank was nice and protective of me. My husband is not.

I'm flattered Frank thought I was "hot". In reality, I want to be considered beautiful and cherished...not a sex object.

Chapter 31
No Way Out

All of my thoughts and emotions are a jumbled mess except for my conviction that divorce is bad, wrong, and absolutely not an option.

Growing up, I remember two different family friends going through a divorce. For one couple, it was a long, drawn-out, expensive battle that lasted for over two years. The other one, the husband cheated on his wife. I didn't understand when the Catholic Church questioned her ability to help with the teens simply because she was divorced. She experienced the rejection of a cheating husband, and then the church ostracized her as well.

The thought of fighting a two-year battle makes me nauseous. However, oddly enough, the bigger deterrent for me is the church doesn't condone divorce. What can they do to stop it? And since we were never married in the Catholic Church, would they really have any jurisdiction over our divorce? I know a divorce would bring overwhelming shame to my family...the lifestyle I am living now would bring massive shame as well if it were revealed.

The bigger question is why do I care so much about what the church says about divorce? I haven't set foot in a church for years. The truth is, I don't want to make God mad. I am worried that a divorce would cause Him to rain lightning bolts down on me. I never gave a second thought about God punishing me for my sexual promiscuity.

When I let the truth of my emotions begin to arise, the fear of rejection and loneliness are way too much to bear. So, I quickly shove those feelings and thoughts down and convince myself to stay put. It doesn't matter if it was in the church or the courthouse, I gave my word, "Until death do us part." So that's what it will be.

"Hey, Lisa, you know Brian, the guy I work with?"

"Yea, I remember you talking about him."

"I want to invite him, his wife, and their little boy over for dinner this weekend."

"That works for me. How old is their little boy? Do any of them have food allergies?" I asked, starting with the mundane questions; scared to ask if this dinner invite is just for dinner or if he has other thoughts in mind.

"No allergies. I think their boy is under a year, so we don't need to worry about feeding him."

I finally muster up the courage, "Are you planning on offering them more than dinner?"

"Um, NO. First of all, his wife is really frumpy. Second, he is a minister at his church. There is no way they would be into swinging."

I release a sigh of relief: a normal dinner party.

"That's a harsh thing to say about his wife."

"Just telling it like it is."

Honestly, I'm excited to have a dinner party that won't end up in sexual relations. However, the fact this man is a minister has me very curious. Why is Andres friends with him? Andres hates everything that has anything to do with God or the church.

"Brian is a minister at his church?"

"Yea, but he doesn't really act all weird and religious. He has introduced me to a lot of the big wi and he is just cool. I thought it would be nice to have him and his wife over."

"Oh, it doesn't bother me. I just wouldn't expect you to befriend a minister."

"He doesn't push it on me, so I am okay with it."

I am a little worried about having this man over to our house. Not that he would go snooping around, but we have so much porn, it's embarrassing. Also, what are we going to talk about? Will Andres freak out if Brian wants to say prayers before dinner? I'm also coming to the realization that it's very exhausting to pretend our marriage is ok. I am afraid this man and his wife will see right through the façade.

The week continued on like any other week. Work, Capoeira, Andres searching FunAdultFriends.com and most nights ending with the request, "Hey, wanna watch a movie?" That line makes me cringe. However, the one thing that fascinated me all week is we are going to have a minister and his wife over for dinner.

I don't know what it is about this man's faith that has me so intrigued. Maybe part of it is I am used to the priests of the Catholic Church who don't marry. It could be that I don't understand why a minister would want anything to do with a couple that has no sign of God anywhere in their lives. Well, Saturday night should be interesting.

I made a pot of the Brazilian stew to share a taste of our cross-culture experience with them. I have some strawberries for their son, Boaz. Brian and Grace are so kind and easy to talk to. The guys went off to talk about electronics while Grace kept me company in the kitchen.

"Lisa, what do you like to do for fun?"

"The main thing is Capoeira. After that, work, and taking care of Andres, there isn't much time for me."

"I understand. I don't work outside the home, but ever since Boaz came along, I've had to be more intentional about taking time for myself and my girlfriends."

"Can I ask you a strange question?"

"Sure," she said.

"Does Brian help you with Boaz? Like, if you want to go hang out with your girlfriends, does Brian watch him?" After I ask the question, I wonder why I am so comfortable asking something so personal after just meeting this woman. "I'm sorry. If that's too personal, don't feel you have to answer."

"Oh no, it's not too personal. Sometimes he does. Other times my parents watch him. Also, at many of the women's events at the church, there is child care so he can go play with the other kids."

A feeling of loneliness washes over me. She seems to have a full army of friends and supporters in her life, starting with her husband.

"You are always welcome to come with me to our Ladies Night at the church. We meet on the third Saturday night of the month. It starts with a pot luck dinner; then one of the female pastors does a Bible teaching; and then we fellowship. It would be a great way for you to meet some new friends, and we can get to know each other better."

I have to focus on swallowing the lump in my throat before it turns into tears in my eyes. I remember back to the youth group I went to a few times during high school. It was a similar format: pizza, a short Bible teaching, and then the game of choice, usually broom ball or dodge ball. It was so much fun. Honestly, an interaction like that is exactly what I need in my life right now.

"That sounds fun. I'll have to see if that works into my schedule." I know Andres doesn't like to spend Saturday nights alone. So even if he said yes to the idea, when it comes right down to it, I most likely will never go.

We enjoyed the rest of the evening with the guys talking business and cars. Grace told me about growing up in Southern California and how God brought her and Brian together. There was a curious peace about this couple.

As they are leaving, Grace says, "Lisa, I would love to have you join me for Ladies Night in a couple of weeks. Let me know if you can make it"

Once they leave, Andres gives me a curious look.

"Grace is inviting you to Ladies Night? What? Are you and the pastor's wife gonna go get crazy?"

"Ummm...no. The women at their church get together on the third Saturday of the month, have a potluck dinner, and talk."

"Now that sounds like a wild and crazy Saturday night."

"Stop. It actually sounds like it could be kind of fun. I went to youth group a few times in high school and really enjoyed it. Besides, I would like to make a few new girlfriends."

"Church girlfriends? How fun can that be? I guess if you want to waste a Saturday night partying at the church, more power to you."

"That's rude. Seriously, are you ok if I go? It's a Saturday night."

One of the things I have learned is to point out all of the details and get a double confirmation from him.

"Sure, whatever. If you want to, that's fine."

I'm excited. A little nervous, but looking forward to getting to know Grace better and maybe even meeting some other women.

The Thursday before Ladies Night, I stop by the store to get the makings for the red velvet Bundt cake I plan on bringing. I'm really getting excited. While I'm at the store, my phone rings. It's Grace.

"Hi, Grace. That's crazy timing! I am at the store getting the stuff to make the cake I was planning on bringing Saturday night."

"That is awesome. You just answered my question. I was calling to confirm you were still planning on coming."

"Yes, I'm really looking forward to it."

The idea of possibly making some new friends excites me. At the same time, I don't know how I am going to fit in with "church girls." If they ever found out the porn and sex that goes on at my house, it would not be good. If I do build any new relationships, they would be my friends. I don't see Andres and me going out to dinner with any couples from church.

Also, will they want to be my friend if I don't go to church there? I can't commit to going to church every Sunday morning. I still stand on the oath I made when I was growing up. "I won't go to church on just Easter and Christmas and take the seat from someone who goes every week."

Such mixed emotions. Maybe this wasn't such a good idea. Also, Andres said he was fine with me going, but what if he gets a wild hair? It wouldn't be the first time he changed his mind and altered my plans.

Lisa, STOP IT! You are over thinking this whole thing. It is a Saturday night event with a group of ladies. It is something you have longed for.

Chapter 32
Ladies Night

"What are you wearing tonight?" Andres asked me as I'm getting ready. "If it was a real Ladies Night, that short black skirt and your high heels would look hot."

Oh my gosh! What a pig. I'm going to a church function. Growing up, it was skirts below the knee, covered shoulders, and no cleavage.

Honestly, I was just asking myself the question, *What am I going to wear?* My wardrobe has gotten a bit risqué. I guess my new jeans and the yellow gypsy top will have to do. At least the top covers my cleavage and midriff.

"You look like you might actually fit in with the church ladies."

Andres is getting on my last nerve. I can't wait to get out of here so I don't need to hear his snide comments any more.

"Hey, do you want me to drive you to Ladies Night? I am just going to hang out tonight since you are busy. I don't really have any plans."

Oh boy. Here comes the guilt trip. He has known about this for two weeks. He had plenty of time to make his own plans.

"It's not that far. I can drive myself; thanks for offering."

"I'll take you. I don't have anything else to do since you are leaving me on a Saturday night." Now it's a statement, not a question. I can feel him getting possessive of me. "Yea, I'll drop you off and then go for a drive and get a bite to eat at Alfonzo's."

I hate it when he does this. Alfonzo's is "our" restaurant. Hearing he is going there alone makes something inside of me twinge. The fear of missing out on something starts racing through my head. All of a sudden, Ladies Night at the church doesn't seem so appealing. This is all part of his game.

Lisa, stick to your guns. Keep the plans you've made.

At least he isn't going to meet up with some couple, or spend the night sexting with some woman on FunAdultFriends.com. The battle on the inside of me is raging.

Lisa, do you hear yourself? This relationship is not good for you. Yes, I know. I also know I can't get out because we are married...and divorce is not an option.

I close my eyes and lightly shake my head to get the voices to shut up.

"Whatever. You can drop me off and then pick me up when it's done," I concede.

The conflict in my head and heart is almost too much to bear. The shame and condemnation are constantly there. The desire to be cherished and chosen continues to exist no matter how hard I try to ignore it. The feelings of manipulation and rejection continue to crush me. I just want an escape from all of it.

Lisa, take a deep breath. It isn't that bad. At least your husband cares enough about you to want to make sure you get to your final destination safely, I lie to myself.

"Hey, Andres, it's time to go. I don't want to be late."

"Hold on a minute. It won't be a big deal if you are late."

It is a big deal to me, but he doesn't understand. I should have just driven myself. In fact, I am about ready to get in my car and do just that... in my mind. I don't know if I would ever have the courage to actually be that bold against him. Someday I might be brave in the moment, but the retribution would be ugly.

My thoughts of defiance against him are interrupted. "I thought you said you were ready to go. Come on."

I grab my Bundt cake and we head off to Ladies Night.

Andres pulls up to the front of the church to drop me off.

"Yea, I never thought I would drive into the parking lot of a church, that's for sure. Have fun. Don't go "all Jesus" on me. I'll be back to pick you up at 9:30. Don't make me wait. And bring me a piece of your cake since you wouldn't let me have any earlier."

He is so annoying.

"I'll meet you here when we are done. I'll see what I can do about getting you a piece of cake."

I breathe a sigh of relief as he drives off. Taking a deep breath, I walk in. I'm nervous because Grace is the only person I know. I'm greeted by the two ladies at the welcome table. I sense the same warmth I had from Grace the night she and Brian came over for dinner.

"Welcome. I don't remember seeing you before. Is this your first time at Ladies Night?"

"Yes. Grace invited me."

"Oh, you must be Lisa! It is great to meet you. She mentioned you would be coming tonight. We are so glad to have you. She said you study a Brazilian martial art and spent some time actually living in Brazil. I would love to hear more about your experience."

That took me a little off guard. It's strange Grace had shared so much about me with this woman. At the same time, it's nice because it feels like I've been heard. Well, I guess I can share the appropriate parts and hide the rest.

"Oh, I am sorry if I was too forward. My name is Betty. Grace is one of my dear friends. When we were talking about tonight, she told me she had invited you, so I asked about you. Your life experiences sound VERY fascinating!"

Well, fascinating is one way to put it. The Brazil thing is cool; however, the rest is more frightening than it is fascinating.

"Brazil was a special experience. I am happy to share," I responded with the smile I've learned to use covering up what's really going on inside me.

"Great! I believe we will be sitting at the same table. After the study, I want to hear all about it."

Does she really want to hear all about it? I can share about the cultural part, the drumming group, the Capoeira. But if I tell her ALL, it would also include the joining of FunAdultFriends.com, the arguing over porn, and the beginning of the toxic swinging lifestyle that my life has become.

Filter, Lisa, filter! Only tell the parts she expects to hear about. You are in a church. You don't want the whole place to get struck with lightning. Then your secret will get out for sure!

"Grace asked me to text her when you got here. Hold on a sec."

As Betty was tapping away on her phone, Grace found her way to the welcome table. "Lisa! It's so good to see you. I have been praying nothing would keep you from joining us tonight!" She greeted me with such love and excitement.

She has been praying for me? She must be a good pray-er. I was really worried Andres would change his mind and do something to alter my plans for this evening; that didn't happen.

"Come on, let's head in. What did you bring?"

"It is my 'famous' red velvet Bundt cake."

"That sounds delicious!" She led me into the big room and over to one of the dessert tables.

"Put it on this one so it is closer to our table. That way we can make sure to get a piece. Now let's head over and grab a seat. You can put your stuff down and I will introduce you around."

We headed up to the front. It feels like I am sitting at the VIP table.

Grace is so kind to me. Not overbearing, but very interested in making sure I am included and comfortable. It's like she is truly glad I'm here. It feels good. Being introduced to various women, I find myself nervous and awkward about how much of myself I am willing to share. Getting to know these ladies is fun. At the same time, I am afraid I might say something that would start unraveling the truth of my hideous life: the truth that I am not enough for my husband; that I am sleeping around with other men and couples; that I am depressed and extremely lonely.

Lisa, you can do this. You are good with the charade and hiding those things you don't want others to know.

We mingle for a few moments.

Then Grace says, "Come on, Lisa. Come sit down."

As soon as we get to our seats, she heads up to the microphone.

"Hello, ladies! Welcome to Ladies Night!" The room becomes quiet as her voice booms over the sound system. "Please take your seats so we can pray over the food and then dig in!"

Women scurry quickly to their tables. I become acutely aware of the conflict raging inside of me. I feel peace, love, and acceptance—something I long for.

At the same time, there is this taunting voice whispering in my head, "Lisa, with all of the porn, and all the men you have slept with, you don't deserve peace and love. You are not enough. The only reason these women are nice to you is because they don't know the truth. Once they find out you are a slut and a disappointment, they will treat you the way you deserve to be treated." These words make me shiver.

As Grace starts to pray, I hear her say the name Jesus. The tormenting voice in my head seems to go silent. What is going on? I feel like I'm in the middle of a tug-of-war, while everyone around me seems to be acting totally normal. It doesn't make sense, but I'm grateful I no longer hear that evil voice.

"...God bless these women, the conversations, and the food. Please open the hearts of those women here who don't know You to experience the love and forgiveness of your Son, Jesus Christ, that they may be reconciled back to You. In Jesus' name we pray, Amen!"

As Grace finishes the prayer, the whole room replies in unison, "Amen!"

Grace gives additional instruction on how to navigate the food tables to avoid complete chaos, and then heads over to me.

"Come on. Let's hit the dessert table first. I want to make sure I get a piece of your red velvet cake. It looks delicious!"

The conversation around the table is full of laughter. Taking turns, we heard about Karen's potty-training exploits, Jan's family reunion plans, and the scrapbooking get-away these women have planned.

Then Betty turns to me, "Lisa, I want to hear about the time you lived in Brazil. What was that like?"

Usually, I am really excited to share about my Brazilian experience. But as the spotlight turned towards me, that tormenting voice starts chattering again in my ear, "Don't slip up and tell them the truth of what happened there. That was when your husband started seeing women who were really beautiful and realized you weren't enough to please him. Are you going to tell these church ladies that you and Andres joined FunAdultFriends.com? I bet none of these women even know that website exists. They aren't promiscuous like you. They are good. They know how to make their husbands happy so their man doesn't need to look elsewhere."

Who is this voice and how do I make it stop? Since everyone is waiting for me to respond, I start sharing about the village, the drumming group, the food, and the Capoeira. I can feel myself being less enthusiastic about sharing than usual. That voice really has me rattled. A wave of shame washes over me. If these ladies only knew what my husband and I do; if they only knew the porn that was in our closet; if they knew who I really was, I would not be good enough to be invited back next time.

Being so in my head, I don't even remember what I shared about Brazil. I was saved by a woman walking up to the podium.

"Happy Ladies Night!! We are so excited each and every one of you, precious daughters of our Heavenly Father, are here with us tonight. The food was amazing. The smiles and laughter I have experienced tonight are even better!"

Precious daughter of our Heavenly Father? She must be referring to everyone else in the room. I am not a very precious daughter. I haven't been to church in years, and I am just failing at life. How can that be precious to anyone, let alone God?

My thoughts were interrupted by Grace nudging me. "Stand up, Lisa. She is asking for people who are here for the first time to stand up."

Really? I'm kind of nervous to stand up in front of all of these women. Grace prods me once more. As I stand up, a woman with a wireless microphone comes running over to me. "Welcome. We are so glad to have you with us. Please tell us your name, who invited you, and one unique thing about you," the woman at the podium instructed.

"Um, hello, my name is Lisa. Grace invited me tonight. One unique thing about me…I lived in Brazil for a year on a cultural exchange program."

As I'm standing, I hear that slimy voice again, "The thing that is really unique about you is that you sleep with other people's husbands."

I want to just run, but the spotlight is on me. That voice keeps taunting me.

The emcee brought my attention back. "Wow! Brazil! That sounds so exciting. Lisa, we are so glad to have you with us. May God bless you because you chose to be here tonight."

As soon as she asked God to bless me, that taunting voice went away. That is so strange, but I am grateful!

The woman at the podium moved the evening along. "If you all can grab your Bibles and turn to Romans 8:1."

When Grace noticed I didn't have a Bible, she turned to share hers with me. It's strange to be reading the Bible. I remember we had one growing up. It had a black leather cover with gold edged pages. The only time it was ever opened was when someone in the family was born, died, or got married.

"I am reading out of The Passion Translation. 'So now the case is closed. There remains no accusing voice of condemnation against those who are joined in life-union with Jesus, the Anointed One.'"

No accusing voice of condemnation? I thought back to those voices that had been taunting me earlier in the evening. Their accusations were torment. But what they said was true. I'm not enough to make my husband happy. I am sleeping around with other men and living a life that feels so dirty.

My thoughts are interrupted.

"This is the gift Jesus gave us by dying on the cross as payment for our sin…all of our sin, past, present, and future."

Whoa, wait a second. What does she mean, "our sin, past, present, and future?"

It was like she heard my thoughts.

"You might be asking, 'What do you mean by future sin?' Well, The Word tells us in Romans 3:23 that we all fall short of the glory of God. In other words, none of us are perfect...even after we accept Jesus. That is why we need a Savior. The Bible goes on to tell us in Ephesians 2:8-9 that salvation is a gift from God. There is nothing you can do to earn it. You just need to believe in Jesus and accept Him as your Lord and Savior; that is how you accept the gift He is offering. Once you do that, you begin your relationship with Him."

This whole message is really blowing my mind. I made a note on my paper. "God doesn't hate me. Jesus is a GIFT to bring me back to Him." But I am not good enough for God to want anything to do with me. I mean, He is GOD, and I...well, I am a mess. I have made so many wrong choices.

"So, it comes down to a choice, to accept Jesus into your heart as your Lord and Savior," she continued.

She makes it sound so easy. It can't be that easy. I mean, if I accept Jesus as my Lord and Savior, I don't think I can keep doing what I am doing. Will Andres hear what is being taught and want to accept Jesus, too? Will that be enough to make him want to stop swinging? If he doesn't, do I leave him? I made a commitment to this man, "until death do us part." Also, I thought God said divorce isn't an option.

This devotional has brought so many questions, but one definite answer. An answer I am pretty sure will make Andres flip his lid! I think I need Jesus. I don't know why Jesus would want me. If what these ladies are saying is true, He does; and He died for me to have a relationship with Him. And along with accepting His gift of salvation, all of my sins, guilt, shame, and condemnation are washed away; AND I get to spend eternity in heaven, too. I feel like Jesus is getting the bad end of this deal.

Lost in my own thoughts, I missed the rest of what the leader was teaching. Grace looks over and can tell my mind is churning. She lightly put her hand on my back and says, "Lisa, take a deep breath. It is going to be ok. Jesus really does love you."

I sigh. How does this woman always seem to know the right thing to say to me?

You don't know how wrong my life is. I don't know how it can ever turn out "ok."

"Nothing is too big for God," Grace encouraged.

With that, the floodgates open. Despite trying so hard to hold back the tears, I hit my breaking point. I want to run out of the room so the women at the table wouldn't see me cry; however, my legs won't move.

The women at my table are so sweet. One got me a box of tissues. Grace put her arm around me, but not a single one of them pushed me to speak. I can feel this wall of love and protection come up around me. And then I feel this gush of love pour down over me. All I can do is sit here and weep.

The voices are muted. I hear a soft, beautiful melody playing as I sit in the warmth of the love that engulfs me. At this moment, everything is ok. Actually, it is more than ok. It's filled with much joy and peace. Something I haven't experienced in a very long time.

As I bask in this special place, I very clearly hear the voice of the woman leading the devotional.

"If you don't know Jesus, or if you have walked away, tonight He is calling you into a relationship with Himself. If this is you and you want to accept Jesus into your heart and accept Him as your Lord and Savior, please say this simple prayer with me.

> *I know I am a sinner in need of a Savior. Jesus, I believe You are fully God and fully man. That You came to earth, suffered, and died for my sins. I believe You were buried and rose from the dead on the third day. I accept You as Lord and Savior of my life. Come into my heart. Come into my life.*

"If you just said that prayer, welcome to the Body of Christ! The angels are celebrating, and we are, too!"

I heard Grace's soft voice, "Did you just accept Jesus?"

"Yes," is all I can muster. It's like a heavy warm blanket is on me and I can't move. Not that I want to. This is the comfort, protection, love, and caring I have been longing for...but it is beyond anything I could possibly imagine.

As I sit basking in this amazing experience, everyone around me begins praising Jesus, singing, "There is None Like You." Although this experience is completely foreign to me, I love it. I want more of it.

The words of the song start pouring out of my mouth as I stand with the other women at my table, raising my hands and singing. The peace and joy I feel is amazing.

As the worship ends, the woman at the mic booms out, "Praise God!! He is so good. Well, now it's GAME TIME!!! If you didn't bring a board game for your table to play, we have some up here, or you can share the ones people have brought."

I love playing board games—something Andres does not. I'm so excited. What an amazing night. It feels like it was planned just for me.

After a couple rounds of Scattergories, Grace turns to me. "Lisa, do you have a Bible at home? Now that you have accepted Jesus as your Lord and Savior, it is time to build a relationship with Him. That's done by reading His Word daily and being in fellowship with other believers."

"No, I don't."

"I didn't think so, so I got you this."

She extends a beautiful turquoise leather Bible towards me. Her kindness and generosity brings tears to my eyes again.

"Start by reading a chapter a day in the book of John," she said, flipping through the pages to show me where it was. "The book of John will begin to teach you about who Jesus is. Call or text me anytime with questions."

"Thank you...for everything. Honestly, I don't really know what just happened here tonight, but I can't thank you enough for inviting me."

"I am so happy you came. Please realize: it was Jesus that invited you. He just used me to do it."

That's a strange comment. At that moment, a streak of terror races through my mind. "What time is it?"

"It's 9:28."

"Good. Andres hates it when I am late. I need to grab my plate. I hope there is still a piece of cake left for him."

The peace and joy I've been experiencing quickly vanishes at the thought of Andres. How will I be able to experience this again? A new level of fear sweeps over me. What is Andres going to think about me bringing a Bible home? Maybe coming tonight wasn't such a good idea.

Chapter 33
The Road to Nowhere

There he is, front and center, waiting for me. "Did you bring me some cake?"

"Yes, today is your lucky day. There just so happened to be one piece left on the plate. It is kind of like a little miracle."

"Well, I don't need to rely on miracles. If you really love me, you would have saved me a piece at the beginning, not waiting to see if there were any leftovers."

Deep breath, Lisa. Pick your battles. "Did you go to Alfonzo's for dinner?"

"Yea. It was really good. I sat at the bar and met this woman. She was pretty and interesting."

My heart sinks.

"I was telling her about you, and she is interested in getting together with us."

Jesus, I need You now. Please stop this. "That's interesting."

"Yea, you will really like her. She's a spunky ginger. We laughed and talked the whole time I was there."

I'm in shock. While I just had an encounter with God, my husband was out picking up another woman to bring home.

What has my life come to? How do I reconcile this? I can't divorce my husband because that's a sin. On the practical side of things, if I divorced him, what would I do? Where would I go?

My anxiety levels are skyrocketing, and my heart is racing. I look down to make sure my Bible is tucked away in my purse. I don't want Andres to see it. How do I get back to that place of comfort, protection, love, and peace I experienced just minutes ago?

"So how was your 'Ladies Night?'" Andres jeered. "Did you all party with Jesus?"

As a matter of fact, yes, I did party with Jesus…and actually did a lot more than that!

"It was fun. Grace's friends are really nice."

"Well, what did you do?"

I don't feel comfortable sharing what really happened. I can't. I want to, but he won't understand. He'll make fun of me. And I definitely can't tell him about my Bible; he will flip his lid!

"Grace introduced me to her friends; we ate, did a devotional, and played games. Pretty mellow."

"Wow, that sounds REALLY exciting!" he mocked.

I really wish I could share my heart with my husband without being belittled.

"It was actually just what I needed: some good, girl time."

"Yea, wait till you get 'girl time' with Rachel, the red-head I met tonight. Now that will be some real 'girl time'."

My stomach wrenched. I don't want another woman, man, or couple in our sex life. I want to be loved and cherished by my husband. Sadly, I don't see a way out of this mess. Then I hear Grace's voice in my head, "Nothing is too big for God."

I don't know. This is pretty big.

Andres turns up the stereo which is fine by me. Now I can get lost in my thoughts and not have to talk with him the rest of the way home. I'm mentally preparing myself to perform my "wifely duties" because I know he is worked up from his evening with Rachel.

Morning comes too quickly.

"Hey, Lisa, hurry and get up. We need to get ready and pull out of here in the next twenty minutes or we'll get barricaded in our neighborhood by the traffic from the stupid mega church across the way."

Ugh. I am exhausted and was looking forward to sleeping in this morning. Why did he have to wake me up like this?

"Can't we wait and head out in forty minutes after the traffic dies down?

I am really tired."

"No, I want to go now. I need some coffee, and we can stop and get donuts."

I know the chance of him letting me sleep any longer is slim to none. He wants coffee. I roll out of bed and throw on some clothes and a baseball cap.

"Hurry, Lisa. We gotta beat the stupid church crowd."

"I am hurrying. Let me at least brush my teeth."

Through my annoyance and sleepiness, I feel a wave of warmth and love rush over me. It's that same feeling I had last night. Although it didn't paralyze me like it did at Ladies Night. It's distinct and palpable. I know it is Jesus telling me good morning. It's comforting to know He is right here with me. It puts a smile on my face.

"Lisa, come on. NOW! We are going to miss our window of opportunity."

The peace surrounding me evaporates with Andres' startling command.

"Coming!" I yell as I grab my shoes and run down the stairs.

He is waiting for me at the door.

"Why are you wearing those jeans? They make you look frumpy."

Really? It is Sunday morning. You woke me up and are yelling at me to hurry, and now you want me to be all gussied up and sexy for you? Jesus, please make this stop!!!

"Well, I could go up and change, but then we will miss our 'window of opportunity'," I sass back.

"Just get in the car."

As we head out of the neighborhood, we can start to see the stream of traffic increase from church letting out. "Sweet! We made it just in time to beat the church folk. It is going to be a good day," Andres said victoriously.

As we pull up to the coffee shop, Andres asks, "Can you just go in and get our usual? I'll hang in the car and wait."

"Sure," I said, knowing there is really no other way to answer his request.

When I come out with the two cups of coffee, I notice a huge grin on his face.

"What are you so smiley about?"

"Oh, while you were inside, I texted Rachel. She is up for coming over next Saturday night for appetizers and drinks...and well, we will see where that leads."

Heavy sigh.

Jesus, help!

"Oh, come on. Don't you trust me? You'll like her...and she is hot."

It's not a matter of trusting him; it's a matter of not wanting to live that way anymore, and he refuses to hear me.

"Whatever is fine."

"Oh, so now you are going to pout and be in a bad mood? Get over yourself. Everything isn't about you and what you want."

I know arguing won't get me anywhere.

"I want to get out of town and just drive."

"Um, ok. I thought we were going to get some work done in the yard today."

"Yea, I don't feel like doing yard work today. I want to get out of town."

"But the yard is a mess, and the side of the house is definitely a two-person job."

"Why do you always have to be such a buzz kill? The mess will be there when we get back. I just don't want to do work today."

All week he complains about how bad the yard looks, then doesn't want to clean it up. Plus, we don't have the money to pay someone to do it. I don't get this man's logic—or lack of it. What I do know is, if he wants to go for a drive, that's what we are going to do. I am annoyed because I feel gross and totally not prepared. I didn't even get a shower this morning because he was rushing me to get out of the house.

As I feel myself getting worked up, I catch a glimpse of the turquoise Bible shoved in my purse from last night. Then the lyrics of the worship song we sang echoed in my head. "There is none like You. No one else can touch my heart like You do…" The peace from last night immediately came over me. Jesus!

"Ok, where do you want to go?" I give up any fight, knowing I don't really have any other choice.

"I don't know. I just want to drive."

That's what my life feels like right now—that I'm on a drive with no real destination: ignoring warning signs and avoiding things that need to be addressed. I want to get off of this ride.

Andres enters the highway and finds his way into the fast lane. It is a gorgeous day. The windows are down, the music blaring, and the weather is perfect; but my heart is heavy.

As we drive, Andres' phone dings with a new text message. He quickly grabs it and tries reading it while he is driving.

"Sweetie, why don't you give me your phone and I can read your message so we don't get in an accident?"

"No, I got it."

"Who is it from?"

"Oh, just somebody from work. You don't know them."

It seems a little fishy, but I'm not in the mood to push it. I am just trying to go with the flow and figure out how I can get the yard work done myself over the next week before it gets any worse.

Andres exits I-70 and turns onto a two-lane highway. He loves doing land speed tests on the back farm roads. Coming around the bend, he downshifts. The car revs and lurches forward. I can feel myself getting pressed back into the seat as he moves to straddle the middle yellow line. The speedometer is passing the 100 miles/hour mark.

"Honey, can you please slow down a little?"

"You're fine. I know what I am doing."

"I know you do, but I am scared. Can you please slow down?"

"There is nothing to be scared of. I've driven this road a thousand times."

Knowing semi-trucks use this road often concerns me. If we encountered one at this speed, we won't make it. While holding my breath and the sides of the seat, inside I am screaming, "Please make this stop!"

Then Andres' phone signals a new text message. He takes one hand off the steering wheel and reaches for his phone so I can't see it. My heart races even faster. I am grateful he didn't try reading it. But what is he keeping from me?

His phone chimes again; he hits the accelerator harder. I want off of this crazy ride!

As things continue to intensify, we hit a rise in the road. I feel the car lift off the ground and start to sway as it touches down. It's happening in slow motion.

Jesus, please help me!

Andres is trying to get the car back under control while releasing a barrage of cuss words. The car decelerates and the tires grab the road again.

Lisa, breathe. You are going to be ok. You didn't wreck.

I can't tell if our near miss is going to cause Andres to mellow out or go off. He seems to be slowing down. Then his phone chimes again.

"Someone really wants to get a hold of you," I comment.

That did it. He slams the car down in a lower gear and we're off again recklessly accelerating.

"Why do you have to ride my case? It's nothing. Just stay out of it."

Stay out of what? What is he hiding? I don't get it? I have given him everything I possibly can, and it isn't enough. Is it another woman? My life is so out of control right now.

"That's it. You have just ruined the whole day. We're going home," he said, slamming on the breaks.

WHAT?!?!? How have I ruined the whole day? I know better than to argue with him. At least we'll get off this road and hopefully make it home safely.

He pulls up the emergency brake and causes the car to spin 180°, and accelerates back towards home.

As we speed down the road, I see a tractor on the road ahead of us. Andres doesn't slow down as he passes him. I am sure it was just as scary for the farmer as it was for me. As my anxiety levels continue to rise, I hear Grace's voice in my head, "Lisa, take a deep breath. It's going to be ok. Jesus loves you."

Just hearing those words begins to bring back the peace I had at Ladies Night. I'm able to breathe, despite the chaos around me.

Jesus, please just get me home.

Chapter 34
The Battlefield

We pull into the driveway. Andres grabs his phone, gets out of the car, and slams the door without a word. I sit for a moment, thanking Jesus for getting us home safely. It's strange how quickly I find myself talking to Jesus. I notice when I do, the atmosphere around me changes.

After a couple of deep breaths, I get out of the car. Cautiously I head inside because I don't want to have another encounter with Andres. I feel the tug in my heart to go read the Bible Grace gave me. I head to the back patio and pull the special turquoise book out of my purse. I think she said to start reading the book of John. I remember from my Catholic elementary school days that John was one of the Gospels—the books that tell the story of Jesus' life.

As I read, I feel a cocoon of peace around me. It's like nothing hurt me. It feels so good.

"In Him was life, and that life was the light of all mankind."

I need life right now. Everything around me is dead. My marriage, my self-esteem, my friendships...everything seems so bleak. My peace is interrupted by the slam of the door leading to the garage. Then I hear the car engine rev and the tires squeal out of the driveway.

He didn't attempt to come find me or even leave a note as to where he was going. In some ways, I am grateful because I don't want to deal with him; in other ways, it hurts. He didn't even have the courtesy to let his wife know where he is going...especially in the mental state he's in right now.

Lisa, just let it go.

I keep reading the first chapter of the book of John, learning the world didn't recognize who Jesus was. It makes me feel a little better that I'm not alone in my struggle to understand what is going on inside me with this new relationship with Jesus.

As I read, I feel this urge to text Andres, just to see where he's going and make sure he's ok. A part of me wants nothing to do with him. The other part of me is reasoning, "You are his wife, and you should care about his well-being."

I grab my phone and fire off a quick text.

"Hey, Babe. I heard you leave. U OK? Where are you going? I love you." Send.

Then I hear the familiar chime of Andres' incoming text messages ring from the kitchen.

What? I'm confused. He never goes anywhere without his phone. Could his phone really be in the kitchen?

I'm still curious about the text messages he was keeping from me when we were driving earlier today.

Lisa, it isn't any of your business...just let it go.

But it is my business...I am his wife. He has never shielded his phone from me, so why now?

I know looking at his phone would destroy any trust between us. But wasn't that already broken when he wouldn't let me read his incoming text message earlier today? I don't know what to do. Maybe he has a big surprise planned for me, and my looking at his phone will ruin it. That's hopeful thinking.

I grab his phone and open it up. Under the message I just sent; I see a series of messages from "Rachel - Hot RedHead." My heart sinks.

"Hey, Sexy man. I can't stop thinking about you. Dinner was good, but dessert was even better. I can't wait for some more of your sweetness; even if I do have to share you with your wife."

I stand there in complete shock. Did my husband sleep with this woman while I was at Ladies Night? Did he really just meet her last night, or was their meeting planned? My head is reeling. If I confront him, I know what he is going to say. "You get to sleep with other men, so why can't I sleep with other women?" This is different. He is cheating on me; and if he did sleep with her, he is lying to me, too.

My marriage is a complete travesty. Despite the mess, I don't think I can actually divorce him. I shouldn't have gone to that Bible study with Grace. That was a stupid decision on my part. What was I thinking, leaving my husband on a Saturday night? It's my fault for not being there for him.

With that, I hear the garage door open. I quickly lock his phone and place it back on the counter. Do I address him about it? Do I act like I don't know? What can I do to make my husband love me?

He storms in from the garage.

"I left my phone."

"I know. It's right here. I just tried texting you and heard it."

He grabbed it and turned to leave again.

"Please be careful. I love you."

"Yea, whatever."

I don't get it. I try really hard to be a loving wife and give him everything he wants and asks for. I just want him to love me. I wonder if I am asking too much of him. Am I really that hard to love?

I go back to the patio and try to focus on reading my Bible, but the words are just mush on the page. I don't know who I can talk to about all of this.

It's been years since I had a session with Brenda. Even if I did call her, I would have to make an appointment and bring her up to speed with all that's going on. We don't have the money to pay her right now.

I don't want to tell Linda about what is going on. What mother wants to hear about the perverted sex life of her child?

And I can't tell Grace, because, well, right now, she is the only friend I have—I don't want to scare her off. I am so alone.

Sitting in the sunshine with The Word of God in my hand, my mind feels so clouded. Then those evil voices start chattering in my head.

"See, you are so lame. You chose to go to that church thing, and your husband found a better woman. There is no way you can compete with her because you are worthless. You choose church over your husband, so your husband found a real woman. Look, you can't even read your Bible...so now you really have nothing. You ARE nothing."

Tears start to stream out of my eyes. "What can I do to make this STOP!!!" I scream.

"There is one way out," the slimy voice answered. "There is one thing that will end all of this. Go grab that big knife that is on the counter."

As if in a trance, I make my way into the kitchen and grab the large cooking knife. It's like an out-of-body experience. I have never thought of committing suicide...EVER! Nevertheless, here I am with this huge knife held to my wrist.

"Turn it to go with the big vein in your wrist so you will get a good cut," the demonic voice instructed.

As I rotate the knife, I hear a sweet and loving voice speak to my heart.

"Lisa, put the knife down. I love you. I cherish you. I have an amazing plan for your future. Delight yourself in Me, and I will give you the desires of your heart. You are precious to me."

I can't help but obey the sweet voice of God. As soon as I pull the knife away from my wrist, the taunting voices are silenced. The peace and love I felt at Ladies Night envelope me again. Cleansing tears flow from my eyes.

Even with the peace of Jesus surrounding me, I know I am not in a good place. I need help. I'm trying to assess what just happened. I know what I heard and felt were real; but it was like nothing I have experienced before. Will a counselor actually believe me? Will anyone believe me?

Feeling the presence and love of God surrounding me, I start searching the internet for a therapist. The next step seems so clear.

I jump as the garage door interrupts the peace and quiet. I had totally lost track of time. I have no idea how long Andres has been gone. I hope he cooled off while he's been away. How much do I tell him? A lot depends on his mood. I don't think I can say anything about the voices and all of that— but I think I need to tell him about why I am going to start counseling.

Anxiety creeps into my stomach as I wait for him to come in. I hate this part—I have no idea which Andres is going to walk through the door. Will I get the angry, accusatory, scary Andres; or the cooled off, apologetic Andres? Most of the time it was the first one; occasionally the second. When he comes back with remorse, it gives me hope this marriage can actually be all I imagine it to be.

I take a deep breath as I hear him walk in.

His greeting is one I didn't expect. "Did you read my text messages?"

I don't know if I should lie to him or not. That thought in itself is so wrong—I am contemplating lying to my husband. Afraid of his reaction if I tell him the truth, I go with the lie.

"I heard your phone when I texted you, so out of reaction, I picked it up. I wasn't trying to read your text messages, really."

"So now you are checking up on me. I can't even trust you to stay out of my phone. You totally violated my privacy. This need you have to control me is the thing that is causing all of the issues in this relationship."

Guilt washes over me. Why am I so needy? Is wanting my husband to love and cherish me asking too much? I guess if I am not lovable, it is asking a lot. The confusion and second guessing myself sends my mind on a wild goose chase trying to make sense of all of this.

"What if I was planning a surprise for you? You would have ruined all of it because you are so insecure. You drive me crazy!"

"I have a question."

"WHAT?"

"Was dinner with Rachel planned?"

"Really? What? Now you are going to accuse me of cheating? First of all, how many times have you slept with some other guy and I've never complained about it? It's only fair that I can do the same with other women. Second of all, if you weren't such a downer, I wouldn't have to go looking elsewhere for fun. And that question just confirms you DID read my text messages. On top of being lame, you have completely violated any trust we had in our relationship."

With that, he grabs his phone and heads out the door.

No, don't go! I didn't mean to mess up our relationship. I take it all back....or do I?

As soon as I hear his car squeal around the corner, the peace of God begins resting upon me again. I don't know what I am going to do. I'm exhausted from the emotional turmoil and scared for the future of my marriage. I feel bad for reading his text messages. That was a total violation of trust. My one poor decision could cause my whole marriage to fall apart. How can I earn his trust back?

Instead of pacing around the house, I decide to go for a walk. As I lock the door, I realize I didn't leave a note. I don't think Andres will be back any time soon. However, if he comes back and I'm gone without letting him know where I am, things will get even worse.

I go back inside and write a quick note.

"Andres, I'm going for a short walk. I'll be back. I have my phone in case you need to reach me. -Lisa"

I don't want him to think I left him. I know he has abandonment issues. I just need to get out and clear my head.

The walk is good. I can feel my anxiety waning. What can I do to get my marriage back on track? What can I do to earn back his trust? I am kicking myself for reading his text messages. He is right; it really is none of my business.

Chapter 35
The Beginning of the End

Trying to keep my mind occupied, I turn on a movie and stretch out on the couch. Where is Andres? It makes me nervous when he is this angry and gets behind the wheel. I hope he makes it home ok. What if he went to see Rachel? If he did, she would probably be able to calm him down and reassure him— something I have clearly failed to do.

I start dozing off. The emotions of the past few days have wiped me out. As I drift off to sleep, I experience the sweetest dream. I'm in a beautiful meadow filled with wildflowers. The colors are extremely vibrant. The sun is warm on my shoulders and face.

As I walk through the tall grass, I begin twirling around and dancing... so carefree. In this dream, I am ok to just be me. The peace and freedom are overwhelming. I take a deep breath and let it out; I feel the release of the last bit of stress in my body.

"Come, dance and be with Me!"

I recognize the voice. It has the same characteristics of the voice that told me to put the knife down. So sweet. So inviting. So loving.

I want to stay in this heavenly place forever. Then it strikes me: "I don't want to die. I want to experience so much more before I go to heaven. I want to have children. I want to spend more time with my parents..." I can feel the anxiety rise up in me again.

"Just be with Me. Walk with Me. Abide in Me. If you choose Me, I will give you an abundant life!"

"Yes! Show me how to walk with You. Show me what I need to do to make You happy, to please You, Lord."

"I am already pleased with you. I already love you. I could never love you any more or any less than I do right now."

How can Jesus be pleased with me? I am a horrible wife. I haven't been to church other than Ladies Night in years. I haven't been a good daughter to my parents...how can He love me?

"Lisa, you need to realize I know the true you. I created you. You are My masterpiece, which is why I am so pleased with you and want to walk with you and be with you. You don't have to "do" anything to earn My love. Just be My precious daughter. Just be."

"I don't know how to just be. I am always striving to be what the people around me need or want me to be."

"There is no more striving to be enough. You are already enough. If you choose to follow Me, I will guide you from the people and places that are not for you; and I will walk you into the life and calling I have created you to have," the loving Voice continued. "I will do this for you. You just need to obey Me."

"What will You ask me to do? I want to follow You, Jesus. At the same time, I don't want to upset Andres. Will You make him change?"

"My sweet daughter, I am calling you. Will you follow Me?"

As I was responding, the slamming door startles me awake, signaling Andres' return.

"I see you are really distraught about what you have done to this marriage. You are asleep on the couch. That makes a man feel really good."

"I am emotionally exhausted. I just…"

"What do you think I am? JUST FINE?!?!?" he interrupted.

"I know we both are going through a lot right now. I'm scared."

"What are you scared about?"

I don't know how to tell him. I don't think there is an easy way.

"Earlier today, I had a knife to my wrist. I had these voices taunting me. I never…"

"You WHAT?!? That is the most selfish thing you could ever do. I mean, what would I do if you killed yourself? How would I face the people at work if they knew my wife committed suicide? How could you do that to me?"

I am dumbfounded. I'm distraught and just contemplated taking my life and he is worried about himself and how he would look to the people at his work.

As my heart sinks, I hear the sweet Voice again, "Keep walking with Me. I will never leave you."

Andres' yelling pulls me back into the moment.

"You are such a selfish, controlling, manipulative woman. I can't take this anymore. I need a woman who will support and trust me. That's it. I am done."

"What do you mean you're done?"

"Like I said, I'm done. I want a divorce. I can't take you and all of your drama any more. It's just too much. And now you are trying to kill yourself. I can't take it...I can't take YOU! I'm out."

With that he grabbed his keys and phone and left again; for the final time.

Even though the words cut deep into my heart, not a single tear dropped. Did he really just ask for a divorce? The moment he said that word, I felt something in my heart close towards him. I felt a strength begin to well up inside me.

"Ok. If you want a divorce, you got it."

Chapter 36
A Way of Escape

Is this really happening? Am I really getting divorced?

The feeling of fear tried grabbing a hold with just the thought of the "D" word. Just as quickly, peace and a feeling of strength take over.

The words Jesus spoke to me in my dream played in my head.

"If you choose to follow Me, I will guide you from the people and places that are not for you; and I will walk you into the life and calling I have created for you."

Is that what He meant? Did God just escort Andres out of my life?

I have no idea what to do. I want to get out of the house before he comes back. I am pretty sure my parents will let me stay with them. I should call and ask. Then I have to admit I was wrong and that my marriage failed. They would probably be happy to hear it was ending. I can't believe I didn't listen to them in the first place.

After the third ring, I go to voicemail.

"Mom, Dad...it's Lisa."

What do I say now? I didn't think this conversation out before I dialed.

"Um, Andres and I are getting a divorce. Can I come stay with you? Please call me back."

My head is spinning. Life is such a dichotomy right now—everything is going so fast, and at the same time, moving in slow motion. Although I should be sad and devastated, there is a part of me that is relieved.

As I pace around my room, not quite knowing what to do next, my phone rings. I jump. I can feel the adrenaline release hoping it isn't Andres calling to yell at me. I look at the caller ID; it's my sister. Why is she calling? She never calls.

Trying to hold it together, I answer in a wavering voice, "Hi, Anna, is everything okay?"

"Oh my gosh, Lisa, I can't believe it. I just heard the worst news..." her almost hysterical voice leapt through the phone.

My heart begins to race again. I can't take on any more difficult news right now.

Before I can say anything, Anna's tone takes a drastic change.

"Lisa, are you ok?"

"Um, no. I am not." I burst into tears. "Andres and I just got in a huge fight and he asked for a divorce. So, I am getting divorced."

With that, Anna switches into business mode.

"Ok, Lisa. It is going to be ok. Let me ask: are you physically safe?"

"Yes. He stormed out of the house, so I am alone for now."

"Ok, we have a little bit of time for you to get everything you need and get out before he comes home. Do Mom and Dad know?"

"I tried calling. I left a message because they didn't answer."

"Well, that's one heck of a message," she said, trying to add some levity to the situation. "It might be a bit shocking. However, I am sure they will be more than happy to have you stay with them. You know they just want you to be safe."

Her caring words and reassurance give me a huge sense of ease and help me focus.

"Ok, so I am going to stay on the phone with you until we get everything you need and get you out the door. First of all, go grab a duffle bag or a suitcase."

Anna proceeds to walk me through packing everything I will need for at least two weeks.

"Make sure you grab any jewelry or other items of high value out of the house."

I am grateful for Anna's help right now. I still have no idea why she called me. The one thing I do know, I couldn't do this without her. Her kind, yet firm guidance is exactly what I need to stay focused and walk out of this toxic relationship. The timing of her call reminds me of how Grace would say the thing I needed to hear at exactly the right time.

Anna gave the next instructions.

"Ok, I am going to stay on the line. Set the phone down and put that bag in your car. Come back and we will get all the files you need."

"Ok," I say obediently.

As soon as I head down the stairs with my bag, a wave of anxiety and nausea hit me.

God, please don't let Andres come home. I don't want to run into him as I am packing and leaving.

Honestly, I don't ever want to see him again. Especially not now. I feel myself begin to shake as I approach the garage. I wrestle my bag into the trunk of my car.

I take a deep breath and run back upstairs.

"Ok, Anna. The bag is in the car."

"Great job. You're doing awesome. We are almost done." She is so reassuring. "Now I want you to grab the files for any bank accounts, investments, loans, mortgage information, car titles; anything like that so you have the documentation."

WHAT?!?!? Oh my gosh, this thing just got real.

Obediently I follow her instructions and put all of those files in a box.

"Done."

"Good. Just like before, I am going to stay here on the phone. You run down and put the box in your car."

"Ok. Be right back."

I grab the box and head down to the car again. This time I can move quicker because the box isn't as cumbersome as the duffle bag.

I run back up the stairs with excitement because I sense the escape from this toxic relationship is almost complete.

"Ok, the box is in the car, and still no signs of Andres."

"Nice. Finally, you need to take the computer. I am sure there are files and saved passwords on that machine that you're gonna need."

She stays on the phone with me while I unplug the cables and prepare for the final two trips down to the car.

"Ok, it's all unplugged and ready to go."

"Great. I am going to try to get a hold of Mom and Dad so they know you are coming. As soon as you get the final things in the car, call me back and I will stay on the phone with you until you get to their place."

"Ok. Anna, thank you. I don't know how I would have done this without you. I still don't know why you called. You have been a Godsend."

"You are welcome. Now get going. I want you to get out of there before Andres gets back."

"Ok. Thanks for calling Mom and Dad. I'll call you when I am leaving."

"Sounds good. I love you, Lisa. Everything is going to work out. Stay strong."

"I will. Bye."

As I hang up the phone, the reality of what I am about to do hits me. I am getting ready to leave my house for the last time. This marriage, this nightmare is truly over.

I begged for the swinging to stop. I wanted the emotional abuse to stop. I asked Andres many times, but he didn't listen. So, God made a way of escape for me.

It's so ironic. The whole reason I never would get a divorce is because I thought divorce was a sin. God actually used the "D" word to start a course of action and events designed to remove me from the toxic environment that stole so much from me. As soon as God opened that door, He also gave me the strength and encouragement to walk through it to freedom.

As I stop and look at my house for the last time, one tear escapes, mourning the loss of what could have been. As the garage door begins to roll up, the light floods in, just like the new light flooding into my life.

I get in my car, start it up, and pull away from this life that has taken me down such a difficult path. I call Anna.

"Hi, sis. We are outta there...free and clear!"

From the Author

Dear Precious One,

Thank you for reading this book. I realize that time is something we never get back, so I am honored that you spent your time to experience Lisa's story. I hope you were blessed by it. Most of all, I hope you are encouraged to believe that you, too, are a precious child of God.

Lisa saw many red flags at the beginning of the relationship which she chose to ignore. Andres was controlling her through anger, lying, and isolation from her family. If you noticed, he never respected her "no."

Although Andres never hit Lisa, he did emotionally and sexually abuse her. She endured things she never should have. I point this out not to bash Lisa, but to highlight this for you. If you are in a relationship where this type of manipulation is happening, please seek help. Speak with a counselor, a pastor, or a teacher. Lisa did have her counselor, Brenda. Unfortunately, she never shared the whole story with her.

I also encourage you to follow Lisa and come into a relationship with Jesus Christ. Whether you are single, in a destructive relationship or a healthy one, there is NOTHING more fulfilling in life than to have a relationship with our Lord and Savior. Start speaking to Him. Say the prayer she said and be saved.

I know I am a sinner in need of a Savior. Jesus, I believe You are fully God and fully man. That You came to earth, suffered, and died for my sins. I believe You were buried and rose from the dead on the third day. I accept You as Lord and Savior of my life. Come into my heart. Come into my life.

Next, find a good Bible-based church to continue to learn and grow in this life-changing relationship. God loves you so much. He will lead you, but you must follow Him. He won't force you to do anything against your will.

Blessings,
Tracy

If you are experiencing abuse or thoughts of suicide, please reach out. Here are hotlines in the US. You can also search your local area for organizations who can help.

National Sexual Assault Hotline – 800-656-4673
www.rainn.org

National Domestic Violence Hotline – 800-799-SAFE (7233)
www.thehotline.org

National Suicide Prevention Lifeline – 800-273-8255
suicidepreventionlifeline.org

Methods of Manipulation and Abuse

Below are some common methods of manipulation used in unhealthy relationships. In most situations, it starts out in subtle ways that intensify over time. If you are experiencing these abusive behaviors in your relationship, seek help. You can search for counselors or a "warm line" in your area online. Get help. Get out.

Emotional Blackmail

Emotional blackmailers use your feelings as a way to control your behavior. Using fear, obligation, or guilt, they threaten to withhold love, approval, or confirmation. This causes the second person in the relationship to question and change their thoughts and behaviors.

Examples:

- "If you leave me, you will never see the kids ever again."
- "If you really loved me, you would {fill in the blank}."
- "But this is what family does."

Gaslighting

Gaslighting is a method designed to erode a person's perception of reality. This is done by a combination of lying, distracting, minimizing, blaming, and distortion. The person being gaslit may begin to second guess everything: their memories, events, and perceptions. After experiencing gaslighting, the receiver may feel confused and wonder if something is wrong with them.

Examples:

- "You're making that up. It never happened."
- "Why are you always so sensitive?"

- "You're overreacting." Or, "You're being irrational."
- "I know what you are thinking."
- "Why are you upset? I was only kidding."

Guilt Trip

Using the power of guilt or misplaced responsibility to manipulate someone to change their emotions and behaviors.

Examples:

- "Look at all I have done, and you haven't done anything."
- Bringing up past mistakes.
- Using passive-aggressive behavior.
- Showing disapproval through facial expressions, body language, or tone of voice.
- Making sarcastic comments about your choices or accomplishments

Love Bombing

When the abuser shows their partner extreme displays of attention through compliments, affection, and gifts. Many times, this is seen at the beginning of a relationship to win over the other person. It can almost make the relationship "seem too good to be true." Many times, it will happen after a fight in an attempt to draw the other person back into the relationship.

Examples:

- Requesting a lot of your time early on in the relationship
- Texting and calling many times a day
- Moving to the next level quickly in the relationship; i.e. they say "I Love You" quickly
- Requesting for you to spend time with them versus your friends
- Consistent gift giving
- Introducing you to important people early on in the relationship

Isolation

This method of abuse cuts off the fostering relationships with family and other friends, making it difficult for people on the outside to see the dynamics really going on in the relationship.

Examples:

- Requiring large amounts of "one-on-one" time with the abuser
- Constantly checking in on the location and activities of their partner
- Refusal to interact with friends and family
- Offers excuses and alternative plans to get out of seeing friends or family

Negging

A method of emotional manipulation where a person makes deliberate, backhanded compliments and insults to undermine another person's confidence. This creates an increase for the need of the manipulator's approval. It can be disguised as constructive criticism or comparisons.

Examples:

- "You look good in that dress. I guess black really does hide your fat."
- "What made you think that was a good outfit?"
- "You could actually be pretty if you wore some make-up."
- "Your spaghetti was almost as good as my ex's."

About the Author

Tracy Fagan is a fireball. She has personally experienced the transformational power of Jesus Christ. She loves to spread the good news of Christ's love through books, speaking, and teaching.

She is the founder of Kingdom Publishing, a Christ-centered book publisher and educational resource for writers. She uses over twenty-eight years of marketing experience, creativity, and encouragement to help others fulfill their God-given assignments and bring their books, ideas, and businesses to life.

She loves her native state of Colorado as well as experiencing different cultures through travel. You can find her hiking, skiing, working out, or swing dancing; but many times you will hear her laugh resonating before you see her. She is a proud mother to a beautiful adult daughter and her precious kitty-cat.

Connect with Tracy through her websites and on social media.

www.TracyFagan.com
www.Kingdom-Publishing.com
@Kingdom.Publish
@Kingdom.Publish

Tracy Fagan's Others Books

When God shows up, things change. This anthology series shares stories of the miracles in people's lives when God shows up. Each book is filled with powerful testimonies of when our personal and loving God reached out to touch the lives of each of these authors.

God Met Me Here ISBN: 978-1733307819
God Met Me Here 2 ISBN: 978-1737515661

All books are available at
www.Kingdom-Publishing.com
or at various online retailers.

Research shows just 15 minutes a day of gratitude can have major impacts in all areas of your life. This journal will challenge you to be grateful for things from A to Z.

ISBN 978-0692610503

Moms are special, in fact, "MOM" is "WOW" upside down! This book offers children of all ages the opportunity to create a book of appreciation for the woman who has healing power in her kisses, encouragement in her hugs and love in her eyes.

This beautiful gift book is a great way to give mom that special gift that tells her how special she is. Celebrate Mom using every letter of the alphabet.

ISBN 978-1732287983